T0171713

No Cappuccino in the Afternoon

the Afternoon

A Collection of Short Stories

Michael Palmer

authorHOUSE

AuthorHouse™
1663 Liberty Drive
Bloomington, IN 47403
www.authorhouse.com
Phone: 833-262-8899

Published by AuthorHouse 06/27/2023

ISBN: 979-8-8230-0891-4 (sc)
ISBN: 979-8-8230-0895-2 (e)

Library of Congress Control Number: 2023909600

Print information available on the last page.

Cover photo by Charmaine Miyoko Palmer.

This book is printed on acid-free paper.

Contents

Dedication

This book is dedicated to Kasumi Furukawa,
who was willing to share his story with me about that Monday morning.
I will forever remember our conversations
and forever cherish his friendship.

Preface

My friends often ask me how I come up with the ideas for my stories.
I've thought about that a lot.
Here's my take on that.
Some ideas originate from random encounters with strangers:
A conversation in India,
And one in Paris.

Some from an experience a long time ago which suddenly and unexpected resurface:
A summer camp,
Shooting a gun.

Some from early childhood experiences which have had a lifelong impact on me:
A road trip to Florida.

Some later in life which were just as impactful:
An evening in Calcutta,
A story told in Japan.

Some definitely on the lighter side:
A traffic ticket in Croatia,
A busboy in California,
A can of paint in upstate New York,
A bazaar in Istanbul,
The Pyramids at Giza.

Some very personal:
A visit to a cemetery in Italy,
A ride in a U-Haul.

And one which was the idea for the title of this book
But then many are just formed from thoughts that just seem to pop
into my head and have no connection to anything or anyone in my life.
However they arise, I hope you enjoy them.

Acknowledgements

Thanks to Annie Barrete at AuthorHouse for her assistance
in making this book a reality.

Thanks to the copyright holders of the lyrics
to The Gambler and The End
for giving me permission to use those lyrics in my story
You've Got to Know When to Hold 'em and This is The End, My Friend.

Thanks again to Bob Jackson for his
masterful proofing of my second manuscript.

To my "brother" Keith Wells for the journey that we
traveled together to complete our second books.

Thanks to all my friends for their support and
encouragement (and editorial comments).

To the real Koda, who was the inspiration for all the stories
about a dog. You will always have a special place in my heart.

And thanks to my wife, Charmaine, for pushing
for that important word change.

No Cappuccino in the Afternoon

I had just landed at Marco Polo Airport near Venice, and with my large suitcase in tow, I decided to stop at a small café before heading to the car rental.

It was a long flight, from New York, a night flight, made longer by my cramped seat in economy class and the over-weight guy next to me watching action movies across the entire ocean.

I looked at the clock. It was 10:30. It was the morning.

Since it wasn't yet the afternoon, I could order a cappuccino. At least that's what I had read on the flight. "No Cappuccino in the Afternoon, And Other Italian Oddities", an article explaining some interesting aspects of Italian culture.

As for coffee, only a tourist would order a cappuccino after noon. A dead giveaway. Milk in the afternoon, according to Italians, is bad for digestion. That's when you drink espresso.

The cappuccino was so smooth. The best I had ever had.

"What's this?" I asked, holding up the coffee cup.

"Lavazza," he replied, raising his arms to acknowledge a given, at least for him.

He was short and stocky. Dark hair, dark eyes, light olive oil skin tone. A few hours beyond a five o'clock shadow. Typical for Northern Italians.

It was my first Lavazza. I vowed it wouldn't be my last.

"The coffee on the airplane tasted like dish water."

"Yes, but this is Italy." He smiled. "No dish water here. Just the best coffee. Il meglio, the very best."

I'm going to love this place, I thought. Why did I wait so long before coming to Italy?

"Quanto?" I said with a New York accent, as I finished my cappuccino.

1

"Due euros." He held up two fingers just to make sure I understood.

Putting two euros on the counter, I looked for the tip jar. But there was none to be found, so I put 50 cents on the counter.

He looked confused, then smiled and put the 50-cent coin back in my hand.

"No," he said. "Not here."

Oh yes, I thought, the article. No tipping in Italy. Yes, I had a lot to learn.

"Insurance, do you want insurance coverage on the car," it was the young lady behind the counter at Euro Cars. Her English was perfect.

"Do you think I need it?"

"Have you been to Italy before?" she said as she rolled her eyes ever so slightly.

"This is my first time."

"And where are you driving?"

"To Florence."

"It's called Firenze."

"Oh."

"On the motorway? Are you driving to Firenze on the motorway?"

"Yes."

"Really." She rolled her eyes again and smiled. "Then I definitely suggest you take full coverage."

"Okay, sign me up."

"You won't regret it, believe me."

As she handed me the keys to the rental car, I thanked her and then commented.

"Your English. It's perfect. Where did you learn English?"

"Denver… Denver, Colorado." She started to laugh.

"Huh?"

"Came to Italy right after college. Fell in love with the country and with my tour guide. That was ten years ago. Never went back. Don't intend to."

"Wow, what a story."

"And you?"

"Just a tourist. A tourist, from the big apple. New York City."

"Well enjoy, Mister Big Apple. Enjoy Italy."

The Fiat Panda 500 was smaller than I had expected. Five-speed. I had not driven a standard since college. Struggling to reacquaint myself with a clutch, I eased the car out of the lot and pulled out onto the motorway.

I decided to stay in the far-right lane. Slower there. Not as stressful, I thought.

Everyone was passing me. Cars, trucks, buses, motorcycles. I expected to be passed by a moped scooter any minute.

The navigation system on my iPhone started beeping. Then a voice. Speeding. Speeding. Jesus, I thought if I'm speeding, what about everyone passing me. Then I remembered the article, Italians are crazy drivers. They don't observe driving rules, or speed limits.

On my way to Florence, 260.44 kilometers. Christ, I thought, why is America not on the metric system like the rest of the world? I drifted out of my lane as I mentally wrestled to convert the kilometers into miles.

I glanced in the rear-view mirror. A speeding bright red Ferrari was closing in on me. Lights flashing too. I quickly moved back into the slow lane. As he passed, he gave me the most classic of all Italian gestures, with his fingertips touching and pointing upward. Not sure how to respond, I gave him the peace sign, even though I wasn't sure that was appropriate.

I had been driving for two hours and was getting hungry. It was 1:30, approaching the latest time Italians eat lunch, and more importantly when restaurants close. 2 o'clock. And then they wouldn't open until 7, or 8 for dinner.

Modena Centrale, the large green exit sign caught my eye. According to my readings, a city noted for its auto-making and home base of both Ferrari and Maserati.

Taking the exit, I saw the sign for Osteria Simone. 4 kilometers.

According to my Italian friends in Manhattan, osterias are casual dining places serving regional specialties. Eat at those, they all said. Cheaper and better.

The parking lot was full. Cars double parked. Some triple parked. I remembered, no driving rules. That must apply to parking as well.

The osteria was not nearly as full as the parking lot. Why, I wondered. A place to park for the day perhaps.

No menu on the table, just a board at the entrance with the Speciali del Giorno, the specials of the day. Lasagna Modenese stood out.

"Lasagna." I said when the waitress came to my table.

"E bere?"

"No … no beer," I replied.

"Bere… not beer. Bere, what would you like to drink?"

"Oh yes, bere." I tried to act like I really knew what she had said, but of course I didn't and I'm sure she knew.

"Wine, red."

"Vino rosso, si." She smiled as she walked away.

Jesus, I do have a lot to learn. Clearly that crash course on Italian wouldn't take me very far. But, it was a free app, so I really couldn't complain.

The lasagna arrived.

I was confused.

Where was the red sauce and globs of cheese? Instead, I was staring at green noodles layered with creamy meat sauce.

"Lasagna Modenese," the waitress said as she placed a portion of bread on my table. I guess she could tell I was expecting something else.

"Grazie," I replied. Then I noticed that I had no butter, no butter for the bread.

"Mi scusi … er … excuse me, could I have some butter?"

"Butter, why do you need butter," was her reply. Now she looked confused.

"For the bread, for my bread."

"Oh. No butter. There is no butter for the bread."

"Huh? No butter?"

"Scarpetta," she replied, making a scooping motion with one hand. "Fare la scarpetta."

I was stumped. "Fare la scar…" I mumbled.

"Si … si, la scarpetta, to make the little shoe."

"What? What little shoe?"

"The bread. A little shoe to mop up the last of the sauce on your plate. No butter, just a little shoe."

"Oh," I said. "A little shoe. No butter."

"Si, signore, a little shoe."

As I reached for my glass of wine, I thought to myself, well at least I didn't screw up this. But then I wondered if I did.

I was done with my meal and was considering a cup of coffee. Yes, a nice cup of coffee. Sugar and cream. Who cares if they know I'm a tourist? I could use a nice cup of coffee. I signaled for my waitress.

"Cafe," she asked as she approached.

"Si, cafe, per favore."

That felt good, I thought, even sounded good. Yes, I'm starting to get the hang of this. If my Italian friends back home could only see me now.

She returned, holding a small coffee cup, a very small cup.

Placing it in front of me I realized it was an espresso.

"Espresso?" I said, sounding surprised and looking confused.

"Si, café … espresso. Same."

"Oh," I replied, but then I noticed a couple at the next table drinking a real cup of coffee. I casually pointed at them.

"Cafe?" I asked.

"Oh, no. Americano. That's Americano coffee. You asked for a cafe, an espresso."

"Oh." That's all I could say. "Oh," as I sipped my espresso.

Back on the road, Florence was close. But I had no intention of driving in the city. Its maze of one-way streets, strictly enforced pedestrian-only areas, narrow roads and lack of parking was enough to discourage this driver who thought nothing of driving in New York City. No, New York City would be a walk in the park compared to Florence.

The Amerigo Vespucci Airport, Florence's only airport, only 8 kilometers from the city center, was my destination to drop off my rental car. After navigating a series of confusing roundabouts, I finally pulled into the Euro Car return lot.

The cab to the city, to my hotel was 22 euros, plus 2 euros for my large suitcase. I wanted to tell the driver that in New York City, cabbies don't charge extra for luggage, but then decided it really didn't matter. Just another Italian oddity.

My hotel overlooked the Arno River, which for more than two thousand years has separated the north and south sides of the city. The north with its religious buildings, large open squares, and luxury shops and the south with modest hotels, narrow streets, artisan shops, and lovely gardens.

I was on the south side, a few steps from the Ponte Vecchio, one of twelve bridges crossing the Arno, and the only one not destroyed during World War II.

Every evening I walked across the Ponte Vecchio on my way to the Piazza del Duomo, which was home to Santa Maria del Fiore, the third largest church in the world. In the large piazza, I enjoyed espresso and wonderful Italian ice cream, Gelato al pistacchio.

My planned week was almost over in Florence. A week of museums, art, monuments, palaces, gardens, churches, and food. Oh, the food. I even stopped missing butter.

Next up Rome, Naples, and then Sicily. I was surprised at how quickly I had adapted to the Italian oddities, and especially not drinking cappuccino in the afternoon.

I guess I was falling in love with the country. Now if I could only find that very special tour guide.

The Encounter

He came at me out of the dark alleyway. Not fast, but not slow either. I just stood there. It was like I was frozen. I wanted to run, but my legs wouldn't move.

I wasn't expecting him.

He was big and appeared to be very strong.

"What do you want?" I said in a shaky voice.

He didn't respond to my question, but instead continued to advance toward me. Slower now. Much slower.

I could see in his eyes that he wasn't afraid. In fact, his eyes suggested he had been waiting for someone. In the dark, in the alley. Just waiting.

And I just happened to walk by.

I looked around. Across the quiet street. Up and down the sidewalk in front of me.

Except for him, I was alone.

Two of us. On this quiet residential street, at 11 at night.

I had decided to take an evening walk. I couldn't sleep.

Why didn't I just read a book or something? Why did I have to go out?

In my hurry to leave my house, I forgot my cellphone. I even forgot the small flashlight and the pepper spray that I usually take with me on evening walks.

I was definitely not prepared for this encounter.

It was a moonless night. The single streetlight at the end of the block cast long shadows of the tall oak trees that lined the street.

It was early fall and while the leaves were turning, few had fallen.

A slight breeze created an unsettling rustling sound as the leaves danced above me. It was like they were trying to tell me something. Trying to warn me? Telling me to flee?

7

That was the only sound. The rustling leaves.

I could feel my heart beating in my chest, in my throat. It was racing.

Suddenly I felt lightheaded, and my knees buckled.

I reached out behind me.

Steadying myself against a large oak tree, I turned once more to him.

"What are you doing here?"

Still no response, but he stopped approaching.

He was about five feet from me. Looking at me, from my head to my toes.

I was confused. Anxious too. What did he want? What was he thinking?

Living alone had not been much of an issue for me. Moving into the city from the country was an adjustment, however.

"Watch out." My parents told me. "Life in the city is nothing like life on our farm. Be careful."

After graduation I took a job with a bank in the city.

I had been here about 6 months.

Up until this evening, the only issue I had faced were the whistles and cat calls from city construction workers.

"You'll get used to it," Charmaine told me. "Just ignore them. Don't encourage them. They're Neanderthals."

Charmaine worked at the bank. She grew up in the city, so she was a great source of information and advice when I needed it.

"But be careful at night," she told me. "Don't go out alone."

And yet here I was. Out, alone and at night. I didn't listen.

A sudden strong gust of wind separated some of the dry leaves from the branches above me.

As the leaves drifted down to the sidewalk, I looked up.

The falling leaves reminded me of little helicopters. Slowly spinning as they fell around my feet.

For a moment, I forgot about him.

For a moment, I was alone, safe in my thoughts with the twisting, turning leaves. I smiled as a few landed on my shoulder.

My thoughts drifted back to our family farm. I was so happy there, but I couldn't shake the feeling that I had to leave. Change, I convinced myself, something different would be good for me.

So, I left our 800-acre vegetable farm in southern Colorado and ended up here, tonight, on Sycamore Street in the city of Chicago.

Here in Chicago, holding on to an oak tree and wishing I was back in Colorado. On our farm.

He started moving again. Closer and closer. His breathing quickened.

I felt like this was the moment. The moment he would attack.

I panicked and stepped back, twisting my ankle on the curb.

Losing my balance, I fell backwards out onto the street.

I was on my back, crying.

The street was still wet from the afternoon rain.

My head was pounding. My vision was blurring.

I was having a damn panic attack, again.

And then it happened. It was so quick that I didn't have time to react.

He was on top of me. I could feel his hot breath on my face.

He was all over me, and as hard as I tried, I couldn't push him away.

Suddenly, I felt something cool, then something wet on my face.

I wanted to scream out, but then my vision cleared, and I could see.

"Wow, that's quite a story."

It was my twin sister, Alice. She had come to Chicago to visit me.

We were sitting on the large couch in my living room.

"Yes, indeed. I was terrified, but then …"

"I can only imagine what it must have been like. Alone, at night. Jesus, Sarah."

"Yeah."

"And what were you thinking at the time?"

"Mainly trying to figure out what to do."

"But, Sarah, you must have thought he was going to attack you."

"Yeah, that thought ran through my mind."

"Why didn't you run?"

"I assumed there was no way I could outrun him. And I was having one of my panic attacks."

"Oh my god, Sarah, are you getting those again?"

"Occasionally. But fewer now."

"Have you thought about moving back, back to the farm."

"Oh no, I couldn't move back. I'm comfortable now in Chicago."

Suddenly, sitting there, I experienced a flashback. A flashback to that night on Sycamore Street.

I looked across the living room and … I could see him there. Emerging from the darkness.

Coming at me. Not fast, but not slow either.

Dry leaves were falling all around me.

Then I saw those eyes. He was looking at me.

I could hear his breathing.

He was all over me.

I felt his breath. It was hot like that night.

Finally, I felt something cool, then something wet on my face, just like that evening on Sycamore Street.

"My god, Sarah, he's so big," Alice replied, as I came out of my trance. She was laughing.

Laughing at Koda, the stray dog I had befriended that night on Sycamore Street.

The scared dog who was lost.

The scared dog who was frightened.

The scared dog who was looking for comfort.

The one with the cool nose and wet tongue.

Now he was my dog.

Settling on the floor, at my feet, Koda looked up at me with those big grey eyes.

"He sure is Alice, so big and so friendly. I love him.

Peggy Sue

. . . .

It was a brand-new car, a truck, actually.

After decades of driving my run-down truck, I decided I deserved a new one.

"What's this?" I asked the salesman. I was pointing to a large blank screen in the middle of the dashboard.

"Oh that? Why that's a navigation screen."

"A what?"

"A navigation screen. It'll show you how to get somewhere."

"My God, those guys in Detroit have thought of everything."

Of course, I had no idea what the salesman was talking about. A navigation screen? Never seen one. And why would I want something to show me how to get somewhere. I just got there somehow. No need for this screen thing.

"I guess they didn't have them back then," the salesman laughed and looked in the direction of my trade in.

A '55 Ford F-150. With its unique V-shaped dip in the front upper grille. A rounded hood and big friendly headlights. A curved one-piece windshield.

Looking like a hot-rod with a long bed in the back. At the time I bought it, the F-150 half-ton truck was America's favorite pickup truck. Affordability and durability the salesperson said. And that's why I bought it.

"1362," I replied.

"What?"

"One thousand, three hundred and sixty-two dollars. That's what I paid for it."

"Well, that would probably pay for three tires on your new truck."

"Really?"

11

"Yeah. This model starts at $29,920 and doesn't stop until around $65,000. And an earth-shaking 430 horsepower."

Turning back to my Ford F-150, I mumbled, "straight six with 101 horsepower."

The salesman placed his hand on the hood of the new Ford F-150. He stroked it like it was his first love. Perhaps it was.

"This new model is a beast with brains. A relentlessly tough, high strength, military-grade, aluminum-alloy body, and torture-tested high-strength steel frame with all of the latest technology."

"Oh."

"And I bet your sweetheart will love it too."

"Peggy Sue," I mumbled.

"Your wife?"

"No."

"Huh?"

"My wife said I loved Peggy Sue more than her. She was probably right."

"Excuse me, you…"

"Peggy Sue, that's what I named my '55 Ford."

"You named …"

"Changed the oil every six months, like clockwork. My wife said I spent more on oil than I did on her."

"Huh."

"Yeah, she was so upset with me she ran off with my best friend."

"I'm sorry …"

"I think she was attracted to his car. A bright red convertible something." 'Really, I'm so sorry can I …"

"But I was fine with that, as I still had Peggy Sue."

"Yes, of course."

"Yeah, Peggy and I have been through a lot."

"I'm sure you …"

"Like the time the house burnt down."

"Your house burnt …"

"Lost everything. Well almost everything. Didn't lose Peggy."

"My goodness that must have …"

"Well, it was a blessing in disguise."

"Huh?"

"Peggy and I hit the road. Drove all the way to Louisville, Kentucky."

"You did…"

"Yeah. Peggy and I wanted to see where they built the F-150s."

"That must have been …"

"Like going back to her birthplace. Where Peggy was born."

"Born?"

"It was very emotional, for both of us."

"For both of …"

"But probably more so for her, if you know what I mean?"

"No, I don't think I …"

"Like going back to the womb, the factory where it happened."

"I'm sorry, but I think I have another customer."

"Mary Jane."

"Huh?"

"Mary Jane."

"No, actually Joan Reed."

"No, Mary Jane."

"But …"

As I slowly opened the bag I had brought to the showroom, the salesman gasped.

"Is that?" was all he could say.

"Yep, money from my insurance company."

"From the fire?"

"Yep, a blessing in disguise."

"I guess."

"How much for that shiny red one over there?"

"Well, it depends on what you want for your trade in … I mean Peggy Sue."

"No. Don't think I'll trade her in."

"Oh?"

"Yeah. I think she and Mary Jane can be the best of friends."

"Mary Jane?"

"Yep, that new shiny red F-150. Mary Jane."

It's a Matter of Time: Part 1

"The biggest mistake you can make in life is thinking you have time."

He was sitting, legs crossed, on a tan tatami mat. Lotus position. I was struggling to do the same. My back was aching, and my legs had fallen asleep hours ago. But I certainly couldn't complain because I wanted to be here.

His right hand reached out to us, palm upright, facing outward. The way of a teacher.

A long sleeved pleated black robe covered most of his white cotton kimono. A bright yellow shawl was wrapped over one shoulder. Its end touched the tatami mat. As tradition required, he did not wear footwear that would cover his feet, but instead wore white socks.

In ancient times, Buddhist monks were told to gather the materials for their attire from worn and discarded clothing, but his dress was an exception. Perhaps representing his high place in the sect.

He had been speaking for over three hours and was coming to the end of his offering. Not one break did he take. I marveled at the endurance and focus of this 'Roshi,' this Zen Master, whose age I guessed to be close to 90.

There were about ten of us. Students. In an old Buddhist temple high in the mountains overlooking Nara, Japan. Listening. Taking all of it in as best we could, his two-day seminar on the meaning of time.

It was Sunday, late morning. The end of the two-day seminar.

I was an American studying in Japan. When I heard about this opportunity to hear a Zen Master, I quickly applied. To my surprise, I was accepted.

The first day consisted of chanting, special foods and drink. To open the soul to the teaching of the Buddha we were told. Except for the chanting, we were not to speak. Just contemplate and listen. Cross legged, of course, with our hands folded in our laps. A sign of meditation, according to the way of the Buddha.

That night I slept on hard tatami mats. Just a thin blanket and small pillow. Nothing but a tall glass of mint flavored water by my side.

I woke in the morning, before sunrise, with a terrible neck ache, but still excited to be here.

It was raining outside. Just a drizzle, but with the distinct smell of a gentle morning rain. That smell of the air being cleansed.

His eyes were closed, his outstretched hand steady as it had been throughout the morning. And while he spoke almost in a hushed voice, his words carried effortlessly through the closed temple.

"Time is free, but it's priceless."

I arrived early Saturday morning. Passing through a large wooden entry gate, flanked on either side by scowling guardian gods, whose presence scared off evil spirits, I entered a courtyard.

In front of me, a large wooden structure, the main temple, at least three stories in height. Its impressive, curved roof, reaching skyward. The eaves extending far beyond the outer walls, covering the verandas circling the temple, supported by enormous wooden columns. It was one of the oldest temples in Nara. One befitting the old capital of Japan.

Nara, once the home to powerful and politically ambitious Buddhist monks. Now a scenic city, noted for its freely roaming deer population and, of course, its renowned Buddhist temples and Shinto shrines.

A series of wide wooden steps led to the only entrance into the old temple, which opened into a large dimly lit interior room. At the entrance, the shoes of all who wished to enter. Neatly placed, almost precision like, just like everything else in this country.

I suddenly realized I was hungry. Only a small bowl of rice and a cup of green tea for breakfast.

The Zen Master coughed. My attention quickly shifted from my empty stomach back to the sound of his voice.

"You can't own it, but you can use it."

It was April. Cherry blossom time. When the blossoming National Flower of Japan makes its annual journey up the Japanese archipelago. When the whole country embraces the arrival of the symbolic flower of spring, a time of renewal, and a reminder of the fleeting nature of life itself.

When families and friends gather under cherry trees to eat and drink and celebrate the white and pink blossoms.

The temple courtyard was adorned with cherry trees. Many of the trees were shedding their blossoms. The fallen flowers covered the ground like an early spring snowstorm.

The large Buddha statue behind the Zen Master was surrounded by burning incense sticks and offerings of fruit and flowers.

The incense drifted in my direction. The breath of the gods, according to Buddhist beliefs. The tall sandalwood sticks, with their unique sweet creamy wood fragrance, had been burning all morning. When one burnt to its final small pile of ash, it was quickly replaced. The smoke was constant. The gods continued to breathe.

The Zen Master coughed again, and then he looked directly at me.

"You can't keep it, but you can spend it."

The temple was in the center of the courtyard. Its entrance facing south, consistent with Chinese feng shui, as any other direction would be regarded as unlucky.

This entrance placing, however, to ensure luck, seemed inconsistent with the teachings of Buddha, who considered such practices as fortune telling, magic charms, and lucky days to be useless superstitions. Buddha actually forbid his disciples to practice such things. But of course, that didn't stop the ordinary Japanese temple worshiper from engaging in superstitious behavior.

My legs were numb, my back was on fire. I wondered how I could stand at the end of his presentation. Perhaps I would have to crawl out.

I suddenly had a vision of me crawling over the tatami mats, to the temple's exit, down the wooden stairs, past the row of neatly placed shoes, to the courtyard and finally coming to rest on the fallen cherry blossoms.

I let out a slight chuckle. The Zen Master stopped talking. Now he was looking at me. So were those around me.

They were all waiting. Waiting for me to say something, to do something.

I bowed, my head almost reaching the tatami mat. My back cracked. A loud crack.

Then I heard him. The Zen Master was laughing. His way of forgiving me, perhaps. I smiled.

He stood up and walked over to me. Holding out his hands, he reached for mine. He was smiling at me. A sympathetic smile.

Holding on tightly, he helped me to my feet. His strength surprised me. Coming close to me, he whispered, "there is no need to crawl out, walking is best." He winked, and then returned to his position in front of the giant golden Buddha statue. But he remained standing.

He cleared his throat. Looking around the room, his eyes stopping to engage each of us. I felt his warmth, his love as his eyes rested on mine. Standing, he motioned for all of us to do so. He was ready for the punchline. The meaning of time.

"And once it's lost, you can never get it back."

It's a Matter of Time: Part 2

The U-Haul was fully loaded. All 750 cubic feet of it.
It was time to leave.

"You gonna miss this place?"

"Probably."

Sean and Brittany were leaving San Diego after almost three years. They took to Southern California and the beach life with gusto. The first thing Sean did after settling in was to purchase a surfboard. By the time we were packing the U-Haul he had four.

The plan was to drive to Denver. When I heard Sean would be alone in the U-Haul because Brittany and her mom were driving their car back, I jumped at the chance to join him.

"Are you sure dad? I'm driving straight through. That's about 1,000 miles."

"1,078 to be exact."

"What?"

"And 15 hours and 44 minutes. I checked it out. And yes, I'm sure I want to go."

"Okay, but don't say I didn't warn you."

Warn me. No way. Not going was not an option. Ever since they moved out of Colorado after graduation, my time with Sean was limited. Understandably so. So, when this opportunity arose, I jumped on it. And in the back of my mind, that feeling of the inevitable. Approaching eighty. Who knows about the future? Yes, I was thinking about that more now. I guess that was understandable as well.

But I was also thinking about the past and a conversation in Paris.

"Think about it dad, almost sixteen hours in a U-Haul. That's a long time."

Oh, time. That's an interesting concept, I thought.

When I was a young boy, I thought time was forever. Almost like it stood still. The days so long. Then as a teenager, I could hardly wait for the time to pass so I could get my driver's license. But that too seemed like such a long wait.

After college, time seemed to speed up. Where did those four years go, I remembered saying to a friend at graduation. He didn't know either.

My career as a college professor went by quickly, too. I used to think it was all those deadlines. Researching, publishing, lecturing, grading, promotion. Each semester, quicker and quicker. Me getting older, while my students stayed the same age. Odd sensation. Not so noticeable at first, but by middle age it was obvious. We were like in two different worlds. My time sensitive comments now received blank stares. Oh, of course, the first moon landing means nothing to you. Nor Kennedy's assassination. As for those jokes, which at first ushered a chorus of laughter, now produced a sympathetic groan at best. Time was now rushing by.

Starting a family at first seemed to stop time. But only for a short break in its unrelenting march. I remember Charmaine asking after the birth of Sean, "do you think we'll ever have a good night's sleep again?" Probably not, I answered. But the good nights' sleep did come again, and time continued its ever-increasing journey.

Family time passed quickly. Those Christmases in Hawaii. Watching Sean playing in the sand, then boogie boarding, and eventually surfing. How quickly that all took place. Like a flash. His school years rushed by too. Schooling in Japan, learning Japanese. Did he really do that? Was I there? It's almost a blur now. As for his years in college, that was a blink of the eye. And soon he was working and married.

Then my retirement. Forty-seven years at the same university. Strange, I remember everything about my very first lecture, the long room with the fireplace at the back, the wooden floors, the old windows looking out onto a busy street, the one student in the front row named Jed, even my lecture on the importance of financial markets. That feeling standing in front of over 100 students. Nervous, perhaps even scared, but so proud, so happy. But what about the lectures that followed? Nothing. Why couldn't I remember them with the same intensity? Did they all blend into one? Where did those forty-seven years go?

Time. A very strange concept.

There was that one afternoon in Paris, talking to a stranger in a small cafe.

"You Americans," he said with that magical French accent, "you don't understand, or appreciate time."

Reaching for my second cup of coffee, I replied. "Why do you say that?"

"Look at you? I bet you're thinking ahead. What will I do for dinner this evening? What is my work schedule for next week? Where will I take my next vacation?"

I didn't offer an objection. I couldn't.

"Americans have an expression. What is it? Oh, yes, time is money. So, let's hurry, finish up and move on to what's next."

My God he was right.

"Perhaps you're right," I said. "But what about you? What about the French?"

"Ah, oui les francais," he shot back. "Time is something to be enjoyed, it's a moment to be savored. Like sipping a good cup of coffee, talking to a stranger, making love to a woman. Do not rush the moment. Embrace it. Give it meaning. Comprenez vous?

Feeling guilty for how quickly I finished off my second cup of coffee, I replied, "yes, I think I do understand."

But did I, and if I did was it too late? I wondered as I climbed into the U-Haul.

"You ready, dad?"

Ready, I thought to myself. Yes, I am, for all 1,078 miles, for all 15 hours and 44 minutes. This time I'm really ready to appreciate the moment.

Turning slowly to Sean, I said "oui, je suis, Sean."

"What did you say?"

"Oh, sorry. Yes, I am, take your time, I'm in no hurry."

A Morning on the Lake
with my Big Brother

The sun was still below the horizon, but the morning sky was slowly revealing itself.

We tip-toed out of the cabin and ran down to the boat dock. My older brother and me.

A line of birds flew over the lake. I wondered where they were going at this early hour.

We jumped into the rowboat and untied it from its moorings.

As we drifted away from the old wooden dock, I turned to my brother.

"Do you think they heard?"

"Naa, they're both sound asleep."

"Are you sure? How do you know?"

"Don't worry, it's fine."

That was my older brother. He was 18 and I was 15. He was always so sure of himself. I wished I was like that. So confident.

There had been no wind last night, so the water on the lake was so smooth, so calm. Just an occasional ripple when an early morning bass broke the surface.

"Did you get yours?" My brother asked.

"Yes, I did," as I held up four cigarettes I had lifted from our dad's pack, "matches too."

"Good. I'm sure he won't notice."

"And you? Did you get the good stuff?"

"Of course, I did."

My brother slowly pulled out of his backpack a quart bottle of Jim Beam and held it up above his head like a Super Bowl trophy. It was full.

"Jesus, a whole bottle. Don't you think he'll notice?"

"No way, the liquor cabinet is full. No way, he'll notice one missing bottle."

"But a whole bottle."

"Don't worry. It'll be fine, you'll see."

That confidence again, I thought. How I envied that.

I was rowing. The oars slipped in and out of the water with little effort. Hardly a splash. Just a faint whisper as they broke the surface.

While our summer at the family cabin was fun, we had planned this special getaway for over a week. We even followed the weather reports to pick the best day.

"No storms, we don't want to go out in a storm, "I told my brother.

"Don't worry," was his reply. That confidence again, I thought.

The sun was peeking through the high hills to the east. It sparkled as it rose through the branches of the tall evergreens. The lake reflected a light orange film. Dawn had broken.

"This is probably as good a place as any," my brother said.

Pulling the dripping oars into the boat I looked around.

We were about halfway across the lake. The cabin directly behind us. Perhaps fifty or so yards. I squinted but couldn't make out any movement.

"Probably still sleeping," I said.

"After that party last night, I suspect so. Perhaps they'll sleep till noon."

They had their friends over for an anniversary celebration. Ten of them from town, about an hour away. We were upstairs working on the details of our getaway.

"Hey, give me one of those cigarettes," my brother was holding out his hand and fluttering his fingers.

"Here you go, one Lucky Strike cigarette."

"Christ, why did you swipe the unfiltered smokes?"

"That was all I could find."

I took a long drag and coughed. Then I gagged. My brother was laughing.

"Hey little bro, slow down. Hold that smoke in your mouth before drawing it into your lungs. Let it cool."

I watched him. He took a long, slow drag. Then the smoke drifted from his mouth into his nose, like a reverse waterfall. He finished with three perfect smoke rings. Jesus, he looked so sophisticated, so cool, when he did that.

I tossed my cigarette into the water.

"I'll never get the hang of this."

"Probably best if you don't. All you're doing is putting a killing stick between your lips."

And there it was again. Advice from my big brother. I loved when he did that. It showed that he cared about me. Really cared.

"Shall we open the Jim Beam?"

"Absolutely. I'm ready."

Of course, I wasn't really ready. My drinking history consisted of a dozen or so beers and a couple of sips from a bottle of cheap red wine. Hardly a seasoned drinker.

Removing the cap on the bottle, he spoke, almost like giving a sermon, "I present to you Jim Beam, the 86-proof bourbon whiskey from the great city of Clermont, Kentucky. Aged for four long years in American White Oak Barrels. The…"

"Stop, stop, that's enough. Give me that bottle."

He handed me the square bottle with its amber liquid. I took a whiff, and detected a sweet, oaky aroma.

Then to my lips, where I had my first taste of bourbon. A hint of caramel, oak, and vanilla. And smooth, like honey as I swallowed. So smooth. So that's bourbon, I thought.

"I could drink this all day," I said to my brother.

"I wouldn't recommend that."

I took another long swallow, and then handed the bottle back to my brother.

The sun was rising in a clear blue sky. The sound of ducks broke the morning silence. I was starting to get a buzz from the bourbon.

I guess that's what gave me the confidence to ask.

"Can I ask you a personal question?"

My big brother had a look of surprise. I rarely did this, ask him personal questions.

"Sure, what do you want to know?"

I looked up at the sky. The sun's rays struck me in the eyes. Jesus, it was bright. Then I dipped my hand in the cool water. I guess I was debating whether to ask. Or simply trying to find the right words.

"What is it, little bro? Ask me."

"Have you ever? You know, have you?" I said in a voice so low that I barely heard.

"Ever what?"

"You know, have you ever…"

"Hey just spit it out. It's just the two of us in the middle of this lake."

"Done it." There I said it. Shouted it out too.

"With a girl? You mean all the way?"

I lowered my voice again, "yes."

I could tell he was uncomfortable. He hesitated, and then spoke.

"Why do you want to know?"

"Did you want to do it?" I replied.

"What?"

"Did you feel like you wanted to. To do it?"

"Yeah, I guess. Why?"

Now I was uncomfortable. I looked down at my hands, they were squeezing the wooden oars. I was trying to avoid looking at my big brother.

I knew that I had to say something.

"Well, I've never …" was all I could say, still holding on to the oars.

"Never what? Never what little bro?"

He moved closer, sitting on the tackle box directly in front of me. He removed my hands from the oars and held my hands in his. I looked up, and then I said it.

"I never wanted to do it. With a girl."

"So?"

"What does that mean?"

"Why should it mean anything?"

"I mean, could I be… you know, could I be?"

"Different? In not liking girls?"

"Yes, that different."

We both sat there, in silence. I glanced over to the dock. Dad was standing there; he was too far away for us to hear him. He was waving at us to come on in. I looked at my big brother, waiting for an answer. Hoping for an answer.

"It wouldn't matter." He finally said.

"Really?"

"Yes, not to me. You're my brother, and it wouldn't matter."

Then I realized, that was the first time he called me brother, not little bro. I wanted to cry.

"Really, it wouldn't matter if I was?"

"Hell no, it wouldn't. And I would bust anyone who said otherwise."

I started crying. He continued.

"I would love you no matter."

And for the first time, he told me he loved me. My crying eased into sniffles.

He took a gulp out of the bottle of Jim Beam and handed it to me.

"Let's drink to that," he said.

And we did, a couple of times. I was smiling now.

"We probably should get back in," I said, "dad's on the dock."

"We need to get rid of the evidence before we do."

He slipped the bottle of bourbon over the side. We both watched as it sank below the surface.

Back at the dock, dad tied the boat to the moorings.

"Early morning boating?" He asked.

"Yeah." My brother spoke first.

"Yeah," I replied.

"What were you two doing out there?"

"Just talking."

"About girls," my dad said. He was smiling.

More of an assumption, than a question, I thought. Then I turned to my big brother, and then turning back to my dad, I replied.

"Girls …yes, I guess you could say that."

"And fishing, how was the fishing?"

"Not good. They weren't biting."

As my brother and I got out of the boat and walked up to the cabin, I wondered if my dad noticed we did not have fishing poles.

I also wondered if he noticed that my brother had his hand around my shoulder.

Sheriff Gotham

The smell of fresh coffee filled the air. I opened my eyes.

The morning sun was gently warming my small tent. I struggled to get out of my sleeping bag. My back was aching from the hard ground. But at least it didn't rain last night.

The chirping of birds mingled with the sound of the fast-running river. The river that we crossed yesterday to get to this side.

Zipping open the tent, I saw fire rising in the pit. Jim was standing there, warming his hands.

"Morning."

"Morning Jim. How long have you been up?"

"Just enough time to fire up the coffee."

The cast iron coffee pot was resting on the red-hot embers. As usual Jim was brewing up his cowboy style coffee. Tossing a hand full of coffee grounds into the boiling water.

"Like strong mud," Jim would say.

"More like wet cement," I would reply.

But it was good, and we both agreed it was like jet fuel. And it got us going.

Going was what we had been doing for four days short of a week now. Jim and me, and our two horses.

Going after those three escapees. Damn, how the hell did they break out of their cells? I was of the opinion it was an inside job. But of course, I had no proof and didn't expect anyone to come forward.

"Hardly enough for one joint," Jim had argued.

Looking at the baggie we had removed from the taller one's back pocket, Jim was right, but then he neglected to notice the condition of the three of them.

"Probably consumed most of what they had before they got to Whitefish," I replied, as we took the three of them off to jail.

Their crime, possession of pot, at least a small amount of pot.

"Another cup of coffee?"

"No thanks Jim, I'm okay. We should move out if we're going to catch these guys."

"Okay sheriff, let's saddle up."

Sheriff. I still wasn't used to that.

But I was. The sheriff of a small town in northwestern Montana. Whitefish, in the heart of the Rocky Mountains. Population, just shy of 8,000. More dogs than people, the locals would claim. I never counted but I had no reason to doubt them.

Sheriff Gotham, they called me. Not because it was my name, but because I had come west from New York City. I didn't much mind the nickname as long as my monthly paycheck cleared The National Bank of Whitefish. And besides, I was ready to leave the Big Apple. Ready for something else.

"How can you leave? You're a New Yorker." My friends had pleaded. "I can't believe you're doing this."

"Time for a change."

"But Montana. Do you even know where that is on a map?"

"Sure, I do."

Of course, I couldn't tell them that I didn't know when I first read that job posting for a sheriff. $55,710 starting salary, small house provided.

Well, I wasn't going there for the money. I just wanted to get away. I was fifty now, unattached, and looking for something new.

"I was escaping," I joked with my friends. But was I really joking? Was I really just tired of the Big Apple?

"Think they're headed for Canada?" Jim's question jarred me back to our current situation.

"That's what I'd do."

Sixty miles to the Canadian border. Sure, that's what I'd do. Of course, the route would be difficult through this remote wilderness. Rivers to cross. Black bears to contend with. And on foot as the three of them were. But they did have a head start.

When I first got to Whitefish, I couldn't sleep at night. It was too damn quiet. Missing were the night sounds of the big city. Police and ambulance sirens, honking horns, sounds of early morning delivery trucks, even loud parties that went on until the sun rose.

"We must be getting close."

"Sorry?"

"To the border. Not far now."

Jim knew these mountains and valleys. He grew up here. Also, knew the preferred route to Canada. Even after five years, I was still a novice. And still after five years, I looked in awe at everything around me. The deep blue sky. The majestic mountains. The pristine lakes. The endless forests, the majestic elk, and the occasional bald eagle. Beauty everywhere I turned. And the cool crisp air, like this morning.

"Sure beats New York," Jim would say.

"Well, they both have their good and bad points." I would reply.

"Bad points? What are the bad points here?"

At first, I would answer the pineapple pizzas, the bitter coffee, and then, of course, the fierce snowstorms. But after a while I came to prefer the juicy dark red elk burgers, the taste of huckleberry and bourbon pecan pies with the bitter coffee, and I even came to enjoy the howling snowstorms. Much to my surprise, Whitefish slowly replaced the Big Apple.

Then of course there was Cathy. We struck up a conversation at the local diner. She was a waitress. After six months, she moved in.

The terrain was flattening out now. The tall mountains were off to our west. The run to the border was easy now, for us and them.

"Looks like an early winter," Jim said, pointing to the west.

The tops of the mountains were dusted with snow, and it was only early September.

"Time to get out the snow shovel," I muttered.

God, I remember my first winter here. The snow piled up. My driveway was impassable. I couldn't even open my front door.

"Got to get yourself a sturdy snow shovel or at least a good snow blower," my deputy said. It was Jim and I could tell he knew I was lost.

"Jesus, Jim, back home the superintendent took care of the snow. And my parking was underground."

"Well, not here. You're on your own. And you better get a lawn mower while you're at it."

Lawn mower, snow shovel. This was part of my new life in Whitefish, Montana. Certainly, different from my lifestyle in my apartment in the big city overlooking the drab apartment complex next to me.

"Well, they came through here recently."

The tall grass was matted down. Their trail pointed straight north to Canada.

"Time to pick up the pace," I hollered. "They must be close."

The horses started to gallop. God, did I love this. And so different from the police cars in the big city. Sure, the chases, and the flashing red and blue lights were a rush, but nothing like this. This was a different kind of rush. A better one too.

The cool wind whipped at my face. I didn't mind it. It was refreshing and my beard was blocking most of the cold. My Montana beard. Couldn't grow one in New York.

"Not permitted, too unprofessional," I was told. In Montana no one cared.

Life in the big city. When my application was accepted for this job, I wondered if I would miss it? My favorite cafe on the corner, New York style pizza, going to Yankee's baseball games, Friday night dinners with good friends, strolling through Central Park, and my job as a captain in the NYPD.

My horse was in full stride now. My butt bounced on the saddle with each gallop. I didn't much mind that either, at least after a few months of toughening up. "All part of the job," Jim would say.

Jim came with the sheriff's position. He had been a deputy for as long as anyone could remember. Born and raised in Whitefish. Never left. And didn't intend to leave.

"Aren't you curious?" I once asked him. "Wouldn't you like to see what's out there?"

"Nope, everything I need is right here. Right here in Montana."

I never asked him that question again. But nearly five years later, I was starting to understand his answer.

My first month in Whitefish, Jim invited me to go fishing.

"Have you ever fished?" he asked.

"Does the fish department at a grocery store count?"

"Jesus, what do you do in the big city for fun? To relax?"

Good question. What did I do? Going to an occasional baseball game? A movie? A new restaurant?

The next day we were in his small boat on Whitefish Lake. A beer in one hand, a fishing pole in the other.

"What you think?" he asked, a big smile on his face.

We had been in the boat for an hour. Two beers and not even a nibble.

"Is this all there is?" I asked sarcastically.

"Be patient. You'll see."

Just then he hit. The line tightened. My heart started racing. And then he leaped straight out of the water, spinning, and splashing back to the surface. My first trout, and not wrapped in brown butcher paper from the corner grocery store. Like that first trout, I was now hooked.

We were within a half a mile now. Canada was just ahead, but still no sign of the three fugitives.

As we got closer, we could see the small wire fence which had been erected to mark the border. Not meant to discourage crossing, but simply to indicate the separation between the two countries.

And there they were. The three of them. Young guys, probably in their mid-twenties. On the other side. Laughing and hooting at us. It was all a game to them, and, as usual, they won.

"Well, they beat us to the crossing," Jim said.

"Hardly worth the effort," I replied. After all they were three young guys hitchhiking through town who were found with a small amount of pot in their possession. We caught them, put them in jail, and someone let them out.

"Any ideas, Jim?"

"Huh?"

"As to who let them out? Any ideas?"

"Nope." He turned away quickly in the direction of the three guys, hoping I didn't see the smile on his face, nor the slight wave from the fugitives.

"Well, we better head back."

Turning the horses to the south, a three-day ride ahead of us, I wondered again, what am I doing here.

Then I remembered that in three nights I'd be back in Whitefish, back in my comfortable house, back with Cathy, probably having dinner at the diner, elk burger and huckleberry pie of course. Bitter coffee too. Dusting off the snow shovel. And at night sleeping soundly without any big city disruptions. Yes, I'd be back home.

Before we commanded our horses to gallop, Jim turned to me.

"This weekend?"

"What?"

"Fishing. I hear the trout are really biting now."

"Thanks. I wouldn't miss it for all the pizza in …"

"The Big Apple?" Jim burst out in laughter as he finished my sentence.

"Yeah, that place. Gotham." I was laughing too.

The Special Coat Hanger

. . . .

I was sleeping. Not a deep sleep, more of an anxious sleep.

Suddenly the plane started shaking.

God, I hate flying, I thought to myself.

The shaking got worse, and I felt a hand on my shoulder.

"Wake up, we're about to land"

I slowly opened my eyes and looking to my right I saw Harry.

"You better fasten your seat belt."

Reaching down in search of my seat belt, I noticed the knuckles on both hands were white from grasping the arm rest.

I hope Harry hadn't noticed. Probably not, or else he would have teased me about it. Harry was that way. A fearless adventurer. He had been talking about going to Calcutta for over a month. And when the boat docked in Madras, he said it was time.

I really had no intention of joining him. But Harry wouldn't take no for an answer.

"I've already booked our hotel. It's right in the heart of the city," he had argued.

Looking out the window as the plane descended, I saw the lights of the city through a bluish haze. It was midnight.

"Jesus, Harry, look at all those lights."

"Those aren't lights, they're fires. It can get cold at night in Calcutta."

"Oh."

The taxi ride to our hotel took about 45 minutes. Along the way, I noticed what appeared to be rubbish covering the sidewalks. Lots of it. Stopping at an intersection, I was able to see that what I thought to be discarded trash, were actually people, sleeping on the sidewalks. Miles of them, some covered with blankets, some with cardboard. Men, women, children, families.

Closing my eyes, I wondered what in the hell was I doing here? Why did I let Harry talk me into this trip? Shipboard life was so comfortable. But this. Jesus.

The taxi slowed as we approached the entrance to our hotel. A security guard waved us in through an old metal gate. I then noticed the high concrete wall surrounding the hotel.

"For security," the doorman said.

Glancing at Harry, I whispered, "To keep them out, or keep us in?

"If we're lucky, we might find out," Harry replied.

"Jesus Christ, Harry, it's always an adventure for you. As for me, I need a drink."

Sitting at the outside bar, with my second gin and tonic, I again noticed the concrete wall.

"Harry, that must be at least ten feet tall."

"Probably so people can't see in."

"And it's like our own isolated world in here. I don't even feel like I'm in Calcutta. We could be anywhere. Miami. Paris. London."

Harry rose quickly from his chair. "I've got a solution. Let's go for a walk"

"But Harry, it's dark out there and I'm tired."

"Bull shit," shouted Harry. "Get your ass up, we're going for a walk."

The security guard at the front gate rolled his eyes as we stepped out into the darkness. I shrugged my shoulders in reply.

The sidewalk in front of the hotel was partially lit by the hotel lights. The bluish haze which I noticed during our landing, reached the ground. It was almost like being in a dream. But it wasn't. Smoke from the fires I wondered. Burning wood, or burning something else?

As my eyes adjusted to the darkness, I was amazed to see so many people. Many were simply walking. Alone. Silently.

I glanced towards a mother encouraging her young child to drink the water seeping from an open pipe near the sidewalk. Two young guys were arguing about something but stopped as we approached. A beggar, with his outstretched hand, slumped against the concrete wall. I reached in my pocket for a coin.

"No," Harry shouted, "it will just encourage more."

A bus lumbered by. It was full to capacity, some passengers riding on the top holding on to the luggage railings.

We reached the newly built train station and went inside.

"My God, Harry, families have taken up residence in here."

"A train station during the day, an apartment complex at night," Harry replied.

"I guess."

Walking back to the hotel we decided to take a bridge spanning the Ganges River. A two-way traffic of pedestrians, cars, cows, bicycles and trucks in competition with one another to reach the other side. Below, in the river I could see some late bathers. Some fires on the shore too, adding to the blue haze.

A block from the hotel, a small girl, in tattered clothes, stepped out of the darkness. Walking towards me, I noticed metal objects in her hand.

Coat hangers. Christ. She was carrying a handful of old coat hangers.

Stopping directly in front of me, blocking the path to the hotel, and holding out the coat hangers. She looked up at me.

"Do you want to buy some?" she asked.

"You're selling coat hangers?"

"Yes, I've even cleaned them. They're like new."

"How much?"

Harry let out a disapproving cough.

"Oh, shut the fuck up Harry."

Not hearing the price, I reached in my pocket and emptied all my coins in the girl's hand. She started to hand me all the coat hangers.

"No," I said, "just one. You pick."

"Here, this is my favorite, it's special."

Harry and I parted ways after that trip, and he died shortly after.

Today when I go to my closet, and reach for that special coat hanger, I can still see that little girl. She and that coat hanger remind me of why I had to go to Calcutta.

I only wish I had thanked Harry!

The Summit

The air was getting thinner. It was harder to breathe. I felt like I was gasping for air. I was.

"Shall we hook up the oxygen?"

"No, you should hold out as long as you can. You need to let your bodies adjust to the altitude."

It was Kami. He was our Sherpa team leader.

"Are we at the base camp?" my dad asked.

"Almost, we should be there within the hour."

After 14 days hiking on hilly terrain, I would welcome the base camp, 17,600 feet above sea level. Not that "the steps to heaven" weren't spectacular. Every bend in the trail another photo opportunity — sheer cliffs, herds of passing yaks, beautiful forests, rows of colorful prayer flags, Buddhist stupas, Sherpa villages, teahouses, monasteries, deep canyons, and glacial moraines.

But my dad and I were ready for a break at the base camp. The typical base camp stay is one month before climbers attempt the summit. During that time, we'll be making numerous short hikes up the mountain from the base camp. Increasing the distance climbed each time. All this to get properly acclimated. Failure to do so could result in swelling in our lungs and brain, and death.

"Dad, I think I see the base camp?"

"Yes, I see it too. Look at all those tents."

Dad and I were so excited to see the base camp. Kami just smiled.

By some estimates, during the peak climbing season, over 300 people are at the base camp. While most are climbers waiting their turn to the summit, the community also includes doctors, scientists, support personnel, and, of course, Sherpas.

"Hey, Kami, here's a good place to set up our tent."

"Yes, it is. We will do so and then prepare lunch."

Dad said we'd make the climb with the assistance of a Sherpa team. There were six of them. They were the muscle and navigators for our climb. Carrying our gear, oxygen, water, and food. And safely navigating us through icefalls. After the base camp, they would become even more important, monitoring our oxygen levels, and getting us through the "death zone" to the summit.

Dad and I talked about this climb for a long time. We trained too. Climbing many of Colorado's 14ers. Longs Peak at 14,259 was my favorite.

But this climb would make Longs Peak look like a weekend stroll in the park, Kami said. Yes, it would not be a stroll in the park. Definitely not.

From Kathmandu, we took a short flight to Lukla where we met Kami and the rest of his team. From there we hiked to the base camp. Along the way we stayed in amazing teahouses. At the base camp, we would use our tent and sleeping bags for the first time.

It was early May. According to Kami, the "weather window" for the ascent to the summit is April through early June. Either side of this window is pre and post monsoon season. The weather is generally free of blizzards, rain and windstorms. Generally, but not always. April and May are also the busiest and most crowded months on the mountain.

The month in the base camp went quickly. Now we were ready for the difficult climb ahead.

There would be four camps on our way to the summit. We would spend the night at each one, adjusting to the higher altitude.

Our hike to Camp 1 took us through the dangerous Khumbu Icefalls. With the use of ladders and ropes we managed to traverse the shifting ice, reaching Camp 1 at 19,500 feet as the sun was setting behind the mountain range to the west.

Camps 2 and 3 were grueling hikes as well, through glacial valleys and ice walls, combined with our labored breathing, as the air grew thinner with each step.

Upon reaching Camp 3 at 23,500 feet, Kami broke out the oxygen tanks and those bulky face masks.

"You will need these until we return to Camp 2."

Dad and I were both happy to take them.

"Rest up," Kami said. "Tomorrow, we enter the "death zone.""

"What's that?" I asked, not sure I wanted to know.

"It's the altitude where there's not enough oxygen for humans to breathe. It's where our bodies will start to decay and die."

"So that's why it's called the death zone?"

"That, plus the fact that the majority of the more than 200 climbers who have died on their way to the summit, have died in the death zone."

"How long will we be in the death zone?" my dad asked.

"No more than 20 hours."

We reached Camp 4, the death zone camp, in the mid-afternoon. My heart was pounding from the climb. My legs were numb. It was brutally cold. Dad was exhausted too. We were at 26,000 feet.

"When do we leave for the summit?" I asked.

"At midnight."

Just before midnight, Kami opened the entrance to our tent.

"Ready?" He asked.

Yes, we were. Neither my dad nor I had slept much. Too excited for the last hike. For the summit.

It was a cold, cloudless night. The stars seemed so close, like you could reach out and grab them. We joined another group heading to the summit. In a straight line, the headlamps marching in a straight line, upwards. The only sounds, those of crunching snow and breathing. The "death zone" I thought with each step.

As the sun broke through the clouds, we could see the summit. Just ahead. Everyone was hurting now, but the excitement of the summit made it all worthwhile.

"Dad, can you see the summit?" I asked.

"Oh yes."

And then we were there, my dad and me. On the summit.

"Welcome to Sagarmatha," Kami said. "To the top of the world."

Sagarmatha, I thought, Nepali for Mount Everest. At 29,032 feet, the highest spot on the planet.

"Dad, can Kami take our picture?"

"Of course, he can Sean. Of course."

Kami was holding the camera. I was so excited. Here I was at the top of Mount Everest, with my dad.

Kami snapped a couple of photos, and then looking directly at me he said, "congratulations Sean, on being the youngest climber to reach the top of Mount Everest."

"Yes," my dad said, "that's an amazing accomplishment."

Suddenly Kami was not there.

"Look Sean, you're at the top. The very top."

Indeed, I was, at the top. At the top of my Tobbi Outdoor Kid's Climbing Dome. A steel frame reaching 82 inches above the grass. Not quite the death zone, I thought. The steel frame dome kit that my dad assembled and placed in the back yard. After all those attempts, I finally reached the top of the climbing dome.

"Quite an accomplishment for a three-year-old," my dad said. "Let me take your picture up there on the top."

"Sagarmatha," I replied.

"Saga what?" My dad asked.

"One of these days, you and I and Sagarmatha." I said. "One of these days."

Bahati and Milele Likizo

The sun was at its highest. The blazing, intense sun.

"How much farther?" I asked.

It seemed like we had been walking for days, perhaps we had. I had lost track of time, so I really didn't know.

"Not far. Not far now," was the reply.

He was carrying me. Actually, both were.

"Do we have any water left?" I was very thirsty. That damn hot sun. Why didn't we take more water with us? "Just a short flight," he said. Our pilot, Bahati, assured me that we had enough.

When I first met Bahati, I asked him.

"Your name?"

"Yes, boss?"

"What does it mean?"

"Bahati, is a Swahili name meaning lucky." Then he smiled and I saw the missing teeth.

Well, we would sure need much luck now. Having crashed in the middle of this God forsaken desert.

As he pressed the canteen to my burning lips, I asked him.

"You did file a flight plan? Didn't you?"

"Drink now, you must drink."

"But Bahati, you did file one? Right?"

Bahati never answered. He was looking at the sand covering his sandals. He didn't have to answer, I could see what he didn't want to tell me in his eyes.

"Time to move on," Milele said. He was the co-pilot. Milele Likizo, tall with shiny black skin and piercing eyes. Never smiled and didn't talk much. But he had such a kind reassuring presence about him. I liked him. Just an observer, I thought.

But they were both strong enough. Strong enough to carry me on this makeshift stretcher.

Both legs were broken. Why didn't the plane have seat belts, I asked? "Not needed," Bahati insisted. "We will be fine, boss, just fine."

We weren't expecting that sandstorm. "Hold on!" Milele shouted. Those were the first words he had said since we met at the airport.

The old airplane was struggling against the fierce winds. The smashing sound of sand hitting the airplane reminded me of those violent hailstorms in Colorado. Visibility was down to zero. We were tumbling through the middle of the storm. The two small engines were straining to keep us in the air. Soon they would give up.

Before we had met at the airport, everything was going so smoothly. The African vacation of your dreams, the brochure in the travel agent's office said. The cover picture of those wild gorillas looked so inviting. See them in their natural surroundings, the brochure said. And those pictures, smiling, satisfied tourists with their cameras and all giving the thumbs up. Jesus, why not, I thought.

I had just retired. Do something exciting to celebrate, my friends said. Something different. You deserve it.

I hadn't travelled much. Well, hardly at all. Once when I was a college student in San Diego, three of us drove down to Mexico to see a Jai Alai game. "Only 35 miles to Mexico," my fraternity brothers told me. "Cheap beer too."

That was my only trip outside of the United States.

"Hardly an international experience." the travel agent said.

"Indeed," I replied, but, of course, failing to mention the three girls we had met. Marie was the one I hooked up with.

"Okay, this trip sounds like the perfect retirement vacation," I said. "Let's book it."

"More water, boss. You need to stay hydrated."

What a strange word for Bahati to use, I thought. Hydrated. Where did he learn that one? I wanted to ask, but suddenly I didn't care.

The trip to Africa really began when we prepared for our landing at Kampala in Uganda. The plane descended from the south over Lake Victoria. The sky was full of small fluffy clouds.

Lake Victoria, historic Lake Victoria, I thought. The second largest freshwater lake in the world. The starting point for the great Nile River. For five minutes all I could see was the smooth waters below us. Then off to the right bordering Kenya, Mount Elgon, with a dusting of snow on its top.

The pilot said we were cleared to land at Entebbe airport. The approach reminded me of my many flights into San Francisco. Water, water, water and then just before what looked like a disastrous water landing, the runway.

It was hard to breathe. Probably punctured a lung in the crash, I thought. Jesus, why did the guide talk me into taking this small plane? I should have waited for a commercial flight.

"The next one is tomorrow," he said. "You must leave now."

Inside the Entebbe Airport it was hard to breathe. 104 degrees, the British Air pilot said after we landed. The airport was full of passengers, some leaving, some arriving. No one stopped to read the plaque. I did.

Here on July 4, 1976, 33 Israeli commandos rescued 103 hostages held by Palestinian hijackers aboard Air France flight 139.

The plaque was mounted on the wall, just to the right of the entrance to McDonald's. It just didn't feel right.

I didn't feel right now. My breathing was becoming harder. I felt like I was gasping for air. "Be still, you will be okay," Milele said to me as he adjusted the hat on my head to block out the sun. "It won't be long now."

Long now? How did he know that? How did he know where we were? All I could see was sand. To my left, to my right, in front of me all the way to the horizon. Sand. Christ, nothing but sand.

The gorilla looked at me. I looked back. What was she thinking, I wondered. Another strange visitor?

She was shielding her young. I didn't see them.

"If they are with their young, don't get too close and don't make any threatening moves." I remembered that from our morning orientation. But I wasn't worried. I didn't see her young.

I raised my camera up to my face. The long telephoto lens must have scared her. Did she think it was a gun?

Before I knew it, she charged. Slapping at my Nikon, she then was pounding on me. The last thing I remembered were her teeth. Those sharp teeth, and the taste of my blood in my mouth. Then I passed out.

Kampala was an interesting city. A short taxi ride from the airport. I was first greeted by a chaotic jam of people and buses. And noise and smells. Africa has a smell all its own. An aroma representing a multitude of cultures, of past conquerors, of hundreds of years of history, and dust. Yes, that dust that blew in from the Sahara Desert. Dust was everywhere, covering everything, everyone.

The short flight to the Bwindi Impenetrable Forest was just over an hour. That's when I met Bahati.

"Hi boss," that's how he greeted me. His twin engine airplane was fully fueled and ready to go.

"How old is this?" I asked, "this plane?"

"Don't worry, boss, it'll get us there just fine."

And it did. A wonderful flight to the southwest. Below were forests of tall hardwoods and rising bamboo. Thick ground cover, too. No wonder this place is called A Place of Darkness by locals.

We landed at a small airport. Hardly an airport. No terminal. Just a dirt runway for landing and departing planes.

Our guide met us. "Welcome to the land of the famous Uganda mountain gorilla."

There was a lot more chatter about the gorillas, numbers, size, but I was paying little attention. Looking back at the airplane, I saw Bahati. He was talking to his co-pilot, Milele. They were both laughing.

I couldn't laugh if I wanted to. The pain in my chest was too intense. And this was really no laughing matter. Being transported on this stretcher to who knows where. Broken legs, punctured lung and who knows what else.

"How you doing, boss?" It was Bahati.

"Why do you call me boss?"

"Respect, boss. We need to show respect."

He looked towards Milele, "right, Milele?"

Milele just nodded in agreement. Yes, a man of few words, I thought.

I tried to remember the actual crash. It seemed like a dream. The plane nosed down. The engines had stalled. The ground rushed up. Then the sound of crunching metal. That awful sound.

They carried me to the waiting plane. I didn't feel the pain anymore. I wanted to go back into the brush to see more gorillas.

"No, boss. Not today."

There were only the three of us in the plane.

"Where are the others?" I asked.

"What others?"

"The others, who were on the plane with us, back at the gorilla sighting?"

"No need for them to be with us, boss."

Then I closed my eyes. I was sleeping.

"Hold on." It was Milele.

We were in that sandstorm; the plane was going straight down.

I wasn't concerned, I wasn't even frightened. It all seemed so surreal to me.

They set me down. I was on a cool patch of grass. There was a small pond in front of me. Palm trees too. I got up from the stretcher. The dust storm was over. The sky was blue. The air was cool.

Strange, I thought, I feel no pain. My legs are fine.

I started walking towards the small pond. The water was so calm, so inviting. Then I noticed. My reflection. I couldn't see my reflection in the pool. I reached for the water, but I couldn't feel it.

I turned. There they were. Bahati and Milele. Both were smiling.

"Time to rest, boss." Bahati said.

"Yes, time to rest. Your journey is over." Strange, that's the most words Milele has said since I met him.

I recall asking Bahati, about his name. "Such a strange name. Milele Likizo. What does it mean?"

"Eternal Sleep." he replied.

I turned and looked back at the pond and the palm trees. It was starting to make sense. The fog was lifting from my mind.

"A mirage?" I asked.

"Yes, a mirage, but your mirage."

Suddenly I understood all of it. I walked in their direction. I reached out to shake their hands. I felt nothing.

"Thank you," I said. "Thank you for bringing me here. The journey must have been difficult."

"No boss, it wasn't difficult."

I walked back to the pond and sat down. I still couldn't see my reflection.

I turned to ask them why?

They were gone, both of them and the stretcher were gone

The Gloves

. . . .

The early morning call to prayers had just ended.
Shopkeepers we're opening their doors. Many were sweeping the walkway
in front of their shops.

They were getting ready for the rush of tourists.

We were in Istanbul.

Istanbul. The city that sits physically and culturally in both Europe
and Asia.

Originally a Greek colony 600 years before Christ, conquered and
rebuilt by the Romans, then by the Turks, when it became the capitol of
the Ottoman Empire.

Today, as one of the political, cultural, religious, and economic centers
of the region, Istanbul is one of the 'must visit' places for tourists from all
over the world.

We were tourists.

It would be our last day in Istanbul.

Our ship was leaving in the afternoon.

"Be on board by 3, or we'll leave you here," was the announcement
from the ship's social chair. She said it in a half joking voice, but for some
it might have been an interesting option.

"Jesus, I wouldn't mind that," I said turning to my wife who had
stationed herself in front of a shop we saw yesterday. It wasn't open yet.

"And then how would we get home? She replied. "Have you thought
that one through?"

We were in the Grand Bazaar, or Kapali Carsi, a city landmark, located
in the Fatih district, in one of the oldest covered markets in the world.

I had thought about it, many times, I started to tell her. But as in the
past, I didn't. Why bother.

"And just who will teach your classes?" She continued. "Have you thought about that?"

Oh yes, that, my classes.

I wanted to tell her that after teaching those classes for 35 years, the thrill was gone. Now I felt like a tape recorder on playback. But of course, I didn't tell her.

"Think of your students. Those that enjoy and gain from your lectures. What about them?"

Yeah, those students.

I wanted to tell her that I couldn't imagine them enjoying my classes. After all, they seemed to be spending more and more time in class on their cell phones. Probably TikTok, or something else I didn't understand.

At first, I asked them to put away their phones, but then I decided, what the hell, if they don't care, why should I.

The tape recorder cycled to playback.

Maybe it's time to press the erase button, I thought. Yes, press that button and stay here, enjoying hot tea in small, tulip-shaped glasses, and baklava, the dessert whose origins date back to the time of the Byzantine Empire. Baklava, with its mouthwatering layers of dough caressing pistachios, almonds, and hazelnuts.

Yes, I wanted to tell her, but of course I didn't.

For days we had explored Istanbul, fell in love with it actually.

The people, the sounds, the food, the smells, the …. Well, everything. It was all here.

"Be on board by 3, or we'll leave you here," kept rolling around in my head. And when I closed my eyes I could see it, the Regent Seven Seas Explorer pulling away from the dock, and me waving goodbye. Waving goodbye as I stood on the pier watching the huge ship ploughing west through the Mediterranean.

"If only," I muttered to myself, "if only."

But of course, it was just a dream. And like those dreams before, I would simply be an observer, unwilling to take that leap, and, of course, I would be onboard by 3, probably with a lot of time to spare.

Then back home, I would once again press the replay button on the tape recorder.

"Disgusting," I muttered as I kicked the cobblestone walkway.

Just then I heard the sound of the shop door unlocking.

Looking up, I saw him behind the glass door.

Olive tone skin, a thick beard, wide, almond shaped eyes, and a heavy brow which concealed much of his upper eyelid.

His short sleeve shirt exposed his abundance of body hair, so common among Turkish men. I tried to imagine his hairy chest and back as the shop door swung open.

"Good morning,' he said, in a low, but hospitable tone.

The Turkish way, I thought to myself. Even strangers, like us, are made to feel welcome.

"Good morning," my wife and I said at the same time in return.

"Welcome to my humble shop," was the reply.

After some small talk, as was the custom here in Turkey, the conversation moved to the issue at hand.

"Please, let me help you find something!"

And there it was, he needed to pay close attention to us, his first customers of the day. Because, what we did, or didn't do, would determine the success of his day. Sell to us, and it would be a good day. If we leave empty handed, he was sure to have a bad day.

"Turkey is a land full of many traditions and superstitions." It was the inter port lecturer speaking to the shipboard community the night before we docked in Istanbul.

She continued. "Their superstitions are believed to be based on myths, legends, fables, traditions, and stories."

When asked for some examples, she smiled and started listing them.

"If you walk on the right-hand side of a boardwalk, you'll find a wallet full of money; you should wash your face every morning because at night evil walks on your face; if the bottom of your feet itch, you'll be taking a trip."

As it turned out my favorite was "If you say one thing 40 times, it will happen." I vowed to try that when we returned home.

So, knowing that the shopkeeper was desperate to sell me something, anything, I decided to put that superstition to good use.

It was then that I noticed the box, on a table in a dark corner of the shop.

In the box were gloves, loose gloves, dozens and dozens of them, all in rich vibrant colors.

The shopkeeper noted my interest, and began his pitch,

"These gloves are hand-knitted by semi-nomadic tribes who live in Western Turkey. The wool and natural dyes used in their weaving are locally produced. The designs are a representation of flowers. No two gloves are alike, they are one of a kind."

A pair of these would be perfect, I thought, a souvenir of Turkey. Yes, I would purchase a pair of gloves.

"How much," I asked, "for a pair of these gloves."

"These," he said as he pointed at the overflowing box of wool gloves. "These are very special."

"And they certainly are beautiful," I replied, hoping my compliment might result in a lower price.

"50 dollars for a pair," was his answer.

Jesus, I thought, that's ridiculous. No way am I paying 50 dollars for a pair of gloves.

"Too much," I said.

Then I turned to my wife and said, "let's go, I want to look in a few more shops."

"No, no. Wait," he said as he blocked my exit.

And that's when I knew I had him. Yes, clever me, I thought. I knew he had to make this sale, this sale to me, his first customer of the day, or … or he might as well closed shop and go home for the day.

As he looked at me, I could see the desperation in his eyes. He had to make this sale. It was not an option.

"How much?" He said, "how much are you willing to pay?"

Without saying a word, I rested my hand over my heart, a Turkish gesture indicating I was declining his offer.

As I moved to my left, he moved too, again blocking my way.

This is fun, I thought, like a game, but with a predetermined outcome.

His hand rested on my shoulder, and in a cracking voice, he pleaded.

"Please, what would you like to pay?"

"20 dollars, no more."

And that was it. Game, set, match. The sale was made.

As I pulled a twenty-dollar bill from my wallet, my wife approached.

"We need to hurry," she said. "I told my mom we'd be back on the ship for lunch."

"Ship?" the shop owner asked, "you're from the ship?"

"Yes," she answered, "and we need to get back as we depart at 3."

"Three," you leave at three."

"That's right, we sail at three."

I thought I saw him smile, well not so much a smile, but more of a look of intrigue.

"Then let me wrap these up for you so that you can make it back to your ship on time."

"Yes, please," I said, as I handed him $20.

After a few minutes, he returned with a small box. It was tightly wrapped.

"Here you are, a pair of very special gloves. I hope you enjoy them."

Strange I thought, he doesn't seem upset. Not one bit. Perhaps it's his way of acknowledging defeat.

The loud blast from the horns of the Regent Seven Seas Explorer signaled we were on our way. Leaving Turkey. Next stop New York City, and back to my tape recorder.

Well at least I'll have an interesting story to tell my class. My class in international business. Yeah, how to do business in the Grand Bazaar. Just be the first customer.

I started to chuckle, then my laughter grew more robust.

"What are you laughing about?" It was my wife again.

"Oh, just thinking how I outsmarted that shop keeper."

"Outsmarted? What do you mean?"

As I explained what I had done, I slowly unwrapped the box. I wanted to show her my prize. Excited actually.

As the box opened, the colorful pair of hand-woven cotton gloves fell to the cabin floor.

"I'll get them," she said, as she reached down.

"What do you think," I said, "what do you think of how I strategized that purchase. Clever, huh?"

Suddenly, my wife broke out in laughter. She was laughing so hard that she tumbled back onto the couch.

"What, what's so funny," I said, "what the hell is so funny?"

She slowly raised the gloves, one in each hand. She was laughing, struggling to get out the words.

"Well, to begin with, he did sell you a pair of lovely gloves."

"Yeah, that's what I told you. I got the best of him."

She rose and started walking towards me, holding a glove in each hand.

"Best of him? No, I don't think so."

"Huh?"

"Here, look, you are now the proud owner of two colorful, hand-woven cotton gloves, but …"

"But … but what?"

"Both gloves are for your right hand."

A Floppy Hat, a Plastic Fork and Susan

"I'm here for my 2 o'clock appointment."

She looked up at me, tilting her head ever so forward so she didn't have to remove her reading glasses to see me.

"Which Doctor?"

"Doctor Banks, Mary Banks."

"She's running a little late today. Perhaps 10, 15 minutes."

"That's okay."

"Special day, today. Everyone is running late."

I didn't ask her what was so special about the day as I didn't much care.

"You can wait over there, and someone will call you." She was pointing at a row of chairs against the wall. Others were waiting too. Some looked annoyed. Others looked bored. A few looked anxious. I would be in the third category. Anxious.

Annual wellness physical. The doctor always seemed to find something that needed further investigation. "Suspicious," was the word she used. It made me shudder.

Slumping in the chair, I closed my eyes. Perhaps if I block out everything around me, it won't be so stressful. But of course, I couldn't block out the sound. The coughing person next to me and the two kids running back and forth.

The door leading to the examination rooms opened. It was a nurse, holding a clip board, looking at the day's list of patients.

She hesitated, shook her head, and mumbled.

"Mister… Chile-e-ann… Chese-e-on."

"That's Kill-ee-yan." He rose from his chair and walked slowly towards the open door. Balance problems, I thought, as he hesitated every few steps to steady himself.

"Sorry." She said, clearly embarrassed by her pronunciation failure.

"Not even close," the cougher next to me whispered.

It was 15 minutes after my scheduled time. I squirmed in my chair. My anxiety was overtaking me. Or perhaps it was a panic attack.

"Special day, huh." I spoke up without considering anyone in the waiting room.

"What?" It was the guy next to me. "What's that." He leaned towards me, cupping his ear. "Hearing aids, batteries running low."

"It's a special day today. At least that's what I was told." I raised my voice. Everyone around me looked in my direction.

"Special how?"

"Damned if I know. Perhaps they're having a party back there." There were a few chuckles in the room. Oh well, I thought, at least I lightened up the mood in here.

The door opened again. Someone different appeared.

"Mister Reed?"

"That's me,"

I rose from my chair. The shooting pain returned. Hip pain, spreading down to the front of my right thigh to my knee.

"Wear-and-tear of the hip joint," Doctor Banks told me last year. "Perhaps from too much skiing. I can prescribe medication, physical therapy, or suggest an ergonomic chair."

I selected none of her suggestions and continued to ski. And now the pain was almost constant.

"How are you today, Mister Reed."

"I'm good."

Not sure why I said I'm good. Now not only hip pain, but worsening incontinence and heart burn. Jesus, I was falling apart.

I was ushered into a small examination room.

"Doctor Banks is running late. Please make yourself comfortable." The door closed and I was alone.

Nothing about this room could make me comfortable. Nothing. Ugly light grey walls. A wall diagnostic set, with instruments for capturing blood pressure, pulse rate, temperature and probing the nose and ears.

A storage counter with jars of bandages and sterile equipment. A sink. A computer workstation. Boxes of blue latex gloves. And taking center stage, the adjustable examination table.

I lowered myself on to the examination table. The paper covering crunched as I did.

I glanced at my watch. 2:41. Jesus, it must be a hell of a party I thought.

If I were home at this hour, I'd probably consider an afternoon nap. Yes, that was one of the positives of retirement, not that there were many. Certainly not that feeling of no longer relevant, important, young. Young. My body reminded me every day that I was no longer that.

I closed my eyes.

I had been sleeping. A few minutes, perhaps longer. I couldn't tell. But now I felt someone's presence.

Opening my eyes, I was confronted by two small inquisitive eyes. I blinked and she came into focus.

I would guess she was five or six. Standing a foot or so away from me. She tilted her head and continued to stare directly at me.

"You were snoring," she said.

"What?"

"A funny snore, like a horse."

I sat up. "Really. What does that sound like?"

"Don't you know what a horse sounds like?"

"Can't say as I do."

"Well, you were snorting. Not very loud, but definitely snorting."

She moved back a couple of steps. Probably disappointed I wasn't a horse, I thought.

"What are you doing in this room?" I asked. But she didn't answer. Instead, she asked me a question.

"Are you sick?"

"Sick?"

"Yes, is that why you're here?" She pointed around the room.

"Well, I'm not sure."

"Well, if you are, don't worry. They will make you better."

"Oh."

"Yes, they are very good here."

"That's nice to know."

Her smile was almost contagious. She stood there and I realized she was wearing a big floppy hat and was holding a plastic fork.

"Party?" I asked. "Is there a party?"

"Oh yes. With cake too." She held out her fork. "Would you like some? Cake? Can I get you some?"

"I better not. I think the doctor wants to do some tests." Damn cholesterol, I thought, and then I realized how hungry I was. Cake sounded so inviting.

"Tests. What tests? Did you have to study for them?"

I laughed. "No not those kinds of tests."

Just then Doctor Banks walked in.

"Susan, what are you doing here? Are you bothering Mister Reed?"

"No mom, he was snoring."

"Yes, she wanted to check on me. To see if I was a horse."

Susan started laughing and then she started coughing. She moved to one of the chairs and sat down. I could tell she was tired.

I looked at my watch. Jesus, it was 3:45. I had been in this room for over an hour. I suddenly got angry. My afternoon was wasted. How could the clinic be so unconcerned about my time?

"Doctor Banks, I can't believe you let me sit in this room for over an hour. It's like my time didn't matter."

"I'm sorry, Mister Reed, we were having a …"

"Party. Yes, I know. Susan told me. With cake and big hats."

"Well, not just a party."

"Yes, but you have patients. We're waiting for you."

"I know that Mister Reed."

"Then why the delay? Aren't your patients important?"

"Oh yes, they are, believe me."

She motioned to Susan who came to her side. I looked at the little girl, who looked back at me. She looked like she wanted to cry. I must have frightened her.

Slowly Doctor Reed removed Susan's big floppy hat.

How did I not realize? Susan's head was shaved, and the big, long scar was still bright red.

"Chemotherapy, Mister Reed. Susan finished her chemotherapy treatments today. We were celebrating the end of that."

I didn't know what to say. I couldn't find the right words. I only knew that the pain in my hip didn't seem to matter anymore. Then suddenly I knew what I wanted to say. I got up off the examination table and bent down in front of her.

"Susan, if your offer for cake still stands, I'd love to celebrate with you."

Even Monkeys Fall from Trees

(Saru Mo Ki Kara Ochiru)

It had been a scoreless game and time was about to expire, when it happened, when he scored what he thought was the winning goal.

But it wasn't and the game was over.

Someone was trying to console him, but he wasn't listening.

But then he heard something that caught his attention.

"The Japanese have a saying for it."

"Huh?" he said brushing away the tears.

"Even monkeys fall from trees."

At first, he didn't know what to say, or even how to relate to what he had just heard, but finally he managed to reply.

"But I'm not a monkey."

"Of course not, son. It's just a saying."

"A saying?"

He was confused, but then he was only 7. Confusion defined him sometimes, like now.

But he had scored a goal. A perfect kick.

The ball just made it past the outstretched arms of the goalie.

But of course, the goalie wasn't expecting him to kick it.

It was his very first goal.

Finally, he had scored a goal.

He would be the hero today, he thought as he watched as the ball cross the goal line and came to rest against the back netting.

Hero, I'm the hero, he thought.

He waited for the celebration, for his teammates' congratulations, the high fives.

He waited.

But, instead the once loud, cheering crowd abruptly fell into silence.

A monkey had fallen out of the tree.

He would learn later, much later, that it's called brachiation, or arboreal locomotion whereby monkeys are able to swing from tree limb to tree limb using only their arms.

In simpler terms, it's called arm swinging.

But occasionally, a monkey misses, and falls, falls out of the tree.

Unfortunately, his monkey had fallen from its tree when the soccer ball he had just kicked made its way into the wrong goal.

"What were you thinking?" was all his teammates could say as they stood there, looks of disbelief on their faces. Some were crying.

"Great kick. Thanks," rang out from the opposition players. They were laughing. Some were rolling on the grass surface in front of the net, and they were laughing too.

Laughing at the monkey who had fallen out of the tree.

Time passed, and even as he became an adult, he still hadn't told anyone about that day on the soccer field.

At least not until the day when his son was taking the driving test for his first driver's license.

"I think I'm ready, dad, at least I think so," his son said on their way to the motor vehicle department.

"You'll do fine, son, you'll see," was his reply.

At the time, he wasn't thinking of monkeys, just his son and the driving test.

But swinging monkeys have a way of showing up when you least expect them. Like on a soccer field or during a driver's test.

As the car pulled away from the parking area, he gave his son the thumbs up.

As the car turned the corner and headed out onto the busy street, he heard it.

It was faint, but it was definitely that sound.

Ook-ook … Eeek-aak-eek

Twenty minutes later they returned. His son and the Department of Motor Vehicles examiner. Neither looked happy.

"How did it go," he asked.

"Don't ask?" his son replied, as the examiner handed him an official looking sheet of paper.

At the very top of the page, he could see it.

FAILED

And under that one word, a list of miscues.

He put his arms around his son to try to comfort him, but it wasn't helping. The sobs grew louder.

"Hey, it'll be okay. You'll pass the next time."

"I can't believe it. Why did this happen to me," his son replied through the choking sobs, "I'll never get my license."

Suddenly it all made sense, what happened at that soccer game, and, more importantly, what his dad had told him and the important advice he had given him.

He knew what he had to say and why, and so he did.

"The Japanese have a saying for it."

"Huh?"

"The Japanese. And it goes something like this... even monkeys fall from trees."

"But I'm not a monkey."

"Of course not, son. It's just a saying."

"A saying?"

"Yes, and monkeys do fall out of trees. Not that often, but they do. Sometimes they miss that branch, and just fall to the ground. But... they don't stay there. No son, they get back up in the trees, and start swinging again, from one branch to the next.

And then he told his son, for the first time, he told him about when he scored a goal in his own net. He told him that and also how he scored the winning goal in their next game. How he got back up in the trees and started swinging again.

Three weeks later his son passed his driver's test.

To celebrate, they decided to go out for ice cream, a banana split actually. After all, they were both back swinging in those trees.

The Last Performance

. . . .

The large red block letters on the marquee outside the old performing arts center caught my attention.

ONE NIGHT ONLY
THE MASTER MAGICIAN
CLAUDE DUBOIS

The large poster behind the glass enclosure offered slightly more information.

Claude Dubois, the last performance of his long career. The master of disappearing acts.

I was an American in Paris. I had been here three months working on a book on French 18th century architecture. Tonight, was my last night in the 'City of Lights' before heading home to Boston.

I had grown weary of Parisian nightclubs, and I certainly didn't want to climb to the top of the Eiffel Tower again, so I thought, why not. After all it's my last night in Paris and Claude's last performance. Why not spend the time together.

The woman in the enclosed ticket booth appeared to be asleep.

"Pardon."

Her head was resting on the side of the booth. Eyes were tightly closed.

"Excusez moi." I said, as I gently tapped on the glass.

She shook her head and rubbed her eyes. She looked annoyed that I had disturbed her.

"Sorry… pardon." I tried to sound extra sincere in my apology.

But she wasn't having any of it.

"What do you want?"

My God, perfect English, I thought. She could tell I was an American.

"I'd like one ticket for tonight's performance, please."

"Où veux-tu t'asseoir?"

"Huh."

"The cheap seats or expensive seats? Where do you want to sit?" She was almost shouting.

"I'll splurge. One ticket in the expensive seating."

I was laughing hoping to break the tension. Again, she wasn't buying into my attempt. She frowned as she handed me my ticket. Yes, she was not happy. Not one bit.

"Seventy-five euros."

"What?"

"The expensive seat. Seventy-five euros."

Oh, what the hell. It's my last night. But more importantly, I didn't want to ask her about the cheap seats. Best to leave that discussion alone, I thought, as I pulled out a hundred euro note.

The lobby was empty except for two ladies behind the refreshment counter. They were busy talking to one another. My French was only good enough to understand that they were complaining about something. Their husbands, I think. Or perhaps their aching backs.

The smell of fresh popcorn was tempting, only two euros according to the large menu hanging above the glass counter, but I didn't want to interrupt their conversation.

Passing the refreshment counter without stopping I made my way to the entrance to the theater. A young lady was waiting for me to show my ticket.

"Follow me, please."

More English, I thought. Is it that obvious?

The theater was dark, except for the string of lights on the path leading down to the stage.

"Please watch your step."

Looking down at the floor I could see why. The rug was worn and torn in places.

"Your seat is here in the first row, in the middle."

Her small flashlight lit the way to my seat. I sat down and settled into a deep crevasse. A hidden spring poked at my backside and dust rose into the air. A musty smell settled over the entire theater.

Expensive seat, Jesus, I wonder what the cheap seats are like.

"Enjoy the show. You know it's his last."

"Yes, I understand."

"And no one knows why. Why he wants to end it."

Just then Claude Dubois walked slowly onto the stage. A single bright spotlight illuminated his way. He was short and thin, with blond hair down to his shoulders. His rumpled tan suit and white sneakers seemed more appropriate for a Sunday outing to a Parisian bistro. Yes, I could definitely see him at a crowded café terrace on the Rue Saint Michel.

Claude raised his hand to acknowledge his audience, but I only heard silence in return.

The theater lights came on and I saw why. The theater was empty, except for me and the young girl who had escorted me to my front row seat. She started clapping and I felt compelled to joined her.

Claude looked at me and smiled.

"American?" he asked.

"Yes."

"Then I'll do the show in English."

I didn't know what to say, so I simply nodded "thank you" back.

The next hour consisted of nonstop magic tricks. Card tricks, coin tricks, rabbits out of hats, exploding flowers, disappearing pigeons, levitating chairs.

Finally, Claude walked to the edge of the stage directly in front of me.

"For my final act, the last act I will perform tonight, and the last act of my career, I will need someone from the audience."

He started laughing.

"Perhaps the young man from America would be so kind."

"I'm sure he would, dad." It was the young girl again.

Dad? Now my mind was spinning. What's going on here? A father and daughter act.

"Come on up." Claude was motioning me to join him on stage.

Sure, why not, I thought.

The wooden floor on the old stage creaked as I walked across it. Some of the boards were warped and a few were missing. How many performers and performances had this stage been witness to, I thought?

"And, you are?" His hand was stretched out as I approached.

"Harold, from Boston."

We shook hands. His grip was so firm, yet welcoming.

"Nice to meet you, Harold from Boston."

He let out a soft chuckle and a big smile followed. I sensed a feeling of relief had settled over him. Perhaps it was the realization that he would soon be finished with his magic tricks. For good.

"I'd like you to meet my assistant, Dorothy." The young girl had joined us on the stage.

"Your daughter?"

"Oh no. Just part of the act."

Somehow, I didn't believe him.

Suddenly, a large enclosed cage appeared above us. A wooden box attached to a thick metal cable was descending from the rafters above the stage. Dorothy was off to the side of the stage controlling its speed. She stopped it one foot from the stage floor.

Claude turned to the empty theater.

"Ladies and gentlemen, for my last trick, my very last trick, I will for the very first time perform the disappearance by fire act. I ask for complete silence so that I can focus all my attention on this difficult and dangerous trick."

Moving towards the cage, Claude opened the one side door. The cage was empty except for two chairs. He turned, waved goodbye, entered the cage, and sat down. He then asked me if I'd like to join him.

"I think I'll pass." I replied.

Dorothy, who had been watching, suddenly rushed over to the cage. She was crying.

"Dad, dad, you promised."

Claude looked at her. Then I saw the tears in his eyes. He held out his hand and pulled her up and into the cage. As she sat down the door slammed shut.

The cage slowly rose. Stopping about ten feet above the stage, it started spinning. Slowly at first and then at a dizzying speed.

The spinning seemed to go on forever. I was feeling nauseous just looking at it. But then it started to slow.

As the spinning slowed, a small flame appeared at the bottom of the cage. Soon the entire cage was consumed by fire. The sound of crackling and popping wood echoed against the back wall of the theater.

At first a few small smoldering pieces of wood fell to the stage floor, but then the four sides of the cage came loose and crashed to the stage. All that remained of the hanging cage was its charred floor attached to the metal cable, and the two chairs. Both empty. Claude and Dorothy were gone. They had disappeared into thin air.

Then I heard the sound of applause. The whole theater erupted with applause and cheering.

I turned and looked. In the subdued light I saw nothing but empty seats. Yet the sound of applause continued and grew louder.

The stage floor started sagging. I made my way off it just before it collapsed.

Running through the dark theater, I tripped on the torn carpet. I felt a hand helping me up, but when I turned to look, no one was there.

Out in the lobby now. The refreshment stand was empty. The large menu was resting on top of the shattered glass counter. The two ladies were nowhere in sight.

Out the front to the ticket booth. It too was empty. A faded sign hung from the inside.

CLOSED

The ticket booth was closed. It was boarded up.

On the outside, I looked up at the marquee. Most of the letters had fallen off, but I could make out the announcement.

KEEP OUT
CLOSED FOR DEMOLITION

John Wayne

We were standing on the porch. It was dark. Not completely. There was a soft light coming from the front room.

Was it dark enough, I wondered?

The movie ended at 8. Standing there I suddenly couldn't remember the movie title. But it was a western. A John Wayne western. Why couldn't I remember the title? Boy was I a nervous wreck.

But John Wayne. He'd be fine. He'd be cool.

I was 12. I think she was 13. What was her name? Sue? Yes, that was it. Sue. At least I could remember her name.

My heart was racing. Is that supposed to happen?

"Thanks." It was Sue.

"What?"

"For dinner and the movie."

Oh yes, the pizza.

Why did I order the garlic cheese pizza? I casually lifted my hand to my mouth, and slowly exhaled. Is that garlic I smell? Why didn't I suggest just a plain cheese pizza? How stupid of me.

John Wayne would have ordered plain cheese. Definitely.

"So, you're moving to California after the school year?" Her voice brought me back to the moment.

"Yes, my dad took a job in California." I couldn't recall the name of the city. San something.

"Are you excited?"

"Oh sure, the beach and all that stuff. It should be fun."

Who was I kidding? Moving from upstate New York to California. I really had no idea what to expect. My cousin in the city thought I would see Indians.

"Are you flying?"

"Huh?"

"To California, are you flying?"

This is not going well I thought. I should be paying more attention to what Sue is saying. Sue? Right? Or was it, Lou? My God, my heart was really racing now, and suddenly I felt a trickle of sweat easing down the inside of my shirt.

"No, we're driving."

"That should be exciting. All the things you'll see along the way."

"Well, hopefully, not Indians."

"Huh?" Now it was her turn to be confused

"My stupid cousin thinks I'll see Indians. Wild west Indians."

We both laughed. I thought I felt her hand against mine. But it was so fleeting. So soft. Perhaps just a moth headed to the light from the window. Yes, that must have been it. A moth.

The light in the front room went off. Now it was really dark.

Might this be a good time, I wondered?

I'm sure John Wayne would know. He'd know.

When my friends heard I was going on a date, they insisted that I should kiss her at the end of the evening. A pizza and a movie. Yes, yes, you should kiss her.

Of course, they didn't know about the garlic cheese pizza.

"What are you doing this summer?" I was struggling to find things to say.

"Probably working at my parent's restaurant."

"Yes, of course, that makes sense. Oh. Please thank your dad for that pizza."

My god, how stupid am I? I'm sure she didn't want the garlic cheese pizza. Why did I order it? Why didn't her dad suggest something else? Probably thinking of a deterrent. Yes, a deterrent, one garlic cheese pizza, that's what he was thinking.

"Did you like the movie?" Now she was changing the subject.

"Very much so."

"What was your favorite part?"

Shit, she's cornered me now.

"I really liked John Wayne." Was that the best I could do? I was really sweating now. My shirt was soaked. Thank goodness it was dark.

Just then the light in the front room went back on.

"Oh no, not now," I mumbled.

In the soft light I could see her face. She was confused.

"Is something wrong?" she asked.

Wrong? My God, everything's wrong, I thought. I'm really screwing this up.

"No, nothing's wrong."

"Well, it's getting late. I probably should go inside."

Damn it. It's the garlic. Or perhaps the sweat. I was doomed from the start. So much for my first kiss. Certainly, my mother's kiss doesn't count, and that was not on my mouth. Oh God, my mouth. What do I do with my mouth? Closed, open, wet my lips?

John Wayne would know. If only he was here.

Oh hell, I wouldn't find out tonight. No kiss tonight.

But then, she moved closer. What was happening?

She was really close now. Her eyes were closed. Was that the signal? Was she signaling me?

Okay, close your eyes and move in. Lips? I think I'll open them slightly. Lick them slightly.

Good God, I could smell the garlic. But, it was coming from both of us. So much for her dad's deterrent strategy.

Thinking of John Wayne, I tilted my head slightly and made my move.

Then it happened. At least I thought it did. Wait. What was that in my mouth? She pulled back quickly. Then I saw it. There was saliva all over her nose. I had kissed her nose. Her nose was in my mouth. Damn, her nose. I kissed her nose.

She turned and opened the front door. There was complete silence. No parting words. What could be said?

We left next week for California. That evening was the last time I spoke with Sue. Or was it, Lou? I guess, it really didn't matter.

And for sure, John Wayne wouldn't care. He'd be cool.

Hold the Vegetables

When Josh told the waitress that all he wanted was a hamburger, no bun, and definitely no lettuce or tomato and to hold the fries, Lily knew something was not quite right.

"Really, that's all? What's with that?" she asked.

But Josh was in his own world and all he heard were sounds.

"Excuse me," he said looking up.

"All you want is a plate with a patty of meat on it? Nothing else?"

"I guess."

"What do you mean you guess? I've seen you eat two large orders of French fries in one sitting."

"I know, but ... I'm ...."

"What? On another one of your stupid diets?"

"No."

"Jesus, Josh, sometimes you're so weird."

"Sorry Lily. I'm just not in the mood."

"Not in the mood for French fries?"

"No, not in the mood to talk about it."

"You gotta be kidding. The guy who can't stop talking, doesn't want to talk about it."

"No, I don't."

Lily reached across the table and grabbed Josh by his wrist. He tried to pull away, but she wouldn't let go.

"Come on, Josh, talk to me. What's going on?"

Josh just shook his head.

It was then that she noticed. It wasn't that obvious, but she noticed. She was surprised because this was so unlike him. Josh, her big brother. Josh, who was always so strong around her. Strong and so self-assured.

Few emotions too. Like a giant rock, she would tell her high school friends. Her big brother, Josh.

No, Lily had never seen this before, at least never from Josh. Never expected too either. But now …

One small, almost undetectable, tear was slowly working its way down Josh's cheek.

As it did, Lily let Josh's hand slip from her grip.

With his now free hand, Josh wiped the single tear away.

But he didn't look embarrassed, Lily thought. Strange, more like he was sad. Like her big brother was sad.

Lily's mind wandered, away from her brother's meandering tear, to thoughts about the past.

How long had it been? How long since they had seen one another, Lily asked herself. How long since she had lunch with her big brother?

Then, like a fast-paced movie, the memories came rushing back.

Josh enrolling in their state college with botany as his chosen major.

"Plants? You want to study plants?" his dad asked him when Josh announced his planned field of study. "Why the hell would anyone study plants?"

Of course, their dad was a contractor. Mostly painting houses.

Dad would tell Josh that the only plant he cared about was the Sherwin Williams paint factory on Hollins Ferry Road in South Baltimore. That and the occasional green peas mom would serve up at dinner time.

"Plants. You must be crazy," his dad would add.

But Josh was unmoved by his dad's criticism and instead went on to get a Ph.D. in botany, and then accepted a research position with the prestigious Plant Science and Agronomy Department at the University of Western Australia.

And now 10 years later, Josh was in New York City having lunch with his sister. Little Lil, as he used to call her.

My God, Lily thought it seems so long ago since dad was asking Josh how he expected to make any money looking at plants. So long ago, since he told Josh,

"Well, if you run short of cash, at least you can eat the plants."

Dad was like that, almost all the time, whenever Josh visited.

Criticizing, joking, but all of it was just belittling Josh's chosen career, the study of plants.

No wonder, this was the first time Josh had come home since he moved to Australia.

Sensing Josh's discomfort, Lily decided to change the subject. To lighten it up. After all, they had not seen one another since Josh boarded his flight to Australia ten years ago. Yes, best to lighten up, she thought.

"So do you like Australia?" she asked.

"It's okay," was all Josh offered as he shrugged his shoulders.

"And your work? How's that?"

"It's fine?"

This is going nowhere, Lily thought to herself, but before she could ask another question, lunch arrived.

One small, overcooked meat patty for Josh and a big Caesar salad for her.

"Is that all you want, Josh?"

Lily tried to use her most sympathetic voice hoping that would break Josh out of his almost trance like state.

"Yeah," was all he could answer.

This is painful, Lily thought. Damn painful.

"Come on Josh, we haven't seen one another in ten years and all I get are one-word replies." Her sympathetic voice turning to frustration, almost anger.

"Sorry Little Lil, I guess this was not a good idea. Coming back home after all these years. I guess I should have gone somewhere else on my vacation."

"That's ridiculous, Josh. Besides mom and dad are so looking forward to seeing you."

"Oh, really. How are they? I've been really bad at staying in touch."

"They're okay. Dad retired a few years back. Now he and mom spend their days working in their garden."

"How ironic!"

"What!"

"Dad's finally into plants."

Josh let out a soft chuckle. Lily followed.

It was starting to feel like old times. Brother and sister. Laughing. Talking. Lily liked that.

And it was like that, old times again, but only for about 10 minutes, when Josh returned to his earlier silent, darker mood.

Only ten minutes!

Lily slapped the table in frustration. Her salad bowl clanged against her water glass.

"Jesus, Josh. What's gotten into you? Talk to me."

Josh was focused on the half-eaten meat patty on his plate, pushing it in circles with his fork.

Then, slowly he looked up.

"Not sure you'd understand, or even believe me."

"Try me," Lily replied, almost pleading.

"Okay." Josh replied with a soft moan.

"Go ahead, I'm listening."

"It all started about five years ago. New, cutting-edge research in the department. I was assigned as the lead researcher."

"That's great, Josh."

"Yeah, that's what I thought at first. Such an interesting project, plant communications."

"Plant communications? What's that?"

"Well, it's long been theorized that plants can communicate with one another. I mean, if animals can, why not plants? Why not all living organisms."

"Wow, how exciting."

"Yeah, exciting, until it wasn't."

"What do you mean, until it wasn't?""

Josh's appearance turned grim, the color drained from his face, his hands started shaking. As his grip on his fork tightened, his knuckles turned white. He was staring at his plate.

"Jesus Christ, Josh what is it. Tell me." Lily was shouting now.

The customers around them were staring. Some got up and quickly left.

The waitress started walking over to their table, but Lily waved her away.

Josh lowered his voice and continued.

"We found that plants did communicate with one another."

"Really."

"But what we didn't expect was that plants, when under duress, made audible sounds that other species could hear."

Lily drew closer, leaning across her half-consumed salad. Her mouth opened slightly, revealing a piece of romaine lettuce.

"At first, we thought the sounds were not audible to humans, that we could only detect these plant communications with special equipment. Very sensitive listening devises."

"Jesus, Josh, what we're the sounds like, what were they saying to one another?"

Josh looked up and directly at Lily. More tears had appeared. A lot more.

"They were screaming sounds, Lil, almost like they were crying too. The plants were crying."

"What?"

"Yes, they communicated with one another when under duress, and the sounds … the sounds were awful, terrifying."

"But you stopped listening? Didn't you. Listening to the plants, didn't you?"

"We tried, but it was too late, too late for us."

"What?"

"Our own auditory systems adjusted to the plant sounds. We no longer needed the special equipment. We had no idea that would happen."

"Jesus."

"Lil, do you have any idea what it's like to mow a lawn, or trim a rose bush, cut a tree down, or …"

More tears appeared.

"Or … or what. Or what Josh."

Josh slowly lifted his fork and pointed straight ahead. His hand was still shaking. More violently now.

"Oh no, Josh. No. Please tell me it isn't so. Please."

"Yes, it is."

Lily dropped her fork into her bowl of salad.

"You … mean," she finally said, almost gasping for air.

"Yeah, Little Lil, what it's really like to hear someone eat a salad."

Baseball and Guns

I was holding it with both hands.

"Squeeze, just squeeze."

But I didn't.

Clearly, they were getting frustrated with me.

"Squeeze, damn it, squeeze"

Why is this thing so heavy? I didn't expect this at all. When my dad handed it to me, I almost dropped it. Yes, it was very heavy.

"SQUEEZE."

Now they were shouting.

I was holding a Smith and Wesson, 44 Magnum Revolver. My hands were almost shaking. My God this is heavy.

Turning to Frank, I heard my dad say. Not quite a Dirty Harry, is he? They laughed. All the adults laughed.

Frank owned the gun club. Dutchess County Rod and Gun Club. Isolated in the woods, but only a few miles from our house.

"Squeeze the trigger. Just squeeze," they said again.

I pulled the gun closer to me and peered down the long barrel.

"Where's the target?" I asked.

"There's no target. Just point and shoot." Again, more laughing. Now my friends were laughing too.

Just after breakfast, my dad came into my room. "Get dressed. I'm taking you shooting."

"But dad, I wanted to spend the day with my friends. We're going to play baseball in the field across the road."

Ten years old and all I wanted to do was play baseball. Shortstop, that was my position. I was good in the field, damn good, some said I could go professional. No, I thought to myself, I can't hit for shit.

Although there was that one game where I smacked a triple. God, I remember that triple, the crack of the bat, sliding into third, almost a home run, I'll remember that day for the rest of my life. Forever. But I never hit another triple. Never a home run. Jesus, why couldn't that ball have cleared the fence? It was so close. Just a damn triple.

"Come on, all your friends will be there with their dads. Jimmy, Douglas, and maybe even Eugene."

"I don't think so."

"What?"

Eugene was my best friend growing up, which was strange because he didn't play baseball. We just connected somehow. It was like magic.

"Eugene won't be there," I replied.

Eugene lived with his mother now, in a small home on the edge of town. I never met his dad, but one day when we were sitting under that tall tree in his backyard, he told me what had happened.

"My dad never seemed happy, and certainly not around my mom. He was okay with me. But not with her. Then there was that argument. All hell broke loose. Mom even threw a full dish of enchiladas at him. After a while he got up and said he was going out to get cigarettes. He never came back. Story has it he went back to Mexico with his girlfriend."

Eugene only told me that story once, but I'll always remember his final sentence.

"He didn't even say goodbye."

God, what must it be like to grow up without a dad? I can't begin to imagine.

"Sure, dad, I'll go shooting. It sounds like fun." I fought back the tears as I said it. I was thinking of Eugene.

We were all in the car now. My dad was driving, Frank was in the front. Jimmy, Doug, and I were in the back.

"Why am I always in the middle," Jimmy said in a whining voice.

"Because you're the youngest," Doug answered.

Jimmy punched him in the arm and Doug pushed back. Frank turned around.

"Stop that back there you two, right now." He was angry.

Frank was their dad. He was very strict. Jimmy told me that he hit them. "A lot," he said, "and hard." Sometimes Jimmy would show me the belt marks. The dark red belt marks on his arms and back. Thank goodness my dad's not like that, I thought to myself.

Pulling into the dirt parking lot, the others had already arrived. Two men were comparing guns.

"I once shot the eye out of a bird at 50 yards."

"That's nothing, I once took down two rabbits with one shot. One damn shot."

I was confused.

Why the hell would anyone want to shoot out the eye of a bird, or two rabbits, I wondered. What's the fun in that? I'd rather play baseball. Yes, baseball. Now, that's fun. Not shooting a bird, or two bunny rabbits.

"Pull the God damn trigger. We don't have all fucking day." It was Frank.

He was standing just to the right of me. He was angry. I could see it in his face. I could hear it in his voice. So angry.

"Oh, give him time." My dad said. "This is his first time to shoot a gun."

I guess my BB gun doesn't count, I thought. Well at least I never shot a bird, or a rabbit. Never.

"Shit, everyone wants a chance to shoot. Even my dumb fucking kids." It was Frank again.

I glanced over at Jimmy. He was looking at the ground. What are you thinking Jimmy, I thought? What a monster of a dad you have.

"Hey Frank, there's plenty of time for everyone to shoot," my dad replied. He was angry now.

"Christ John, why don't you discipline your fucking kid. Tell him to shoot the God damn gun."

Frank was really mad now. His face turned red. I thought of the belt marks. I thought of Jimmy staring at the ground. I bet he would be happy if I did it. Yes, he would. Perhaps Doug too.

"That's no way to talk, Frank."

My dad turned to me, "come on son, we're leaving."

"No dad, I want to shoot. I have to shoot." The words came out so forcefully. I even surprised myself.

"Alright then do it." Frank was screaming now. I thought of Jimmy, of the sound of his dad's belt, and then I thought of Eugene's dad."

"Why don't you leave?" Now I was screaming, back at Frank.

"What did you say to me, you little shit?"

Standing there with that heavy gun in my hand, I thought, little shit, Frank, look who has the gun.

The Smith and Wesson, 44 Magnum Revolver didn't seem so heavy now. Yes, this was what a gun should feel like. And why shoot birds and rabbits? That's no fun.

I could feel his breath now. Frank was shouting in my ear. Strange I didn't hear a word. I kept thinking of the gun, the Smith and Wesson, 44 Magnum Revolver. Then I thought of Clint Eastwood in Dirty Harry.

Dirty Harry. That's when I knew what I had to do. Just squeeze the trigger. Just once. Make my day, like Dirty Harry would say.

I wasn't afraid now. I was focused. I glanced up at Frank. His expression suddenly changed. Not of anger, but confusion … then fear. A Dirty Harry fear.

There was complete silence, except for the sound of a rabbit that scurried through the tall grass.

Yes, a bunny rabbit.

The gun jerked up in my hands. A loud booming sound ricocheted through the forest.

The Smith and Wesson hit me squarely on the forehead and knocked me backwards. I fell to the ground. The gun resting at my side.

Were those stars I was seeing?

Jesus, my head hurts.

Looking down at me was my dad. Jimmy too.

"That's quite a bump. We better put ice on that when we get home."

Home? Bump? What the hell happened?

Then I remembered. I could see the bird; I could see the two rabbits. They didn't deserve to be shot either.

Laughing now, my dad reached down and pulled me to my feet.

"We should have told you about the kick on that gun. Sorry."

Struggling to stand, I looked around.

Where the hell is Frank, I wondered? Then I saw him, hiding behind that big tree. He probably thought the same thing I had been thinking standing there with that Smith and Wesson, 44 Magnum Revolver. Yeah, me and Dirty Harry.

Jimmy and Doug were looking at Frank too and laughing. Others joined in.

As I opened the passenger side door and slid in my dad looked over.

"You'll probably never shoot a gun again." He was laughing.

No, I never did, but then there was always baseball. Now that was fun. Real fun. If only I could hit.

The Sailing

The line quickly slipped through my hand. The cold wind was at my back. I didn't much feel it as I was waiting.

"Ten seconds," my first mate shouted above the howling wind. It was hard to hear him.

The first knot slipped through my hand. Another 47 feet to go.

The seas had been especially rough this day. Most of my crew were made unavailable. I wondered during the worst of the day if we should just give up and turn the ship around. Even the large sail was battered by the stiff winds, torn in places and in need of a quick repair, which we were able to do, but with the loss of one climber who fell from the tall center mast.

It was a sign, they said, a bad omen, losing Odin the way we did.

After two fortnights at sea, perhaps they were right. Odin was the best sailor, and certainly the strongest rower aboard and if he couldn't survive, maybe that was a sign that the Saegammr couldn't. Or perhaps the crew couldn't survive.

The Saegammr, a sailing and rowing longship, in search of new lands. With a crew of 32, each one responsible for one of the 16 oar holes on each side when the winds were weak. But now with Odin lost, one of my officers would have to take that empty spot.

"20 seconds."

Soon after, the second knot slipped through my hand. The large blister on my palm broke open as it did.

"Damn it," I yelled.

My first officer didn't respond, although he must have heard. He was too busy counting the seconds, as he should.

There was no rowing today. The pounding waves on the starboard side and the strong wind rendered that useless. Just as useless as my seasick crew.

"Are you sure these are seasoned sailors, strong rowers." I asked.

"But, of course, nothing but the best crew for you. And you will have Odin just like you requested."

"I just want to make sure as this is likely to be a difficult journey."

Difficult journey was an understatement. We were sailing in the fall, unlike our usual sailings in the summer when conditions were likely to be better. When we would have more sunshine.

Rain plagued us most of the way. Even snowed one night.

And our course? Started west, but with the last four cloudy nights we couldn't see the stars, especially the navigation star to the north.

The sun's rising and setting positions up until a few days ago had suggested we were on course, but now that was uncertain given the rain, the clouds, and the wind.

We hadn't seen land since we left Hernam and with the wind conditions today, using one of our ravens was out of the question. Perhaps tomorrow, conditions permitting, we will set him free and see what he tells us.

"30 seconds, times up."

The third knot hadn't passed through my hand. I counted. Another ten seconds and it did.

"Not even 3 knots," I exclaimed as I reeled in the wet rope.

The longship started to sway. Darkness approached. The wind picked up and it started to rain again.

"Lower the sails, we can't afford any more damage," I shouted to the crew.

The one large sail was gently lowered to the deck. While the repair in the wool had held, it was soaked. Too soaked to be much of a protective covering for the crew tonight.

The Saegammr didn't have a below deck, or a hold, which the crew could use to escape the weather. The small area below deck was full of heavy rocks for ballast and, of course, bilge water which had to be bailed out on a daily basis or more often in rough water like today.

Sleeping was done on deck. And tonight, would be no different. Blankets of seal skin were all that protected the crew from the rain and the occasional spray from the pounding waves.

I was at the steering oar at the back of the ship. Someone had to be there all the time. Tonight, it was my turn.

Yes, perhaps we should turn back, I thought. Too many bad omens.

The night passed slowly. The long narrow ship withstood the pounding waves. I was exhausted, but I couldn't let the crew see that.

I almost dozed off when I felt the warmth on the back of my head. Turning I saw the sun rising. The rain was over, the storm had passed. Just a few light clouds above.

Today, I would order that beer be served with the salted fish. It was time and the crew had reason to celebrate. And of course, we wouldn't be turning back, at least not today.

Throughout the day we checked the ship's speed. Finally, up to 6 knots. The wind was at our backs and pushing us to the west. The crew had rowed today as well, probably helped in part by their two helpings of beer.

In the afternoon, we brought out the cage of ravens.

"Time to see if land is near?" my first officer asked.

This would be our first time to use one of the six ravens we had brought with us. Would it simply circle above us or fly off in the direction to a land we couldn't yet see?

"Yes, it's time," I replied.

The raven rose above the Saegammr. Circling at first. Then straight off in a direction off to our port side. After a while, our raven was completely out of sight.

"That direction. That's our new course," I said.

A cheer went up from the crew. Soon they would be on solid footing.

Dusk turned to night. The stars reappeared after their long absence.

"There, there it is. The navigation star."

It hung in the night sky, motionless. The north star. Our navigation star since we first took to the seas. Without that, we would have never ventured far from home. Without that star, we Vikings would be simple land bound people.

"Keep it steady, keep the north star on our stern. That's the course we seek." I was speaking to the first officer. It was his turn with the steering oar tonight.

In the morning we awoke to the sound of screeching birds.

Looking across the bow we saw a dark outline on the horizon.

"Definitely land."

Soon we could hear the sound of waves breaking on the shore. The air smelled of trees and fires.

In front of us we could see a rocky shoreline interrupted by an occasional sandy beach. Beyond the coast, a densely forested area blanketed the land, and in the distance towering mountains reached to the sky.

We directed the Saegammr towards one of the sandy beaches. As the gentle swells followed us to the shore, we saw them. On the out crop of rocks off to the port side.

A group of five, dressed in the hide and fur of animals.

We waved, but they stood motionless, some clutching long spears.

The Saegammr came to an abrupt stop. The bow of the ship resting against the sandy beach.

"Captain, what shall we do now?"

It was my first officer. I heard him but didn't reply. I was too busy staring at these strange people in their strange outfits.

"Captain, shall we disembark?"

"Yes, of course. This is why we sail. To find new lands."

They were on the beach now, just in front of the bow. One reached out and touched the carving of the dragon head on the prow of the ship. Then they all broke out in laughter.

As I stepped off the ship, the gentle waves washed over my boots. It was colder than I expected.

I walked slowly to the group with my first office at my side.

"What do we say?" he said.

"Perhaps we do something first," I replied.

I pointed to the decorative dragon head.

"That. Remove that."

With one quick twist, the dragon head was separated from the bow.

Holding the head in both hands, I moved closer to the one who had touched the dragon.

He stepped forward. I placed it in his hands. He smiled and said something, then he pointed at me.

I pointed at my chest and said,

"I'm Captain Leif Eiriksson. From Iceland."

Champagne Music

In 1933, the California state legislature legalized on-track, pari-mutuel wagering on horse races at private tracks, district or county fairs, and the state fair.

Shortly after, racetracks began appearing throughout California, first among them the racetrack at Santa Anita which opened on Christmas Day, 1934.

In the 1930s, Del Mar, California, was a small town with a population of 4,000.

The small, sleepy town just north of San Diego had become the 'Playground of the Hollywood Movie Stars.' Celebrities flocked to oceanfront vacation cottages, ate in local restaurants, swam in the ocean, played volleyball, and enjoyed barbecues at the beach.

On May 6, 1936, Bing Crosby, filed for articles of incorporation with the California Secretary of State to establish the Del Mar Turf Club. Crosby was a passionate horse racing enthusiast, and so he wanted a racetrack where he and his friends could relax, gamble, and enjoy the races.

Opening day, July 3, 1937, was like a star-studded Hollywood premier. Crosby personally greeted arrivals at the entrance. He even composed a song," Where the Turf Meets the Surf," which is still played before the first race and the last race of every season.

Movie stars flocked to Del Mar during the race season which ran from July until Labor Day.

Among them, W.C. Fields, John Wayne, Lucille Ball and Desi Arnaz, Zsa Zsa Gabor, Jimmy Durante, Gregory Peck, Barbara Stanwyck, Betty Grable, Ava Gardner, George Raft, Elizabeth Taylor, the Marx Brothers, Charlie Chaplin, and even Lawrence Welk, whose "champagne music" aired for more than 30 years on his long-running television show, The Lawrence Welk Show.

It was the summer of 1957.

My best friend, Stew, and I managed to get summer jobs.

We were seniors in high school.

I was a busboy at the Hotel Del Charro in San Diego. Stew was the lifeguard. We both worked in the early evenings.

The Hotel Del Charro opened in 1948. In 1953, Texas oil tycoon Clint Murchison, purchased the hotel and expanded and rebranded it.

The New York Times described the Hotel Del Charro as a "fabulous hostelry" with every guest room having either a private patio, sundeck, or balcony. The "restaurant, built around a huge jacaranda tree, has not one chef, but two, one imported from Scotland, the other from Palm Springs." The pool was described as "Texas-size", crescent-shaped, with private pool-side cabanas. A Texas flag flew overhead, and there was a working Dow-Jones stock ticker machine in the lobby for those who wished to monitor the movement of the stock exchange.

The Hotel Del Charro was clearly not an ordinary hotel and certainly didn't have an ordinary guest list.

Close to the Del Mar racetrack, the hotel attracted wealthy horse-race aficionados. It was also a favorite of Richard Nixon, Lyndon Johnson, Senator Joseph McCarthy, Howard Hughes, and the FBI's J. Edgar Hoover.

During the Del Mar racetrack season, J. Edgar Hoover stayed at the hotel. As a result, every summer from 1953 through 1971, the FBI was headquartered, for at least two weeks, in Bungalow A at the Hotel Del Charro. At Hoover's request, Bungalow A included a direct phone line to Washington which he would use to conduct FBI business.

It was rumored that Hoover stayed at the Hotel Del Charro at the same time as some of the nation's most notorious gamblers and racketeers. It was also suggested that while Hoover tried to avoid the mobsters, who also enjoyed their afternoons at the Del Mar racetrack, there were a few of them he actually got along with quite well.

How Stew and I managed to get a summer job at the hotel remains a mystery to both of us to this day. But when we were offered employment, we didn't ask any questions.

All the bus boys were jealous of Stew. While we got to pour water, serve desserts, and remove dirty dishes, Stew got to impress young girls at the pool and we, of course, could care less about impressing J. Edgar Hoover, or other guests.

But the money, and especially the occasional large tip, was good and we got to consume the remaining desserts after closing every night.

It was one evening in late July. An evening which a decision on my part became the talk among the busboy group for months, perhaps years, to follow. An evening when I responded to a dare in a way that even now, I find hard to believe.

Horse racing was finished for the day and as typical a few of the Hollywood celebrities drove the short couple of miles south to the Hotel Del Charro for dinner.

We were just punching in for the early evening dinner shift. Stew of course was in his bathing suit.

"How was your day, Grubby?"

Grubby was Stew's nickname for me. Stew joked that my five o'clock shadow looked like dirt on my face. Hence, Grubby.

"It was bitchin, the surf was really up. The waves were totally tubular."

"A made in the shade kind of day."

"Yeah. And how was yours?"

"Oh, spent the afternoon at the pad. My dad was at work all day, so Julie and I hung out."

"With classy chassis?"

"Yeah, that's the one."

It was the 1950s and young people had a language of their own. Probably to keep our parents confused, my dad would say.

Suddenly there was a sharp tap on my shoulder. I turned, it was John, one of the waiters.

"Hey Michael, you've got my tables tonight. We're expecting some important people, so don't screw up. Understand."

"Sure."

Stew moved over to the lifeguard station, and I started setting tables. Life's not fair, I thought. Definitely not.

The early dinner crowd was light, but then it picked up. The big hitters were arriving. Limousines the size of freight cars pulled up to the hotel's entrance.

And then he stepped out of his chauffeur driven limo. As he did, I could see imaginary champagne bubbles floating out from the open car door. It was none other than ....

Lawrence Welk.

"Wunnerful, wunnerful!" He said as he entered the restaurant.

The only thing missing was the lively polka music.

"The guy thinks he's real cool." It was Jimmy, another bus boy. "Cool as a cucumber."

As the cool cucumber was shown to my section of the restaurant, I let out an "oh fudge."

"Hey, maybe you can get his autograph?" Jimmy was laughing now. "I bet your mom would like that."

"Oh, get bent, Jimmy."

And off I went to the champagne music table, water pitcher in one hand and a basket of rolls in the other.

"Good evening," I said, but no one replied.

"Celebrities," I mumbled as I left their table. "Too good for ordinary people."

The rest of the evening was the same at the champagne music table. No acknowledgements, no thank you, just an occasional nod.

"Odd," I said to Jimmy.

"What?"

"Nobody's drinking champagne."

It was time for dessert.

"Ice cream all around," Welk ordered.

The waiter asked me to prepare and deliver the desserts to the table, so I went into the kitchen.

All the busboys were there. Even Stew.

"You need to do something. We dare you to do something."

"What?'

"To Mister Cucumber, that odd ball."

I thought for a moment, and then blurted out,

"No sweat, guys. Just watch."

As I dished out the large scoops of ice cream, I motioned everyone to leave.

"Just wait and watch."

The desserts were ready. Eight vanilla ice creams.

I circled the table, carefully placing each dessert, but saving the last for Lawrence Welk.

When I reached him, I said,

"Here's your ice cream, Mr. Welk. Please enjoy."

The other busboys and Stew gathered close to the table, then they started to snicker.

The ice cream in front of Lawrence was not like the others. It was not a large round scoop.

He looked down but didn't say anything. But then he was an adult and didn't understand our language, the language of the 50s.

The ice cream was shaped into a giant square.

I turned and walked away. John the waiter saw what I did and gave me a thumbs up.

We were all in on what I had done, a square ice cream for the square, everyone except for Mr. Cool and his party, but of course, they weren't in on the hip language of the 50s.

As the last of the dinner crowd was finishing up, Stew approached me and said, "what do you want to do this evening?"

"Let's just go cruising. Perhaps stopping at Howard Johnson for ice cream."

"Yeah, 28 flavors. But no square scoops."

Control Room 27

There was that alert, again. He's here.

I was in the control room. On the monitor I could see him. He looked like he was floating, in his spacesuit and he was at the main airlock.

I pressed the button and watched as the heavy door opened. He slid in and the door slowly closed. There was no sound. He was secure in the main airlock.

After a few minutes he could breathe on his own. The airlock had filled with life sustaining oxygen. He waved, and said hello, in English. I replied,

"Good morning, Igor, or should I say dobroe utro."

Igor laughed; he always did at my greeting.

"And how are you, Bobby?"

"Same as always, bored. Just watching all these monitors."

"Well, that's important, you know."

"Are you here for the daily checkup?"

"Yes, Bobby, I need to make sure the equipment is in working order."

"Equipment?"

"Yes, the equipment in your control room."

Oh yes, the control room.

But when had I been assigned to this control room? While I struggled to remember, there are a few things I can recall.

"You'll be fine in there, the person in charge had told me."

"And what shall I do?"

"Well, you're in charge of monitoring all these screens. A very important job, too. We must make sure that everything is running smoothly."

"But why me?"

"We had no choice. We had to move quickly. Best to think of yourself as the commander. You are responsible for the success of this mission. And you monitor what's going on from this control room."

At the time, it made little sense to me. How could I be the commander of anything? I couldn't recall any formal training. But here I was in this control room, surrounded by all these monitors.

"Ok Bobby, everything checks out," Igor had just finished his daily inspection.

"Do you have to leave now, or can you stay and visit for a while?" I asked.

"Sure, a few minutes, Bobby. What would you like to talk about today?"

"What's it like outside? Outside my control room. Tell me again?"

"Well, there are many control rooms out there. You happen to be the commander of this one, number 27."

"Do they all have their own commander?"

"Oh yes, that's important. They need to keep track of what's happening. Just like you, in 27. We can't afford to overlook anything. We certainly don't want to get caught by surprise."

"And, Igor, why the spacesuit today? What's with that?"

"Spacesuit? No, it's just my normal outfit."

"I thought for sure you were wearing a spacesuit. And you came in through the airlock."

"Sorry, Bobby, you must have been dreaming. I just came in through that door over there. Just like every morning."

Struggling to look over my shoulder, I saw the door, the only one in and out of the control room.

"And, Igor, why does this control room have no windows?"

"Bobby, as I explained to you last week, you don't want outside light coming into this room. It might make it difficult to read the displays on these monitors."

Igor stood up and looked at me. He was ready to go.

"What's wrong, I asked. You look sad today?"

"Oh nothing."

"Igor, I can tell something's wrong. I can see it in your eyes."

"Best not to talk about it."

"Please, I don't want you to leave like this. Please tell me."

Then in an almost hushed voice, he told me,

"We … er … lost another commander this morning. Control room 21. It was so unexpected."

"That's three commanders this week, isn't it?"

"Yes, there seems to be more every week."

"Are you able to replace them?"

"Replacing them is never a problem. We often have more candidates than we can handle."

Igor leaned over and patted me on my head. "Take care commander." He was smiling now.

"Igor, how do I say goodbye in Russian?"

"I don't know Bobby; I left that country when I was only 4. You know more Russian than I do."

The rest of the day I monitored the screens. Some had flashing lights, others moving lines. Occasionally, one monitor would make a beeping sound. I decided I really didn't like being the commander of this control room. I would have to ask for a transfer.

The door opened. It was Igor again.

"Good morning, Bobby. Did you sleep well?"

"Is it that time already? Equipment check?"

"Every day, same time."

"Igor, I have a question."

"Sure, what is it, Bobby?"

"Are all the control rooms the same?"

"Well, some are newer than others, but yes, they're essentially the same. Why do you ask?"

"Is this a newer model? My control room?"

"Control room 27 is one of our newer models."

As my plan to ask for a transfer faded with that information, I decided to ask him about the noise.

"But why is it so noisy?"

"Oh that. Not much we can do about those pump noises. They regulate the temperature and other essential functions. Without them, the control room wouldn't work."

"Igor, I've been trying to remember what day it is, but there's no calendar in here."

"Today, why today is Wednesday, December 24. Tomorrow is Christmas.

"And the year?"

"1952, Bobby."

Last Christmas, I remember that now. We spent the day before Christmas decorating the tree. Mom, dad, and me. It was so much fun.

But then the next morning I woke up not feeling very well and when I tried to get out of bed I couldn't.

"Will we celebrate Christmas, Igor?"

"Oh, I'm sure there will be something special for all the commanders."

"And a tree? Will there be a Christmas tree?"

I wondered what happened to that Christmas tree last year, the one we decorated the night before. I was responsible for the tinsel. That was my favorite, the long silver tinsel. But I never saw the tree the next morning. Never opened any presents. Didn't get to take the tinsel off either.

"Not sure about a tree, Bobby. Why do you ask?"

"If there is a tree, I'd like to be in charge of the tinsel."

"Okay, I'll let the head of operations know of your request."

Oh, yes, the head of operations. I met him shortly after last Christmas. A lot of technical talk. I didn't understand a word he said.

Igor smiled, patted me on my head, like he always did, and left.

The rhythmic sound of the control room, usually an annoyance, relaxed me this time. I closed my eyes, and sleep came quickly.

But not for long.

As I opened my eyes, I saw them. All of them. The head of operations and four others, I assumed his assistants, including Igor. The head of operations was talking and pointing in my direction.

"This, gentlemen, is the very latest technology, the Emerson R. It is equipped with portholes for easy access. And, even at over 750 pounds, it is still easy to maneuver, with these hydraulic lifters and wheels. Yes, the Emerson R model is a real game changer."

"Well, we certainly need a game changer." One of the assistants replied. "With nearly 58,000 cases this year, the Emerson R might give us the time we need for a solution.

As I listened, my lungs rose and fell as the air pressure in the control room changed. That rhythmic motion. Constant motion.

"And who is this in 27?"

"Bobby …."

Before Igor could finish, I spoke,

"Jones, sir. Commander Bobby Jones."

"Yes, yes of course. Commander Jones in 27."

"How long has Bobby, I mean Commander Jones been in 27?" one of the assistants asked.

"Tomorrow it will be one year, yes tomorrow on Christmas Day, it will be one year."

Suddenly Christmas last year became clearer. The night before I had that fever. Then chills. My chest felt so heavy, it was getting harder and harder to breathe. Then I couldn't move, my left side was frozen.

"One year, isn't that longer than most?"

"Yes, the usual stay is a couple of months."

"Hopefully, Bobby will be out soon."

"One never knows with this, but thanks to this technology there is now hope."

Hope, what were they talking about? I wanted to reach out to Igor. I tried to lift my hands, but they were blocked. I couldn't lift them.

"How old was Bobby when he joined your facility?"

"Nine. Like most of them, before they reach their teens."

I wanted to scream out. What are you talking about? But the head of operations kept talking.

"Hopefully in a few years, this will all be over."

"And when it is, we can thank this technology for helping."

"Yes, the Emerson Negative Pressure Regulator. A state of the art in life support technology."

"Yes, thank God for the Iron Lung, an important tool in the fight against polio." It was Igor talking.

Polio, Iron Lung? I was really confused now. What were they talking about?

But then I felt safe in my control room, number 27, and I knew Igor would look after me. He always has.

The head of operations looked down at me, actually just at my head. The rest of my body was encased in the huge metal box, which was my control room, Iron Lung 27. The bellows attached to my control room, first creating a vacuum to lift up my rib cage to draw air into my lungs, followed by a positive pressure to compress my lungs and expel the air. The Emerson Negative Pressure Regulator working every minute, of every day, since last Christmas, to keep me breathing, to keep me alive.

"Commander Jones, do you have a wish for Christmas?" It was the head of operations.

"I shook my head to acknowledge I did." Igor bend over and put his ear to my mouth.

"Are you sure, Bobby? That's your wish?"

"Yes," I whispered.

"What's his wish," the head of operations asked.

Igor smiled and turned to me. "Commander Jones said if there is a tree, he'd like to be in charge of the tinsel."

This is the End, My Friend

The traffic was light. I would probably be early.
The car radio was on. It was that song.

"This is the end
Beautiful friend
This is the end
My only friend, the end"

It was the 1967 song by The Doors, the song famously used in the opening scene of Francis Ford Coppola's 1979 film about the Vietnam War, Apocalypse Now.

Just as Captain Benjamin Willard and Colonel Kurtz were engaged in a long, epic battle on the big screen, I too was engaged in a battle.

Mine was a long battle too, but not one fought on a battlefield.

Mine was an epic battle too, but not with physical scars, only emotional ones.

I was alone in my car. But I didn't mind. Being alone was normal for me. Even in this battle, I had been alone, fought alone with no support.

The battle. I can remember the day, the moment, actually the battle began. I would never forget. How could I?

I can trace that very moment back to my early childhood. That moment when I just knew.

It was the first time I didn't want to go to school.

I was only 15, in my first year of high school.

I didn't want to go. For the first time, I didn't want to go to school.

I had come to the realization that they'd always be waiting for me. Waiting as I approached the school grounds.

The bullies.

At first, I dismissed it and later I thought I could handle it. After all, it was only a battle of words.

And for a while, I did. I handled it. The taunting, the laughing, the insults.

During that time, I often wondered if their bullying reflected their own doubts, their own insecurities.

But one day the bullying got worse, much worse. It got physical.

On that day, tired of confronting them, I considered surrender.

And for a while I did, but now …

I had decided I would go to battle.

The driver's side window of my car was down. My arm rested on the open window frame. My shirt was flapping in the breeze. I put my hand straight out. It felt like I was flying as the wind pushed my outstretched arm up and down. Like a bird, I thought. I felt I was flying. Like I was about to escape my cage and become free.

The song continued,

"Of our elaborate plans, the end
Of everything that stands, the end
No safety or surprise, the end
I'll never look into your eyes again"

I looked in the rear-view mirror. My eyes were staring back.

Those eyes that had known the truth for a long time were looking back at me, wondering why I had taken so long.

Of course, not going to school was not an option. No way, my parents said, but of course, they didn't know.

In the months ahead, they asked me how I was doing.

I always said fine, but I wasn't.

When I first went into battle, I felt like Captain Benjamin Willard,

"Part of me was afraid of what I would find," Willard confessed, "and what I would do when I got there."

I felt like Colonel Kurtz "… crawling along the edge of a straight razor… Crawling, slithering, along the edge of a straight razor."

I too was afraid; I also knew that I would have to confront my fears.

I had no choice. It was all part of going into battle, and I knew that eventually I had to get off the edge of the straight razor.

The traffic light turned red. The facility was in sight. I looked back into the rear-view mirror and saw my eyes. I wondered if they would recognize me after. I wanted to think they would. I certainly hoped so.

The traffic was heavy now; the song continued.

"Can you picture what will be?
So limitless and free
Desperately in need
Of some stranger's hand
In a desperate land

I once told my best friend.

"No way," he said. "I don't believe it."

And that was it. No willingness to understand, to comfort me, or to ask me how I was coping.

It never came up again.

In the movie, Captain Willard's assignment to find Colonel Kurtz turned out for Willard to be a personal journey into darkness and self-doubt.

My journey, like Willard's, had also descended into a deep, dark place.

I often wondered if there would be a point when I would not be able to leave that dark place, when I would be trapped.

But I also felt the overwhelming need to try. The need to escape the darkness, to find the light. The need to settle the raging battle within me.

I was in the facility parking lot now. The engine sputtered as I turned off the car. It was an old car, in need of many repairs, just like me, I thought.

Yes, we're both in need of repairs. I chuckled.

The 11 minute and 41 second song was coming to an end. I turned up the volume,

"It hurts to set you free
But you'll never follow me
The end of laughter and soft lies
The end of nights we tried to die

Michael Palmer

This is the end"

Exiting my car was that point that I realized. It was the end, the end of my friend. The battle would soon be over, and I would be free.

So, the decision had been made. I would do it. Like Colonel Kurtz, I would come out of the shadows, out of his cave.

But unlike Colonel Kurtz, my final words would not be "horror, horror." Mine would be "Free, I'm free."

And my freedom would come just as Captain Willard freed Colonel Kurtz by taking his life. By killing him in that dark cave.

But my freedom would come through a different kind of death.

I moved away from my car and walked slowly towards the elevator.

As I pressed button 3, I repeated the last line of the song,

"This is the end."

A smile came to my face. My first real, unforced smile in many years. The darkness was lifting. I was leaving the cave. I could feel it.

The office was almost hidden on the third floor. Only his name on the door. But this was the place. The place where the battle would end. The place where I would find my freedom.

I had contacted him months ago. He explained everything. After that, he said it was up to me. He would wait for me to decide.

And I did. Eventually, I did decide. My decision was yes.

The waiting room was barren, just a few magazines. I thought of Colonel Kurtz living in that dark, barren cave. I suddenly felt sorry for him because I knew what his ending would be. Shot by Captain Willard.

I settled into one of the chairs at the far end of the waiting room.

I wondered how many others had sat in this very chair, waiting, hoping, that this place would end their personal battle.

The song's final lyrics drifted back into my head. The Doors, they were speaking to me.

"The end of laughter and soft lies
The end of nights we tried to die
This is the end."

Then, I realized that unlike Colonel Kurtz, I wanted to leave my cave. That I had grown tired of the "soft lies" and the "nights we tried to die."

The door to his inter office opened. He was standing there, waiting for me. Then he motioned me to join him.

I hesitated. Was I reconsidering? Did I want to stay in that cave?

"Jessie, so nice to see you." It was him and that soothing voice.

"How are you doing?" he asked.

Remaining seated, I simply said "fine."

Fine. My God, my standard answer. I thought of my parents and high school. Fine. I'm fine.

"Would you like to join me in my office?"

I rose and slowly walked to him. His hand was extended. It was a gentle greeting. Our hands hardly touched.

His office was not a typical one. There was no desk. Just two easy chairs, a couch, a couple of floor lamps and a side table. A few pictures on otherwise barren walls.

I suddenly thought of Colonel Kurtz living in that barren cave. A chill suddenly came over me.

Doubts, I wondered, was I having doubts.

"Come sit down, Jessie." He was pointing to one of the easy chairs.

Lowering myself into the chair, I fixed my focus on the floor. Nothing fancy there, either. An old wooden floor scarred by many visitors.

"How have you been, Jessie?" By the tone of his voice, I could tell he really cared, he really wanted to know how I was feeling.

"Not sure ... no wait, I am sure."

"Hesitancy is normal Jessie. It's to be expected."

"No, no, I am sure. I've given it much thought. I'm sure, I'm ready. I want to do it."

"Any concerns, Jessie?" It was that comforting voice again.

"Well ... er..."

"What Jessie? Let's talk about it."

"I don't know what to expect from my friends."

"That's understandable. What about your parents?"

"They're okay with my decision."

"That's good Jessie. Don't worry about your friends, they will deal with it."

I looked up from the floor. He was looking straight at me. I could tell he cared, I could see it in his eyes, that he cared and understood.

"Can I ask you a question?" he said.

"Sure."

"Name. Have you selected a name?"

"Yes, actually that was easy. Probably the easiest part."

"And what name did you select?"

"Jessie."

"Jessie?"

"Yes, I selected Jessie as my name."

"But, why? Why Jessie?"

"Easy. I may be changing my gender, but not my name. I will always be Jessie."

"That makes perfect sense, Jessie."

"Now I have a question for you."

"Yes, what is it, Jessie?"

"When do I start treatment, my hormone treatment?"

"Today, now, Jessie, we start."

"Good, because I'm ready to leave my cave."

"Cave? Your cave?"

"Oh, sorry, it's just an inside joke, one between me and Colonel Kurtz."

The '48 Woody

. . . .

"Do we really need that?" Sam asked sheepishly.

"Better we have one, just in case," Tony replied.

"But this was not part of the plan."

"Plans change, deal with it."

"But ..."

"I said, deal with it. Damn it, deal with it."

"Okay."

Sam and Tony were friends. The best of friends many believed.

They had known one another since grade school.

But their friendship wasn't equal. Not even close.

Tony was the bigger of the two. Stronger. Louder. A bully actually. He called the shots, all of them.

Lowly Sam, many assumed, was just there for the ride, the companionship.

Perhaps Tony was his only friend some wondered.

Rumor had it that Tony let Sam hang out with him because of Sam's special talent. Of course, there was much speculation as to what that talent might be, but no one really knew for sure, and neither friend would talk openly about it.

Tossing the car keys to Sam, Tony shouted, "here, you drive."

The keys missed Sam's outstretched hands and crashed to the pavement.

"Damn it Sam, that's my new key chain. Probably all scratched up now."

"Sorry, Tony, I tried to ..."

"Shit Sam, stop trying and just do it."

"Okay, Tony okay."

"Jesus Christ, I don't know why I let you hang out with me. You're so clumsy. So, fucking clumsy."

Of course, Sam knew why Tony was fine with his friendship. Tony knew too. But it was something they didn't talk about. Maybe they were both too embarrassed to do so.

"I'm not, Tony, I'm not clumsy," Sam replied, but his weak response suggested either he didn't believe what he was saying, or he didn't want to rile up Tony.

"Shit if you ain't. You're the damn clumsiest person I know."

"But..."

"And dumb too. Christ, the dumbest person I know. Clumsy and dumb. That's you."

Sam didn't say anything in his defense. He wanted to. He wanted to remind Tony that it was him, Sam, who did all of Tony's homework in high school. Shit, Tony wouldn't have graduated if it weren't for him. He wanted to remind him, he wanted to scream at Tony, but he knew better, cause Tony would be pissed if he did. And when Tony was pissed, he could be mean. Really mean, and that scared Sam. And since Tony was holding the gun, the last thing he wanted to do was get Tony mad at him. Yes, that wouldn't be good.

The car was a 1948 Ford Woody Wagon Country Squire, a station wagon whose exterior side panels consisted of real wood.

"The last of the real Ford Woodies," Tony's dad reminded the family every time they went for a ride.

Tony's dad loved his new car. And he could talk at great length about his prized Woody.

"Ford grew this wood in their own forest in northern Michigan," he would tell Tony every Saturday when the two of them washed the car.

But Tony didn't care and most of the time he was just going through the motions.

When new, the family car sported a stunning burgundy exterior with a unique wood side paneling.

The interior was light tan leather, and the dashboard, like the exterior, was wood.

A split front windshield, split rear window, clamshell taillight, wide whitewall tires, and bright chrome were standard features.

Indeed, the '48 Woody was a classic.

When Tony's dad died, Tony got the car. His dad wanted him to have it because he believed Tony would keep it new looking just like he did. At least he assumed Tony would.

Sam opened the driver's side door, and slid in. He was shocked, but not surprised by what he saw.

The interior of the car reeked of cigarette smoke. Empty crushed beer cans rattled around on the floor. The tan leather seats were stained and torn in places. The back seat was piled high with discarded clothing and unrecognizable items.

And as for the outside of the car, the once stunning burgundy exterior was a far cry from stunning. The surface was caked with dirt and streaks of mud. The passenger side taillight was cracked, and the rear bumper was dented.

How long since we've been in this car? Sam wondered. Clearly too long.

Unfortunately, Tony's dad was wrong about Tony's willingness to keep the '48 Woody in perfect condition.

Sam just shook his head. Best he didn't say anything about the car, at least for now, he decided.

After some furious pumping of the accelerator, the car finally started. "Jesus Christ, Sam when you going to learn how to start this thing?"

"Huh?"

"God, beats me why I let you drive my car."

Sam didn't say anything in return. But he knew why, and he knew that Tony knew why too. Why he drove Tony's dad's '48 Woody.

Tony couldn't pass the written drivers' license exam. Six times tried and six times failed. Not even close, the license department grader would say as he added up the test score. Not even close. Eventually Tony gave up, and why not, Sam passed, and he could drive.

"So where do you want to go?" It was Sam.

"Jesus, Sam, how many times do I have to tell you!"

'I thought perhaps you might have changed your mind. You know, about ..."

"Shit Sam, does it look like I've changed my mind?"

Tony was holding the gun, actually pointing it at Sam, and pretending to pull the trigger.

"I guess not, but ..."

"Fuck the buts, Sam. I'm doing it, we're doing it. End of story."

Tony's plan was to rob the small grocery store in the next town over.

"A shit load of cash," Tony reasoned. Every Friday, before they close and make their weekly bank deposit.

"Like taking candy from a baby. Shit we'll be rich."

"But what if we get caught?" was all Sam could offer.

"Caught? Fuck we'll be in Mexico before anyone realizes what we done."

Sam wanted to explain again, for the hundredth time probably, that Mexico was 450 miles to the south of them, but Tony wouldn't listen, and of course Tony wasn't all that good at understanding things like that. 450 miles could be 4 miles, as far as Tony was concerned. It was just a number to him. A meaningless number, at least to Tony.

"And we don't speak the language, Spanish. How we going to communicate down there?"

Tony didn't reply, and why should he. Hell, everyone spoke English he thought. They did here, they would there. It was so obvious to Tony. It just had to be that way.

It was like that. Always like that. Tony was in complete control. What he said was it. Settled any and all disputes. Sam did as told and when he was told.

"And after we rob that damn store, we probably should stop for a while to ... er ... you know."

Sam did know. Tony was laughing now and shaking the gun in Sam's direction. "It's been too long since we ...

Tony stopped mid-sentence. Suddenly, he didn't really want to talk about it. About what they hadn't done for a long time.

Sam didn't say anything. As usual, he wanted to. But he didn't.

And he realized a long time ago, why he didn't. It was the only time he was in control. Total control of a situation with Tony.

"We're going to live like kings in Mexico."

"You really think so?"

"God yes."

Sam shook his head, offering a small sign of doubt. Tony wasn't looking.

"And what do we do when we run out of money, the money we stole? What do we do then?"

Tony didn't reply. He realized he didn't have an answer. What were they going to do?

"Hadn't thought about that? Shit Tony, I thought you thought of everything."

For the first time, Sam was challenging Tony. Actually, challenging him, and it felt good. He decided not to back down, so he continued.

"Shit Tony, who's the dumb one now? Where's the fucking plan?"

Tony just sat there, with the gun in his hand, looking confused, looking for an answer.

"You're pathetic, Tony."

Sam's voice was so focused and so forceful, that it even surprised him.

Finally, Tony replied. "Shut up."

"That's it? Shut up? That's your plan? Jesus, Tony, really, shut up? That's it."

"Shut up, or I'll…"

"What Tony, or what?"

"Fuck, I'll shoot you."

"No, you won't Tony, you don't have the guts to do that. You're just a joke."

"Shit if I won't."

Sam slowly steered the '48 Woody to the side of the road. After stopping, he turned to Tony.

"Here, dumb ass, I'll make it easy for you. Go ahead and shoot. I'm not moving."

"But…"

"Go ahead, damn it. Use your gun."

"But …"

"All talk, huh. All talk, Tony."

"But …"

"But what Tony? Damn it, say it."

"I forgot."

"What?"

"I forgot the bullets."

Sam jerked his head back.

"You forgot the bullets."

"Well, maybe. Maybe I didn't want them." He tossed the gun on to the back seat.

Sam started laughing.

"What's so funny?"

"You."

"But I could have, could have shot you." Tony's voice was one of sadness now. Sadness perhaps for what he might have done.

Sam didn't answer. He didn't have to. They both knew. They realized they needed one another; they actually wanted this friendship. They were indeed the best of friends.

Sam eased the '48 Woody back on the road and did a u-turn.

"Where we going, Sam?"

"Back home, Tony, but before we do there's something we have to do. Something we must do."

Tony was smiling now.

"Like you said, Tony. It's been a long time since …"

"I'm sorry, Sam, I forgot. It has been a long time. Too long."

"Too damn long, Tony."

Sam was pointing to the back seat.

"Just look at that mess. Can you imagine how your dad would feel?"

Sam was smiling now. He was in control, as he always was when it was time for his special talent to kick in, his talent at cleaning the '48 Woody.

I'm What?

· ·

At first, Justin thought it was just a small scab from a scrape.

So, he didn't concern himself about it.

But then it seemed to be getting bigger.

Odd, he thought, but then he moved on to other things in his life.

His upcoming marriage for one.

His career, which had suddenly stalled when he was overlooked for that expected promotion.

His aging parents.

And finally, his taxes which were due next week.

So, the growing scab on the top of his head was pushed to the back of his concerns.

But of course, it shouldn't have been.

In his defense, Justin did ask some friends, even his fiancé, Susan, to look at it. After all, he could feel it, but couldn't really see it given its location.

"Just a scratch."

"Perhaps a bug bite?"

"A spider bite. For sure."

But always,

"I wouldn't worry about it."

But then someone said, "loose skin, it looks like loose skin."

Rubbing his fingers over it for the hundredth time Justin wondered if it could just be loose skin.

"Yes, it kind of feels like that," he replied.

But how could that be? Loose skin at the very top of his bald head, he asked himself.

Of course, he needed to start his taxes, so he decided to move on.

But, of course, he shouldn't have. Shouldn't have moved on.

In the days that followed the mysterious area on the top of Justin's head continued to expand.

He could almost see it.

"That's weird," his fiancé, finally told him. "Creepy looking too"

"Creeping looking?" Justin asked. There was a slight panic in his voice.

"Yes, ugly, creepy, kind of disgusting, actually."

"What?" he shouted, as he stumbled in his rush to the bathroom in search of his hand mirror.

Holding the mirror above his head and positioning it so that he could clearly see the top of his head in the large mirror above the sink, he let out a piercing scream.

The hand mirror fell from his shaking hand and shattered on the marble countertop.

"What the hell is that?"

That's all Justin could say as he slumped onto the bathroom floor.

He didn't even notice that he was now sitting on a bed of broken glass.

"What the hell is that?" he said in a dazed voice.

"No idea," Susan replied.

But Justin didn't hear her. He was too consumed by his own racing thoughts, and for the first time, concerns. Yes, concerns about that strange thing on his head.

It wasn't a scratch, definitely not a scab. And it certainly wasn't an insect bite.

It was more like a patch of dead skin, almost transparent, dried out dead skin.

Justin took a deep breath as he rose from the broken glass.

I've seen something like that once before, Justin thought. But when, and what was it?

In his fear of the moment, Justin couldn't recall when or what, but he was sure he had once seen something like this.

Yes, he had seen it once. Just once. He was sure.

"What you gonna do? About that thing?" It was Keith, Justin's older brother, he was tapping the top of his head.

"Huh?"

"Jesus Justin, I mean, your wedding's in two weeks. As your best man,

I have to tell you that's a pretty ugly thing atop your head, brother. Damn ugly."

"Larger too," Susan chimed in. Almost down to your neck in the back."

"I really think you should see someone?"

Justin just shook his head.

He was still struggling to remember when he first saw it. He was a young kid, that he could remember now. And he wasn't afraid, just curious.

But he couldn't remember what it was. How it turned out.

"Yes, Justin, please see someone." It was Susan, she was almost pleading, begging Justin to do something.

"Okay, I'll call Doctor Sperry, first thing in the morning."

And he did, at least his office.

"I'm sorry, but Doctor Sperry is out of the office for three weeks." It was his receptionist.

"Can I see someone else?"

"Is this an emergency?"

Not knowing how to answer, Justin fumbled for a reply.

"Er, well, um … I guess I don't know. Perhaps."

"Perhaps?" was the surprise response.

"It's something, er, something growing, um, on my head."

"Growing?"

"Yes, it's like … extra skin."

"Extra skin?"

"Yes, a layer of dry, skin. Extra skin. Feels like … like … a loose membrane … on my head. Top of my head. It's just sitting there."

"Huh?"

"And it's getting larger. I mean, at first it was just a small area, but now, er, now it covers my head and is starting to appear on my forehead."

"What?"

"Yes, like it's moving down my body. Started with my head … top actually… and moving down. This … er … membrane."

"Membrane?"

"And I'm getting married in two weeks."

"Married?"

Justin suddenly realized he wasn't getting anywhere with the receptionist. But then, she probably couldn't imagine what he was describing. How could she? How could anyone for that matter.

Again, he thought back to that one moment a long time ago.

He was in the front yard. The grass was in need of mowing.

Then he saw it. There in the grass. Like the growing thing on his head. But what was it?

"Can you feel it," it was the receptionist again.

"Huh?"

"The membrane? When you touch it, can you feel it?

"Er, not really. I can kind of move it, but it simply feels like ... er ... like a ... crumpled piece of thin paper. Yes, that's it, a crumpled piece of paper."

"Well, I think we need to schedule an appointment."

Justin wanted to say that's why he called, but decided to be tactful.

"Yes, thanks."

"How about today, at 2?"

"Perfect. I'll be there."

He was early, of course. And of course, he wore a big floppy hat. Pulled it down just above his eyebrows.

Still people stared. Especially the receptionist, especially her, trying to see the mysterious membrane.

She would probably faint if she did, Justin thought to himself.

He chuckled.

Then he noticed it.

Jesus, part of the membrane had broken off, a small portion had peeled away and floated down to the office floor.

Justin reached down and cupped the membrane in his hand.

As he stuffed the piece in his shirt pocket, he looked around to see if anyone noticed.

The receptionist was standing at her desk and looking directly at him. The most confused look appeared on her face. A slightly scared look too. She put her hand over her mouth and sat down.

Another piece, larger now, gently fell to his feet.

Those around him, rose quickly and moved away. Even the person in the wheelchair, quickly positioned himself at the far end of the waiting room.

He could hear them too.

"What the hell is that?"

"Is it contagious? Deadly?"

He wanted to say something. Something in his defense. He wanted to tell them that he once saw this, a long time ago when he was a young boy, there in the tall grass in his front yard.

He wanted to tell them but didn't. He couldn't find the words as a third piece of the mysterious membrane fell to the floor. A much larger piece.

"Justin, the doctor can see you now." It was the nurse.

As he exited the waiting room, he could sense a sigh of relieve from everyone in the room.

Then there was the little boy who started laughing. Others followed.

He wanted to go back and tell them he once saw it. That they didn't have to worry and didn't have to laugh.

But of course, he didn't. He was too embarrassed.

The examination room was small.

He never did like going to the doctor. And especially now. Not with this mystery on the top of his head.

There was a sharp knock on the door. It opened.

He was probably in his 60s. Late sixties. His white coat was spotless and without a crease. A stethoscope hung from around his neck. He was holding papers in his hand, looking at them and then up to Justin.

"So, what seems to be the problem, Justin? Why are you here today?"

"I ... er... have this situation. A ... uh ...condition. And ..."

"Can you describe it?"

"Better I just show you."

Justin removed his hat and set it on the examination table. He leaned forward, and as he did three more pieces of the membrane fell from his head.

"Jesus Christ," was all the doctor could say as the papers he had been holding fell to his feet. "Jesus Christ, what is that?"

"Er, that's why ... why I'm here. This thing that's growing, this..."

"Jesus Christ."

"Excuse me?"

"This is so strange. I must call in another doctor. I'll be right back."

Within minutes, four doctors had gathered in the examination room. Two nurses too. Justin was surprised that the receptionist and a few patients were not there as well.

"What the hell is it?"

"Should we take a sample?"

"You do it, I don't want to touch that thing."

On and on the discussion went.

Finally, one of the young doctors approached Justin. As he did, he snapped on a pair of long blue gloves.

"Let me look," he said with a very gentle voice.

The young doctor pulled at the membrane from Justin's forehead. Rolling the pieces in his hands, he turned to the other doctors.

"I think I know what this is. I think he's …"

But Justin didn't hear the rest of the sentence.

He didn't have too.

He was back in the tall grass in his front yard.

The sun was out, it was warm, and a light morning dew coated the tops of the grass. It was cool to his bare feet.

It was summer, and school was out.

Next year he would be in 4th grade.

It was all so clear to him now. It was like he was there. Standing in the tall grass.

He looked down and saw it, there in the grass. Almost hidden.

He called for his mother.

"What is this?" He asked her. Surely, she would know.

"Oh that."

"Yes, that," Justin said pointing to the tube-like object in the grass. "It's …."

Suddenly, he was back in the examination room. All the doctors had gathered around him. All wearing blue gloves. All touching and examining him.

The young doctor reached out. He was holding a tube-like object that Justin had seen in the tall grass years ago.

Before the doctor could speak, Justin offered up one word.

"Molting."

"Yes, you are," the young doctor replied. "Just like a …"

"Snake," Justin injected. "I'm shedding my skin like a snake."

"But how did you know?"

"My mother told me."

Red Sun

The sun rose in the east, just like it always had, but its color was markedly different. Redder now, like it was angry.

"It probably is," I muttered.

"What is?" she asked.

"Angry at us for what we've done. The sun. Angry. At how we've screwed up this planet."

"Oh, don't be silly. It's probably just a haze from the fires that's causing it. The red color."

"And did you notice the birds?"

"Not really."

"Well, there are none. Where have they gone? Doesn't that seem strange to you?"

"Perhaps they've gone south?"

"For the summer? I doubt it."

"Damn it, don't be such an alarmist. God, I hate it when you get in these moods."

Moods? I wish they were just moods, I thought.

We thought coming here would be so different. That they would care. Certainly, they wouldn't let things get out of hand.

Our trip was long and difficult, but we were willing to do it, for the sake of our children and grandchildren, who deserved better.

"I see where the rains are back in Japan," I said. "Flooding too, many missing, or dead."

There was no response from her. Understandable.

She wanted to stay. She said she was giving up so much leaving. Too much. It was too sad for her, and she had been depressed ever since we arrived.

121

"Record high temperatures in Europe too. 113 in Sicily yesterday. The world is burning up."

"Shut up, will you. Just shut up."

"What's wrong?"

"Everything. You were so insistent we leave. And for what?" She was angry now. Had I gone too far this time?"

"But I thought ..."

"Thought? What were you thinking?"

"I thought it would be better here. I really did."

"And is it? Is it?" She was screaming now. The children were frightened. They started crying.

"Please, the children."

"Oh yes, the children. We did it for them, didn't we? Gave up everything for them."

"I had no idea it would be like this."

"They left their friends behind, had to learn a new language, English. Different culture. More crime, bad influences all around them. I could go on."

"Not all their friends. Some came too."

She looked the other way. I could tell she was crying. Was it because of her parents? They wanted to stay. They did. Why couldn't I talk them into joining us.

"Think about it, we'll all be together in a new land. Your daughter, your grandkids and you," I had argued. Pleaded.

"No, we're too old. Too set in our ways. It will be too difficult. And we are comfortable here. You go."

And we did. Leaving them behind. Yes, that was part of why she was angry and sad.

"Have you reached out to them?" I asked.

"Who?"

"Your parents?"

"No, I can't get through." She was much calmer now.

"For how long?"

"Months now, no communication. I wonder if something has happened to them."

"Perhaps it's just weather related. I read that the sun's recent flare up is creating communication problems."

She glanced at me with that look of screw you. God, I had set her off again. Why did I say something so stupid?

"Sorry."

Again, no response. Yes, she was mad again. But I really couldn't blame her. After all I decided we were leaving. There was no compromise. That was it.

"Stay here. With your friends. With your parents," they all told her. "You won't be happy there. Think of the children. It will be so difficult for them."

I told them I was thinking of the children. That's why we were leaving.

Soon after we arrived, I realized my mistake. This place was just like home. The whole world was going to hell. Few cared and their voices were silenced by the majority. Jobs, way of life, personal freedom, they argued.

Why did I think it would be any different here? But it was too late to return because it was the same back home. Both planets were dying, and nothing was being done to save them.

I sat on my porch overlooking the dry lakebed. Once an inviting lake, it was now just a barren spot in front of me. Once full of fish, it was now an example of a climate change disaster. Once a place for boating and swimming and family picnics, it was now nothing. It had died a quick death, and few cared. There were other lakes, they said. But for how long, I wondered.

The smoke from the fires to the west grew darker and more ominous by the day. They were closing in on us and there was no escape. All attempts to contain them had failed. As I breathed in, I could taste the smoke. My lungs felt the fire. It was just a matter of time, before we would be evacuated, and our house burnt to the ground. But where would we go?

I took a sip of the ice water to cool down. Bottled water. Tap water no longer safe to drink. We had poisoned our drinking water too. Toxic chemicals.

Just then our two kids joined me.

"Dad, tell us again about our home. The one we left."

They each pulled up a chair in front of me. Then I began.

"Well, in many ways it was like it is here. Communities of people.

Perhaps they dress differently, speak a different language, eat different foods. Some may look different."

"So, why did we leave?" They finally asked that question which I had been waiting for. And now the time had come.

"Well, like many parents, we wanted a better life for our children. And it was becoming impossible to have that back home."

"And, why was it impossible."

I paused. My wife was smiling now. Perhaps she was starting to understand, or accept.

"Well, the place was dying. We had neglected it. It was no longer livable. The air, the water, the land was dying. We had to leave."

"But, why here? And how did we get here?"

Well, it's finally time, I thought. Time to tell them the whole story. No more deflecting. No more avoiding the issue.

"Some of us thought this place would be different. We had researched it. So, we decided to come here. We thought it would be better. A better future for all of us."

I could tell by the looks on their faces, that they wanted more. They deserve more, I thought. Okay, time to come clean.

"So, we built ships to transport us to this planet. At the speed of light. From our solar system to this one and then to this planet they call Earth."

"Did we make the right decision?" My wife was looking at me. Still smiling. Perhaps she did not blame me after all.

"No, we didn't." I said. "Clearly, we didn't."

The Last Hurrah

"Well, this is where I live."

"Impressive."

"Twelfth floor."

"Wow, you must have a great view of the city."

"Would you like to see it?"

"Huh?"

"My apartment. You want to come up for a drink?"

"Sure, why not."

"Perhaps watch a movie."

"A movie!"

"Perhaps make love."

"What?"

"Make love."

"Huh?"

"Sex, you know what sex is. Don't you?"

"Of course, six, I know what six is ... I mean sex."

"Cut, cut... Jesus, Tom what's the problem? Can't read your lines today."

"Sorry Ron, I don't know what's ..."

"Okay, let's do it again. Everyone, quiet on the set. Action."

"Sex, you know what sex is. Don't you?"

"Of course, sex, I know what sex is."

"Well, I was beginning to wonder."

"Let's head upstairs and I'll prove it."

"My pleasure."

"No, it will be my please you, ... I mean pleasure, oops, sorry, Ron."

"Jesus Christ Tom, what's got into you today? You're fucking up all your lines."

"I don't rightly know, Ron. Just one of those days I guess."

"Well, let's call it a day. Everyone's tired. Take the weekend to relax. We'll shoot the scene on Monday."

And so it was, another disaster on the set. That seemed to be the norm recently, at least for me.

I was one of those movie stars of the 1950s trying to make a comeback. At least that's what I told my agent, Scott.

"And why the hell do you want to get back in the movies?" It was Scott.

"Bored, I guess. Bored. Nothing to do," was all I could come up with.

"Well, you're not a young chicken anymore, Tom."

"Well, I'm not looking to play the part of a chicken, Scott. A human part would be nice."

"Okay, okay, I'll see what I can do."

And do, Scott did. A major part on the set of the movie, The Last Hurrah.

I played the role of an aging movie star, Kenneth Gordonstorm, who was trying to make a comeback. It was supposed to be a serious picture. A "tearjerker," the director, Ron, said. He wanted the audience to leave crying.

"True to life," Scott said. "You should have no problem with this role."

But I was having problems. Forgetting lines, mispronouncing words, turning the wrong way, tripping over my own feet.

Spending the weekend reading and re-reading my lines, I knew I had to do better. Ron was clearly pissed at my efforts thus far.

"Damn it, Tom. This is a serious look at an attempt to restore the glory of one's youth. We want struggles, introspection, sadness. Most of all we want the audience to feel your struggles, your depression at growing old. At confronting …"

"I know Ron, I'm trying, really I am."

"Well try harder, Tom."

"I will, I will, I promise."

Well so much for promises. The screw ups continued.

One day all the cast members gathered on the set for a meeting. Ron was fuming

"Okay people, time to accelerate our efforts. We are falling behind schedule and it's costing the producers money. Money." He was looking directly at me when he repeated the word money. No surprise, I thought.

Weeks went by and my screw-ups continued. Dropping my coffee cup during a café scene, running into a wall, sneezing in the leading lady's face, the pasta sauce that ran down my chin on to my white shirt, and perhaps the worst one of all, when during a romantic dinner, I got too close to the burning candle and my hair caught fire.

Finally, it was the last day, the last scene of the movie was upon us.

The scene involved me talking to a young actor, Sean. We were standing on a small hill overlooking a lake. The sun was shining. It was a beautiful setting for a perfect ending to the movie.

The scene called for me to be discussing my career and how much I missed it. How much I appreciated the opportunity to return to acting. At the end of the scene, I was supposed to break down and hug Sean and start crying.

Then Ron would say, "that's a wrap."

First, Ron called Sean and me over for a pep talk.

"Okay, let's put everything you've got into this final take. I want to see pure emotions from you two, especially from you, Tom."

The assistant director shouted, "Picture is up. Quiet please. Roll camera."

"Rolling." It was the camera operator.

"Roll sound."

"Rolling." It was the sound operator.

Ron turned to one of the crew members and shouted, "slate it."

In response the slate operator stepped in front of the camera with the clapper board and said, "scene 1, take 1."

The sound of the hinged section striking the clapper board signaled we were ready to shoot the final scene.

"Action."

I took a deep breath, slowly exhaled, and started to speak.

"So, Sean, did you enjoy your first acting experience?"

"Yes sir, very much so."

"Oh, please Sean, not with the sir again, please call me Ken."

"Yes, sir... err ... Ken. I will try to."

"Do you have any questions for me Sean now that we're about done here."

"Yes, how do you do it, Ken? I mean, all those years, auditioning for parts, dealing with rejections, reading those horrible reviews. And the critics? How did you do it? Why did you do it?"

"I guess after a while you can't help yourself. You want, no you crave, that rush of stepping in front of that camera, then seeing yourself on the silver screen, it's like an addiction, Sean."

"But why did you want to make a comeback. Why after all these years away from it? What brought you back?"

"I guess it was in my genes, my DNA. I realized I couldn't let it go. It was part of me. I was empty without it. So, I had to come back. I just had too."

"And … and how do you feel now. Now that we're done filming."

"Sad, Sean. Very sad. It's almost like I want to …"

The closing scene called for me to reach out to Sean now. I was to show my despair, my need for comfort, for someone to hug. And, of course, to cry, softly."

I started to move to Sean, slowly at first, but as I did, it happened.

I stumbled on a rock and went head over heels.

Tumbling down the slight embankment in the direction of the lake, and before I could right myself, I was face down in the water.

Lifting myself up, and dripping from head to toe, I turned to Ron. He wasn't smiling.

He simply looked at me, shook his head, and shouted, "cut, damn it, cut."

And that was it for me. I didn't even wait to be fired. I just cleaned up and drove myself home.

It was at that point that I decided to forget about any acting comeback.

I didn't even want to leave my house. I didn't want to see anyone. I was too embarrassed.

Then two months after hiding from view, the doorbell rang. It was my agent, Scott.

"How are you doing, Tom?'

"Getting by."

"I've called, left messages, but when I didn't hear back, I became concerned. So, I decided to stop by."

"I've been staying home. Not interested in seeing anyone."

"So, you haven't heard?"

"Heard what."

"The movie."

"What about the movie."

"It was released."

"Really?"

"Yeah, they changed the title."

"What?"

"To the Last Funny Man."

"Huh?"

"Yeah, the producers insisted on the change."

"But, how? Why?"

"All those cuts of yours, all those mistakes, even falling into the lake. They kept them. It's all in the movie. They made the movie into a comedy, Tom. A damn comedy."

"Oh."

"And get this, the movie has been nominated for an Oscar, at the Academy Awards. Best picture."

"No way."

"And there's more."

"More?"

"Yes, more. You're in the running for best actor. Can you believe that Tom? Best actor. Can you believe that?"

The Fire

At first it was just a groan. Barely audible.

But over time, it grew louder.

It was a cry for help, my cry for help, but no one heard me.

Or if they did, they didn't respond.

I'm not hurt, at least physically.

How long have I been here? In this place?

Was it days? Hours? Minutes?

I have no concept of time.

How long have I been here, trapped in this space?

It was dark when I first awoke. That's when I realized I was alone. Alone again. That's when I became frightened. Frightened of being alone.

I look around. Some things are familiar, some not.

There is light coming from one far opening, but it is an opening I am unable to go through. I have tried many times.

There are familiar smells too. They bring a smile to my face.

I'm able to elevate myself, just slightly. But then I hit the top of my head. Ouch.

I realize I'm under something. This something is familiar too.

Suddenly, I'm shaking all over. I'm trembling. I am afraid. Afraid again of being alone, like that time in the mountains.

I struggle to remember where I was in the past, in the mountains. Before this place.

The memories come back slowly.

All I saw was fire. Fire all around me. It was hot and the fire was coming closer. I saw smoke too, spinning all around me. The wind was blowing, and it was feeding the approaching fire.

I tried to run, but there was no escape. I was surrounded.

The smoke was burning my eyes and it was difficult to breathe.

The fire kept feeding on the wind. It was hungry. I wondered, would the fire soon be hungry for me.

Being alone in this strange place fuels that fear in me. The fear when I was in that fire, and it is growing, like the fire, and I can't escape.

This dread of being alone is not new. Ever since that fire, it smolders within me. Waiting to awaken. Waiting to return to finish what it started.

The light which had come through the far opening is slowly fading. It is getting dark.

I wonder where the light goes after it leaves me. I wonder if it will return.

Memories of that day reappear.

The fire grew taller, leaping high into the dark sky. I could hear strange snapping noises, like the fire was talking to me, laughing at me. Teasing me. Mocking me.

I waited for the fire. I had no choice. There was no place to run, no place to hide.

I closed my eyes and waited.

Like I'm waiting now as it gets darker. Waiting, as the disappearing light moves on to another place.

I'm shaking again.

Am I losing control?

I desperately want to escape, but there is no out for me, no place to go. I am enclosed in this space, waiting for the fire to return.

My memories of the fire reappear.

The flames were getting closer. I felt the heat. I tasted the smoke. It was burning my throat. I was coughing.

Suddenly, I'm lifted up. I wonder, has the fire consumed me? Is this the end? The end of me? Has the fire won?

As always, my memories of that day end there.

Suddenly, there is that familiar sound.

Could it be?

I am excited, happy, as always when I hear it. That familiar sound.

I hear voices. They are familiar too.

A light returns. But it is a different light. Much brighter.

"Hey Sean. You forgot to leave the light on when you left for work."

"Britt, sorry, I thought you had done that."

"Where is he?"

"There under the coffee table as usual."

"His safe place."

"Look, he's wagging his tail. He's happy to see us."

"Hey Koda … hey buddy, we're home. Did you miss us?"

They were back, I was not alone anymore. I was safe.

The fire was out.

I was safe.

Marguerite's Mirror

Marguerite wasn't much of a talker. At least when I met her.

She once told me that the two things she liked the most in life were her stamp collection and her goldfish. I assumed that was because she didn't have to talk to them, and of course, there was no chance they'd be talking to her.

But when I asked her why, she didn't answer. That was very Marguerite.

Marguerite and I met in college. We were roommates.

It was the fall semester. 2013.

From the beginning it was hard, no, almost impossible, to get her to open up about herself.

All our conversations seemed to be one sided. I, doing the talking, Marguerite, the listening, or at least I thought she was listening, but of course, she rarely acknowledged my babbling, so I really couldn't tell about that either.

But then that was Marguerite.

At first, I thought she didn't like me; later I dismissed her quietness to just being shy, an introvert; it wasn't until much later that I learned the truth.

Marguerite's recall, especially her early memories, resembled a shattered mirror. That was her description. There were pieces, seemly random at times, of events. Other shards, hidden from view, would occasionally come to light, but only to fade away after hinting at her past.

Sometimes I wondered if she intentionally looked away when reflections of her past started to resurface and reveal themselves. Almost as if she didn't want to remember, I thought.

Despite her quiet demeanor, Marguerite and I became friends. Good friends.

I would tell her about my past, growing up in a small community in upstate New York.

"The most exciting event in my life was the annual summer picnic at the municipal swimming pool," I told Marguerite.

When I asked about where she grew up, she only said,

"A big city."

And that would be her only reply as she shook her head, not so much in doubt, but almost in fear, in unspeakable fear.

I never pressed her on her response. Perhaps I didn't want to know. Perhaps, like her, I was afraid to find out. To really find out, what might be revealed in that shattered mirror.

Our first year in college was probably typical for most. Studying, studying and an occasional party.

I made it to almost every party, but after the first one, Marguerite decided not to go. Some undergraduate attempted to engage her in conversation and that was all she needed to avoid future gatherings.

Our second year was much the same, although Marguerite started struggling in some of her elective classes. Her solution was to drop those classes, especially those that required a presentation.

"I'd be lucky to get through the first sentence," she said in her defense to drop those classes.

But then in our third year, she found herself in a bind. All third-year students were required to take a speech class. It was part of the graduation requirement.

Marguerite and I were in the same class.

"What am I going to do," she asked me through her uncontrollable sobs. Of course, I had no answer.

The course syllabus required a presentation by each student. The topic was a particular event in our childhood and how it shaped us in later life.

Marguerite was mortified.

"How can I?" She said, "when I can't even recall my childhood."

For weeks Marguerite struggled with her assignment. The broken mirror refused to reveal much of her past. As before, all she could remember were random, unconnected images.

When the visions did come back, Marguerite would tell me what she remembered.

"I'm with my mother.

"She is holding my little hand."

"She is singing a song."

Then, just as quickly as random hints of her past would show themselves, they would quickly disappear. It was if they were teasing Marguerite, or perhaps protecting her.

"I am skipping along a busy sidewalk."

"People are smiling at me"

"It will be a surprise, my mother says,"

Sometimes Marguerite's flashbacks would bring a smile to her face. Sometimes we would both laugh as past scenes came and went.

But then there were the occasional memories when we wouldn't. Wouldn't smile or laugh.

"I hear a loud noise, then screams."

"I am running, trying to get away from something."

"I call out for my mother, where is she?"

As the class session for our presentations approached, Marguerite became more desperate and more despondent.

"I'm going to fail this class. I just know it," she constantly repeated to me.

The morning of the class presentation, Marguerite refused to get out of bed.

"I'm not going. I'll just embarrass myself. Better to fail the class," she said.

"Come on, Marguerite, it'll be okay. You'll do fine," was all I could offer in response.

"But what can I talk about? Nothing. I have nothing," was her reply.

After much pleading, Marguerite agreed to go to class, but she informed me that she wouldn't be doing any presentation.

"I'll just sit and listen, that's all."

The class was at 8, so we quickly dressed, gulped down our coffee, and jogged across the campus to the classroom.

"I've decided we will do our presentations in alphabetical order," the professor announced. "No more than 20 minutes each. So, let's begin."

That's when I heard a loud gasp and an "oh, shit." It was Marguerite. She had quickly calculated that she was third in line to present.

At 8:40, Marguerite's name was called.

At first, she didn't move, but I nodded my head in the direction of the front of the class and she slowly rose.

Once at the front, she stood there in silence.

The bright sun was pouring through the large window at the side of the room.

Suddenly, there was a loud noise from outside. The glass windows in the classroom shook. Violently.

Marguerite turned to the window.

The look on her face suggested that her shattered mirror was coming into view, was reconnecting.

She remembers, I thought.

Slowly Marguerite starts to talk.

"It's my birthday and my mom is taking me to where dad works to celebrate."

"Mom is excited and tells me that we are going to surprise dad."

Marguerite hesitates, but as the mirror fills in, she continues.

"Mom is holding my hand as we cross one busy street after another. Her hand feels so big in mine, but it should, I'm just a little girl."

"Tall buildings are all around me. So tall they look like they can touch the clouds."

"Mom starts singing a song, one that she sings to me every night before I go to bed, as she does, people passing by smile at us."

"It is so lovely. I am so happy. I want this moment to last forever. This special day in September when my mom and me are going to surprise my dad in the tall building just in front of us."

"Suddenly, there is a loud noise. People around me are screaming."

"Some start to run in our direction. They are screaming, some crying. I get knocked to the sidewalk."

"I don't know what's happening. I call out for my mom."

"I feel her hand lifting me up. Hurry Marguerite, run."

"As we run, I look back. The tall building where dad works is on fire, pieces of it are falling to the ground."

"Someone shouts out. It was an airplane. An airplane hit the World Trade Tower."

"I don't know what he's talking about, as my mom starts crying."

"I stop and look up at her and ask."

"But she can't talk, and never does, never talks about that day, my birthday, September 11."

Marguerite stops talking. No one speaks, not even the professor. There are a few soft sobs.

She walks back to the window and with her back to the class, she finishes her presentation.

"Mom couldn't talk about that day, and neither could I. But today, I could. The mirror is whole again."

Joey

Joey was always late. He didn't mean to be. Time just wasn't important to him. Didn't wear a watch, didn't even own one, so he couldn't tell he was late. Didn't care, either. That was Joey.

The clock struck noon. The twelve chimes broke the eerie silence in the room. It was good to hear some noise. All I had heard for the last 30 minutes was my soft breathing.

It was an old wooden clock on the back wall. Joey was late. I squirmed in my chair, but there was nothing I could do. Nothing. It's Joey after all.

My earliest memories of my time with Joey are fading now. Time distorts and removes.

But a few memories are still with me. Memories of Joey.

That time we planned to go fishing at the pond. We were just kids. Just a short walk. We agreed to meet there at 9 when the fish were first biting. Joey was bringing the bait and I had the fishing poles. I waited under the shade of that apple tree next to the water. I sat there counting apples and watching the trout show off with their graceful leaps. They were ready for those night crawlers alright, but Joey wasn't ready. He showed up at 2 and by that time I had an upset stomach from all those damn green apples.

I looked around the room. Many in attendance were pointing at their watches and shaking their heads. I could hear the mumbling. "Where is he?" I glanced at my watch. It was 1. An hour late. I started to tell the concerned young couple next to me about Joey's tendency for tardiness, but they turned away and slumped in their chairs. Clearly, they were unhappy.

Then there was that time in high school. We were playing for the state football championship. A big game, our coach said. The biggest, we shouted back. Joey was our star quarterback. I was just a lowly lineman.

141

Joey was not there for the coach's pregame pep talk. When coach finished, he looked around the locker room. "Where the hell is Joey?"

Joey showed up as the game was ending. With two minutes to go as I recall. He had spent the day with his girlfriend, Anna Gail. "Priorities," he answered when asked why. We lost 77 to nothing. The coach said, "well at least you guys didn't give up an even dozen." The next year the new coach told Joey not to try out for the team. Not to even think of doing so. Joey didn't care.

It was getting hot in the room. No A/C. The windows were closed. I got up to open the window next to my seat when a guy in a dark suit ran over to me. "Please no, the traffic noise outside. We need to keep them closed." I wanted to ask him if they had A/C but was distracted by the sweat rolling off his forehead. He turned and left, and I sat back down.

My wet shirt was sticking to the back of the metal chair. It was now 1:30. In 30 minutes the baseball game would be on TV. Seventh game of the World Series. And of course, I would miss it, thanks to Joey. But I should have anticipated that. Yes, I certainly should have.

Graduating from college. What a wonderful day that was supposed to be for Joey and me after four years in engineering school. Four grueling years. The day was perfect for the occasion. Sunny and warm. Not a cloud in the sky. Parents and friends filled the outdoor stadium. Ten, maybe fifteen, thousand strong. The speeches went on and on, but we didn't care, it was a wonderful day. Then it came time for student speeches, starting with the graduating student with the highest-grade point average. Of course, it was Joey. The Dean of Engineering spoke glowingly about Joey's accomplishments, "and only one A- in four years of college." Then he invited him to the podium. The guests started applauding, as did the dean, the faculty and all the graduating students. After 30 seconds the applause started to let up and within another 30 it stopped altogether. Joey was not among the graduating students. He was not there. Eventually, he showed up, wearing his cap and gown, but by then we were filing out of the stadium. He forgot what time graduation started, he claimed, and then he added, he had spent the day with his new girlfriend, Samantha. Priorities. Yes, it was Joey.

It was now 2 o'clock. I noticed that a few guests had left. The couple next to me was making noises like they were considering it. I looked at them and nodded. They must have taken that as an okay because they got up and quickly walked to the exit. I noticed that both of their seat backs were soaking wet. Jesus, it was hot. Plus, the seventh game of the World Series was starting, and I was sitting here waiting for Joey. Oh well, he's my best friend, I reminded myself. I needed to be here.

Joey ended up in real estate in Southern California. San Diego. Said jobs in engineering were boring. Became the top salesperson for the company. Only took him two years to do so. Bought himself a flashy sports car. Red convertible. Large house overlooking the Pacific. Too big for one person, but Joey didn't care. Learned to surf. Had it made, his friends said. And at such an early age. Lucky Joey. Then Joey started showing up late for his scheduled appointments with clients. Then he didn't show up at all. His career went into a tailspin, then into the toilet. It was over. His boss was dumbfounded. I wasn't. It was Joey.

At least half of those in attendance at noon were gone. Joey wouldn't care, I thought. Priorities. Everyone has them. Everyone needs them, he would say. And clearly being on time was not a priority for him. It was now 3 and I wondered how the baseball game was going. Damn, why didn't I record it? Joey would have.

After real estate, Joey opened a restaurant. Moved to someplace in Idaho. Sold his red convertible and his house overlooking the ocean and up and moved to Idaho. Took his surfboard, however. It was a vegan restaurant, the Vegan Hut, which seemed strange to me, but then I was never a big fan of vegetables. Meat and potatoes, I told Joey, that's what people in Idaho want. Of course, I had never been to Idaho, or knew any Idahoans, but it just seemed right to me. But I was wrong, and Joey's restaurant was a hit. A big hit. Until that closed sign started appearing in the window. Joey couldn't be bothered to show up on time. Priorities, he argued, got in the way. And this time in Idaho it was Jennifer. However, when the Vegan Hut was forced to close, Jennifer moved on. She had priorities too.

Only a handful of guests remained. It was four o'clock. Still no Joey. I'm sure the game was over and there was a new World Series champion. But of course, I had no idea who it was. God damn it, Joey. Couldn't you be on time just once? Just once, damn it.

I felt myself getting angry at Joey. That was not like me. The only time I remember being angry with Joey, was the first time. Waiting for those night crawlers and getting sick on green apples. Damn green apples. Ate too many. I can't even look at them ever since that day. I avoid them whenever I go grocery shopping. Damn green apples. Damn Joey.

After Jennifer and the Vegan Hut, Joey moved to Arizona. There he started a sky diving company. Bought an airplane, hired a pilot, and a sky diving instructor. Joey just sat back and watched the money role in. It was great, he said, because he didn't have to be there if he didn't want to. The place practically ran itself. Joey now had new priorities; golf was at the top of his list. "Gonna join the PGA," he would boast. But of course, being late for half of his tee times, as he was, probably would have excluded him from that profession. Joey didn't care.

Looking around the room, I noticed I was the only one left. It was 5, and everyone was gone. Even the promise of food couldn't get them to stay. But I stayed because Joey was my best friend, even when he was late.

The sky diving business was a hit. People came from all over Arizona to experience free falling. Joey asked me to come down and we would do it together. He said he never tried it. But I never made it. Never tried to sky dive. But I wish I had. Wish I had with Joey. Just once.

Someone entered from the side door. I didn't recognize him. But of course, there was no reason why I should. I mean I didn't know anyone here as it was my first time to travel to Arizona.

But I had to be here. For Joey.

A man's voice broke the silence. "I'm sure Joey would be pleased to see all his …" He stopped and looked at me.

"Who are you?" he asked, looking extremely confused by what he was seeing. All the empty seats.

"Joey's best friend, since grade school."

"How nice. How nice of you to be here."

Yes, it was nice, I thought. Knowing Joey like I did. The real Joey. Not just the Joey who was late to go fishing, or was late …

No, I didn't want to think about all the times Joey was late. After all, that's why I was here. Because Joey was late again. One last time. But then it was Joey. Late Joey, that should have been his name.

He decided to go sky diving. Before they took him up in the company plane they explained what he needed to do once he jumped. "Sure, sure, I got it," he said as they boarded.

The plane leveled off at 10,000 feet. It was a clear sky. A perfect day to sky dive. No clouds. Minimal winds. Two of them jumped. Joey and his instructor. They held hands at first and did cartwheels. Joey had the biggest smile on his face. He was laughing. He was flying like a bird. He had a new priority.

After 50 seconds of free fall and at 3,000 feet it was time to pull open their parachutes. The instructor hollered, "pull, Joey," as his parachute spread above him. Joey waved. Just a little bit more, he probably thought. Just a few more seconds, a few more feet. But it was too late when he finally did. When he finally pulled the cord to open his parachute. The ground rushed up and Joey and his partly opened parachute crashed into it. Joey was too late. Too late, but, as it turned out, that was not his last time to be late.

From the side door, it appeared. Joey's coffin was being pushed into the empty funeral hall. Joey was finally here, of course he was late. Just over five hours late. But that was Joey. Why should I have expected anything else?

I sat there, thinking of my best friend. Joey and happier days. Then I wondered. What the hell are they going to do with all that food in the other room? I smiled and started laughing. Priorities, I thought. Joey wouldn't care. It was just food.

The Escape

The horizon glowed from the lights of the city. Except for the stars above, it was the only light on this moonless night. But, for now it was my guiding light. My only guiding light.

My mind was racing.

How many miles have I gone? How many miles to go? How long before they notice I'm missing? How long before they would start searching for me, again?

I had been walking for at least two hours. Running at times, too.

The thick sand, which was hot earlier, was now cool beneath my bare feet. If only I had boots, I thought, it would be so much easier. But they took my boots away when they found me.

I had been hiding in a deserted home, well hardly a home. Very little remained of the structure, although it probably wasn't much to begin with. But still it was a shelter for me. Who lived there, I wondered? Was it a family? Were there children living there? If so, did they play and laugh outside before everything changed? And where did they go?

A few pieces of furniture remained. A small table. A couple of chairs; all broken. Some clothing scattered on the floor. And over in the corner, the remains of a dog, whose end must have come quickly with one bullet to its head. Jesus, I thought, how could someone do this to a dog?

There were beds, three of them, just dirty mattresses on the floor, where I managed to get some sleep while I waited for them to find me. Not deep sleep, because I was always listening and waiting.

The food which I had found there was almost gone now. Most of it was rotten. But I had to eat something. I even considered the dog but couldn't get myself to do it. The drinking water, which I collected from the murky pond next to the house, was making me sicker by the day.

147

And I was listening and waiting, almost hoping sometimes that they would find me and take me away from this.

How did I get separated from my group? There was much confusion, panic. It was night. We had just touched down in a small clearing and weren't expecting any resistance. "A piece of cake," our captain said. A hell of a cake, I thought, as the unexpected gun fire greeted our arrival.

Within seconds after we jumped from our Black Hawk transport helicopter, an explosion of gun fire was all around us. Jesus, we were surrounded.

We fired back into the darkness, unable to see them, only firing in the direction of the flashes and the sounds.

The helicopter was hit as it maneuvered to leave. Barely reaching the treetops, it burst into flames and crashed into the dense forest. Its four-bladed rotary wings spinning into the trees as it fell from the sky.

Eleven of us, including the captain, were looking for cover. But which way to run?

In the direction of the falling helicopter, I thought. Into the dense forest. Three of us, and the captain, sprinted in the direction of the burning helicopter. More shots rang out.

Just then, the captain grabbed on to my arm. I stopped running and turned in his direction. He had been hit. Blood was everywhere. Gushing from his head. I tried to speak as he let go of my arm and dropped at my feet. But I realized he wouldn't have heard me. I kept running.

The two soldiers in front of me suddenly stopped running as the bright lights in front of them came on and revealed their position. They dropped their guns and raised their hands in surrender. I fell to the ground to avoid being seen.

Many shots rang out. The two fell to the ground. I heard soft moans, then nothing.

Time passed. I lay motionless. The flames from the mangled Black Hawk were ebbing. The forest was becoming dark again. Time to make a break, I thought. Now before sunrise. Now, or never. I got up and ran.

Once in the forest, I dodged between the trees, trying to conceal my escape. Then I realized I had left my rifle where I had fallen. Jesus, alone, no rifle, lost too. What a mess.

The sun was coming up now as I broke free of the forest. Off to my left were tall snow-covered mountains and off to my right a desert. A desert! This must be a joke, I thought. Why was there a desert here?

But I had to decide. I went to the right, into the desert.

A day of walking brought me to the small village. It was deserted. All the structures had been ransacked, some completely destroyed and some barely standing. I selected the one near the pond, the one which still had a roof and four walls.

Its front door was missing. All windows broken. Floors were covered with dirt. Flies circled around the rotten fruit on the small table. But it was shelter and a place to rest, to sleep. It was a refuge until I could figure out what to do next.

Days passed. I was growing weak. The dysentery from the pond water was taking its toll. The rotten fruit was making me sick too.

Then they found me. I was asleep on the dirty mattress. I felt the barrel of the gun poking me in my side.

"Wake up. What is your name? What are you doing here? Are you alone? The questions kept coming. I just shook my head.

Then the one who was obviously in command stepped forward. "We followed you from the spot where your helicopter crashed," he said.

"Water." was my only reply.

He motioned to the soldier next to him. The one with the canteen.

The metal touched my lips. I was so thirsty. Almost crying, I could feel the cool water touching my parched lips. Then he abruptly pulled the canteen away. "Only a few drops," he shouted. They all laughed.

"Take off his boots," the one in charge ordered. He was looking at me, smiling. He reached for his gun. I thought of the dog in the corner of the room. "Do not try to escape," he said, pointing his weapon at my face.

The interrogation was nonstop. I refused to answer any of their questions, even when they offered fresh food and water in return. "Better than that rotten fruit and dirty pond water," they would say. I just shook my head.

They never beat me. Curious, I thought. Just mental torture. Waking me when I dozed off. Question after question. And the one in command, always waving his gun, pointed at the dead dog, and then a me. Smiling. Sometimes, laughing.

One night they left me alone for a few minutes. They had just finished eating and were exploring some of the other structures. I was lying on the mattress and they probably thought I was sleeping.

I got up. I could hear them talking, laughing. Looking at the table, I saw the canteen. I reached for it. It was full. There were some slices of bread too. I stuffed the bread in my pocket, grabbed the canteen and slipped out the opening in the back.

I ran, not looking back, passing the pond, into the open desert. The sand was still hot from the afternoon sun which had set only an hour or two earlier.

As the distance between me and the village grew, I felt more confident in my escape. But then I heard gun fire and shouting. They knew I was gone. They would be coming for me, again. Their commander would be mad this time. So much for his smiles, I thought.

I kept running in the darkness. Occasionally I would trip on something and fall headfirst into the sand. Spitting the sand from my mouth, I would get up and continue running. I couldn't let them catch me.

The water in the canteen was gone, but I couldn't throw it away for fear they would see it and know my direction of escape. The slices of bread had been eaten. I was running on adrenalin now. But I couldn't stop. I had to get away.

Then, there was that glow of lights in the distance. A city I thought. I pushed on.

My feet were raw and bleeding from the sand. Why didn't I look for my boots, I thought? I started shivering in the cool night air. Who knew the desert would get this cold at night? Perhaps the captain told us, but I couldn't remember. My mind was racing. Why the hell did I sign up for this?

I heard the angry voices behind me. It was them. How close were they?

I fell again into the damn sand. I was exhausted. Should I get up? Should I just let it end here? Like that dog in the corner of the room. At least there was no more suffering for him. And he wasn't thirsty or hungry anymore.

Then I heard the shots. They were closer now. Could they see me? It was still dark.

I got up from the sand and started running in the direction of the lights on the horizon.

Then I heard the dogs. Jesus, they were tracking me with dogs. But at least they were all on foot too. So, I just had to stay ahead of them. If I could.

Damn it, I fell again. This time I hit my knee on a rock. The pain shot through my entire leg. I wanted to scream out but didn't.

I tried to run. Was my leg broken? I could only manage to hop, with a limp. The city came into view. It was an Army compound. I saw the entrance. Soldiers were waving at me. "Hurry up," they were shouting.

Then I heard the gun shots behind me. The sand kicked up on either side of me. Bullets. Jesus, they're close. Don't stop, don't turn around.

"Hurry up, you can do it. Over here." The shouting grew louder. So did the guns behind me. Sand kicked up all around me.

I fell into his arms. The sentry at the entrance to the compound. I made it. I turned to look back. There they were, not more than 30 yards behind me. The commander was waving. He was smiling. His troops were too. He shouted at me. "Next time you won't be as lucky."

I turned back to the sentry. He was smiling. "Congratulations," he said, "you have successfully completed the first level of Escape, the latest video game from Nintendo Switch. Would you like to try level 2?

I sat back in my easy chair and turned off my Nintendo. Perhaps tomorrow, I thought, but now it's family time.

Double Baksheesh

"How much? I asked.
"For what?
"To go … to the top."
"Oh no, not possible."

Wearing a security badge and a gun holstered to his side, he looked as if he had heard this request at least 100 times today. Pissed. Definitely pissed. And it was only noon.

"Kam ath-thaman?" I said, reaching back to my college days when I roomed with Fazie, an Egyptian exchange student. Fazie was determined to teach me his native language. Most of the expressions I remembered were swear words. Not appropriate here. But "how much" in Egyptian was certainly useful.

"Kam ath-thaman?" I repeated pointing upward.

He had a surprised look on his face as I repeated the expression. Perfect pronunciation, thanks to Fazie. I congratulated myself.

"Not possible," he replied again, but this time a very unfriendly tone. He meant it. Or did he?

He was standing next to the sign. In bold letters it shouted out:

IT IS AGAINST THE LAW
TO CLIMB THE PYRAMIDS

Okay, but then it came to me. Another expression, a useful Fazie bit of information. A simple word, but one with a deep cultural underpinning in the Arab world.

"Baksheesh"

The guard's look went from annoyance to surprise.

153

"Baksheesh," he slowly repeated.

Now it was my turn to take the lead.

"Kam ath-thaman? How much?"

In Egypt, as in many other countries in the Middle East, paying someone to do something or allowing you to do something has a long-established footing. Grease payments. 'Baksheesh.' Nothing big. Perhaps paying a policeman so you can park illegally for a while or paying a security guard so you can take pictures inside the tomb of Tutankhamun.

Or, I wondered, climbing the ancient pyramids at Giza.

"10 dollars, and for 20 I'll show you the best way up."

Turning to my traveling buddy, I said.

"Terry, what do you think?"

"Yeah, let's do it."

The guard stuffed the 20-dollar bill in his back pocket and waved us to follow him.

"Follow me. Don't look down."

Taking my first step on the ancient pyramid, I stumbled and fell back. Picking myself up off the fine desert sand, I looked up at the guard.

"Did I mention to look out for loose rocks?" he said.

"I guess I didn't hear that," I replied, dusting the sand out of my hair.

"Anything else you want to tell us before we start?"

"That should cover it," he answered. Grinning from ear to ear.

Okay, so that's the way this is going down, I thought.

"Come on, Terry. Time to show this joker who's up for this."

The climb to the top was difficult. Many times, we had to pull ourselves up to the stone above. And it was hot and getting hotter. Not a cloud in the Egyptian sky.

"Why the hell didn't the pharaohs think of elevators?" I mumbled to Terry as I pulled myself up on to a particularly large stone.

Turning back to see Terry's response, I glanced at the ground below. Then I remembered. Jesus, don't look down. I took a deep breath and waited for my racing heart to slow. The spinning too

"Come on you two. Too much for you Americans? I don't have all day." The guard was growing impatient with our progress. The distance between him and us was increasing by the minute.

Americans. He's mocking us. Christ. What the hell were those swear words? I could use them now. No, I better not. Okay, at least I could whisper them. Perhaps I would feel better if I did.

"Al'ahmag!" Yes, that was it.

The guard spun around, "What did you say?" His hand moved towards his gun.

Oh Jesus, did he hear me? Now we're in trouble.

"Come on, be a man, say it. Say it." He was shouting now.

"Al'ahmag, Al'ahmag, Al'ahmag." "There I've said it. Now shoot me."

Looking down at me, the guard broke out in laughter.

"Fine pronunciation. Well done." His laughter grew louder. "Come on now, to the top."

"What did you say to him?"

"I called him an asshole, multiple times."

"Jesus, do you want him to throw us off this pyramid?"

"Don't worry. I think we may have bonded."

"Right!"

The rest of the climb was uneventful. Finally at the top. The view was amazing. The other two pyramids were dwarfed by the one we were standing on. Five hundred and fifty-five feet at the top. The Great Sphinx directly below us. The city of Cairo in the distance. I caught my breath.

"Did you mean that?" the guard asked.

"What?" I replied.

We were standing close to the edge now. My back to the steep drop-off.

"You know, what you called me."

"Oh that, I was just frustrated, perhaps a little annoyed."

"My father had a saying. When you are angry, the truth comes out."

"Wise man, your father, but I really didn't mean it."

"Okay, let me take your picture."

I handed him my camera. Something didn't feel right. Perhaps it was the scorching heat. Perhaps it was... my mind drifted off.

"Over there, by the edge. That will make a fine photo. One for your grandkids."

The camera snapped. A few times. Not even sure I was smiling.

He walked towards me. I didn't move. My feet were like stone, like the pyramid. Then he handed me the camera. He was smiling. Not a nice smile. A sinister smile, I thought.

"Perhaps you and your friend would like a picture together?"

Oh yes, I thought. That way you can take care of both of us at the same time.

"Terry, would you like your picture up here?"

Terry walked over from the other side of the uneven platform we were standing on. Not much room I thought to myself.

"Do many climbers fall?"

"Why do you ask?"

"Just curious." Sure, I was. Who was I kidding? I wonder if he noticed the panic in my eyes.

The camera clicked.

Having finished our picture taking, we started down. My legs were burning from the climb up. And I was tired. He noticed I was struggling.

"Do you want me to carry you?" He was laughing. "Only an extra 20 dollars." Laughing and snorting now. Jesus, what's with this guy?

"No thanks." Al'ahmag. This time I thought it. Not even a whisper.

We were getting close to the bottom now, then I saw them. Two policemen pointing up at us.

Our feet touched the sand.

"Hey, what do you think you're doing. You can't climb these sacred pyramids."

"We thought it was okay. He said he could take us up."

"Who?"

"The guard. He was just here."

Looking around I saw the guard standing by the sign.

IT IS AGAINST THE LAW
TO CLIMB THE PYRAMIDS

"Him, over there."

The policeman turned to the guard. "Him, no. We only saw the two of you coming down. You and your friend."

"No, you're wrong, he took us up. We paid him 20 dollars."

"Americans. You come here and embarrass yourselves, embarrass us, and then expect us to look the other way."

"Please, we are very sorry for what we have done."

"You think a mere apology will get us to look the other way?"

I guess not, I thought, but I think I know what might.

"Can we pay a fine and just forget this?"

"Americans. You always think you can pay your way out of trouble. We should take you to jail. Get the handcuffs."

"No ... please," I was desperate now and they knew it.

"Well perhaps," one of the guards said.

"Perhaps what? What?"

"100 dollars."

"Okay, okay. Terry, do you have 100?"

As Terry pulled out five twenties from his wallet, I realized what was happening. Baksheesh, of course and all three were in on it.

Handing the two policemen our money, I glanced over at the guard standing by the sign. His mouth was moving. I couldn't hear him, but I certainly could read his lips.

"Al'Ahmag." Then he smiled. I'll never forget that smile.

Never.

The Polar Man

It was bitter cold, and the snow was piling up. We hadn't seen the sun for over three months. It was secluded beneath the horizon.

It was June, the middle of the winter at the South Pole, and we were housed in a giant geodesic dome.

Antarctica, the land at the bottom of the world. Our planet's southernmost continent, the earth's basement. This was my first time here.

It had been nearly 90 days since the last plane left our base. Another 90 days before they would return. Barring a life-threatening emergency, pilots wouldn't attempt to land under winter conditions where temperatures will freeze gasoline and metal becomes brittle.

The wind was starting to blow again. Not that it really ever stopped. Well at least it was drowning out my tinnitus, that constant ringing in my ears.

Outside the sled dogs were barking. The thermometer read 50 degrees below zero.

"Probably close to minus 100 degrees with the wind chill," I said.

"Huskies love the snow and the cold. They'll be fine." It was our group leader. "And they can always go into the storage shed for shelter."

Eight of us were here to study the stability of the East Antarctic Ice Sheet. Thought to have been stable for millions of years, recent monitoring had suggested major melting. One basin of concern, the Wilkes Basin, at the edge of the ice sheet, held enough ice to raise sea levels by 10 to 13 feet.

It was a yearlong study which had commenced in the late summer at the South Pole. Now we were in the middle of Antarctica's winter, the most difficult time to be on the ice sheet.

The personal challenges about being here were both physical and psychological. Physical conditions like the cold and wind were manageable,

159

at least most of the time. The psychological, less so. Homesickness, missing family and friends, and familiar places was a problem we all faced on occasion. But the issue, which was most difficult to overcome, was living in a place where there was just one full sunset and one full sunrise per year. Then in between, the long uninterrupted periods of darkness and light, when the passage of time was difficult to judge.

There are also beautiful things about Antarctica, the stars that blanket the night sky and the magnificent auroras, with their dancing light shows. I could watch them for hours.

But there are unattractive things about this place as well. It is an isolated world surrounded by seas of notorious roughness. The lack of humidity creates an unbearable dryness. Finally, apart from the creatures on its fringes like whales, seals, penguins, and gulls virtually the only life on its interior is the alien one of clouds, fog, and frozen water. At least I thought so.

For decades, Antarctica has been the breeding ground for rumors and conspiracy theories, from giant pyramids to alien spaceships, to the home of extraterrestrial life, to huge underground caverns leading to a staircase to the North Pole.

One of the more bazaar rumors surfaced on July 17, 1945, when the Argentine newspaper, Critica, reported that Adolf Hitler and Eva Braun had escaped Germany and had landed in Antarctica. The Critica also reported that a new Berchtesgaden was "likely to have been built" earlier to accommodate the two fugitives. The Critica article received even wider distribution through reprints in Le Monde, the New York Times, and the Chicago Times.

Another strange rumor involved human like 'polar men' who lived in tunnels beneath the ice. First reported in the 1940s, these polar men, were described as covered in long hair, which protected them from the bitter cold.

The story continued that these polar men evolved from dogs which had been abandoned on the ice shelf by early explorers. Over time these creatures took on the appearance of those who had left them behind. But when needed, they could return to their original canine form.

More ominously, it was claimed that these polar men had fatally attacked early explorers to Antarctica.

All our technical equipment had been set up at the edge of the ice shelf. We did that shortly after we arrived, in early January, the last full month of sunshine. Since we had 24 hours of sunshine to accomplish our task, setting up the monitoring equipment was relatively easy. In addition, the temperatures hovered only around 20 degrees below zero. Comfortable for the South Pole.

Our job now was to monitor and record the readings, and of course, repair, or replace equipment as needed. As repair, or replacement meant leaving the shelter of our station, we were thankful that had only happened two times.

But then.

"Hey Randy, monitor 2 is offline. It was the group leader. "Isn't it your turn?"

"Yeah. Scotty and I are next on the list."

"Well, you two better get going."

Stepping outside, the wind was howling. The door closed quickly behind us.

We stood there for a moment. Adjusting to the cold and the wind.

With our heavy thermal underwear, two insulating layers under a windproof outer layer, our insulated jackets, boots, oversized gloves, goggles, a thick bushy hat, and scarf, we were prepared for the cold and the wind. Still, I could feel it. The cold. The wind. I always did and I didn't like it.

At the South Pole, the moon rises and sets roughly every two weeks. When below the horizon, Antarctica is plunged into complete darkness. Then, when rising to full, the moon bathes the polar landscape in a faint magical silver-like glow.

This evening there was a full moon, but not enough to safely show us the way. So, we used the rope guides to make our way to the storage shed.

The snow crunched like Styrofoam under our heavy boots. The huskies heard us coming and started barking. They had retreated to the storage shed, and it was obvious that they were excited as we approached.

We would have to use the sleds as it was too cold to use the snowmobiles. They wouldn't even start in this weather. Besides we had drained the gasoline months ago.

The strong wind only sharpened the bitter cold, and with the wind chill of minus 150 degrees, we would experience frostbite after only a few seconds if not protected.

However, bundled up, as we were, the harsh conditions were tolerable for an hour or so. But anything approaching two hours, we were pushing our luck. And we certainly didn't want to do that.

Using our huskies and dog sled, we could make the journey to the first monitor in about 15 minutes. Another 5 minutes to reach monitor 2, 15 minutes to repair, or replace it, and then 20 minutes back. Less than an hour and we'd be back in the warmth of our shelter. Less than an hour if everything went according to plan. Of course, that was always a big if out here on the frozen ice shelf.

I had to remember to keep my mouth covered. The last time I ventured outside when the air was this cold it burnt my lungs, resulting in a hacking cough that hung on for weeks. Hand signals, that's how we communicated. Loud shouts through the face covering only when needed.

The sled was loaded with a replacement ice monitoring unit and the eight huskies were paired and tethered to the tow line. The two lead dogs were anxious to start, the other six were comfortably resting in the snow.

Then we were off. Randy, me, the replacement part, and eight barking huskies.

The wooden blades cut gracefully through the fresh snow. Our two headlights showing the way. The tumbling snow appeared like a cresting wave on both sides of the fast-moving sled. Twenty miles per hour, at least.

The journey to the first monitoring unit was uneventful. We arrived earlier than we thought. Perhaps because the wind was at our backs. Going back would be different.

A quick check of the unit revealed it was online. So, we pushed on. Coming ever closer to the ocean waves as unit 2 was positioned near the edge of the ice shelf.

It started snowing. Hard. The direction of the wind changed. Now it was coming directly at us. We were sledding into pounding sheets of blowing snow. Our goggles were fogging up and caking with heavy snow. Just what we didn't need. The visibility was down to a couple of yards.

I signaled to Randy to reduce the speed, to slow the dogs. He saw my glove hand, palm down, quickly rising and lowering, and nodded; he understood. The dogs resisted at first, then their pace slowed.

We would lose some time, but it was better than sliding into the freezing ocean.

Soon the tall pole with the red flag came into view. The pole that indicated the spot of unit 2. We were there.

Stopping the sled, we dismounted. The huskies settled quietly into the snow.

There directly in front of us was unit 2. Almost unrecognizable. It had been crushed. Crushed flat.

As I picked up the smashed unit, Randy threw up his hands indicating what the hell happened here? I simply pointed at the new unit in the sled. He turned to retrieve it.

As he did, my eyes caught something dashing across the ice. In the driving snowstorm it was hard to make out what it was. Like a shadow. The huskies must have sensed something too as they all rose and started barking. Their bark wasn't one of aggression, but more like recognition or acknowledgment. Almost a welcoming bark.

Just my imagination, I thought, as I dumped the broken unit into the sled. Mind can play tricks out here, in the darkness, in the cold, in the wind.

Suddenly a strong gust of wind hit. The sled lifted off the snow and fell on its side. Randy was pinned under it.

I raced to the sled and attempted to push it upright. But it was too heavy. It wouldn't budge. Randy was trapped.

Perhaps the huskies could pull it off him? I clapped my hands. The signal for them to pull. But try as they might, the sled was stuck in the deep snow. It didn't budge.

I got at the back end of the sled. Perhaps if I pushed and the huskies pulled, together we might free Randy.

But no, the sled still wouldn't move.

Then I remembered the emergency phone on the pole. A direct line to the station. I would call for help.

Once over at the pole, I reached inside the metal box for the phone.

It was empty. The phone had been removed.

Then I heard it, a loud grunting noise.

I turned just in time to see the sled rising up, up to its upright position.

As it settled back down into the deep snow, I saw it. Again. That shadow dashing across the ice.

But now I had a better look.

It was tall, very tall. And while it looked human, there was much about it that wasn't. Long hairy arms. A face that looked part husky. And eyes, the likes of which I had never seen. Enormous eyes.

And then it was gone. Off into the storm.

I turned to the dogs. They were all standing, facing the direction where the creature had gone. Their tails were wagging, and they were silent. The only sound was the blowing wind.

Helping Randy back into the sled, I replaced the monitoring unit and after checking to see that it was on, we headed back to the station.

The storm had stopped by the time we arrived. We unharnessed the dogs and entered the station. The warm air kissed our faces as we removed our gear.

"How did it go, Scott?" It was our team leader.

I handed him the crushed unit.

"Jesus, Scott. What happened out there?"

I didn't know what to say. I turned to Randy. He shrugged and turned to the group leader and said,

"Nothing happened. Just a routine swap out."

"But this box?"

"Oh that."

"Yes, that, damn it. That."

The group leader was clearly frustrated. Randy continued,

"You wouldn't believe it, but we think a big human like creature crushed it."

"Hell yes, I don't believe it. But I would believe you two have been smoking something."

Randy turned to me and smiled. Then he turned back.

"Right, you caught us. Guilty as charged."

I turned to Randy, confused by his response. What was he doing?

He walked towards me. We were close now, closer than he had ever been.

I noticed. His eyes were larger than I remembered. And his face, his face suddenly, and only for a split second, took on the appearance of a …. husky.

"Yes, we were smoking," he said. "Weren't we Scott?"

Bug Juice

It was the summer of 1948.

There wasn't much to do in upstate New York in the summer, especially if you were 7 years old and more so if you lived in the town of Moores Mill. Moores Mill, on Route 82, 7 miles south of the larger village of Millbrook, made famous in part, by one of its reclusive residents, the Drop Out, Tune In LSD guru, Timothy Leary.

Moores Mill, the small town, my dad called a hamlet, where we lived with less than 100 other residents. Moores Mill with two gas stations, a small water bottling plant, a chicken farm where we'd buy our eggs, a small grocery store where my dad would sometimes roll dice with the owner, two stop signs but no stop light, a one room school house, where the community would come together once a month for an evening of bingo, a dentist, who owned the town's only television set, and one small pond, which at the time seemed like a gigantic ocean to us kids.

In the winter the pond would freeze over, so we could ice skate. In the summer it was just a pond. No fish. But plenty of water bugs, small long-legged water striders, who were able to skate across the pond's surface. "How do they do that?" I would ask my parents each summer. I never got a satisfactory answer. "They just can," they would always say.

We left the big city, New York City, when my mother found my sister and I throwing toys from the open roof of our high-rise apartment building. "We're moving, John," she said that evening. And so, we did. We packed up our things, minus a few dozen damaged toys, and headed up north, 81 miles on the Taconic State parkway, to the sleepy community of Moores Mill.

This summer would be different, my mom said. "We need to find something for the children to do."

165

Since throwing toys off the roof of our single-story house was not an option, my parents selected summer camp.

Summer camp in the Adirondack Mountains, a camp for boys. My sister went to a camp for girls.

One whole month. Camp Sigorria, perhaps named after some long forgotten Indian tribe, but more likely made up by the camp owners.

Camp Sigorria, a cluster of wood cabins, located near the shore of a large imposing lake. Rumor had it that the girls' camp was on the opposite side. We never found out, and at my age, I really didn't care. Each cabin housed about 8 boys and one counselor, usually a teenager closing in on his twenties.

There was the diving platform at the lake's edge, where we learned to swim out to the floating raft. Many first-time swimmers, me included, took in large gulps of lake water in our early attempts to master the art of swimming. But surprisingly, none of us drowned, and many became pretty good swimmers, while a few simply enjoyed the taste of lake water for the month.

And of course, there was the big open mess hall where we took meals and where I had my first taste of what the camp counselors called bug juice, an unnaturally bright colorful sugary juice drink. This radiating 'Kool Aid' quickly became my drink of choice at every mess hall meal. I loved it.

Games, hikes, boating, fishing, craft making were always on the daily camp postings. At night, campfires, burnt marshmallows, and off-key camp songs, usually with guitar, were available.

The camp counselors would warn us of the bears.

"Better not leave the cabins at night and be on the lookout during your day hikes," they would say. We, of course, thought they were just trying to scare us, but many years later I read up on the Adirondack Mountains, and found much to my surprise, that black bears roamed those hills.

But my favorite event was the one day only Olympic Camp Games. A series of events patterned after the real summer Olympics, but with significant modifications for adolescent boys. So weightlifting, shooting, boxing, and the javelin throw were out.

While I was small for my age, my nickname was Shorty, I was fast. At least I thought so, because while we never had any track meets in Moores

Mill, I was always the first one to get to the swing set during school lunch break.

So, when I saw long distance running on the Olympic Games sign-up sheet, I was in, along with at least 20 other kids who probably thought I should have signed up for the horseshoe or duck calling competition instead.

At twelve noon, the head counselor, shouted out "runners take your mark." Somehow, I got pushed to the back of the group. With all those older, taller guys in front, I couldn't even see the starting line.

"On your mark, ready, set, go." And so, we were off, first heading up the steep dirt road which led back to the mess hall behind us. The road passed through a heavy forest, then around the lake. One of the guys in front of me shouted out, "maybe we'll see the girls." He and his buddies were laughing as I passed them on a sharp curve overlooking the lake.

Then the dirt road opened up. Straight and flat. This is the running I liked the best. Just focus on the straight road ahead. Camp counselors were cheering us on and pointing out the directions ahead. "Down to the camp entrance and then back the way you came," they instructed.

I was panting now. Starving for something to drink. At the camp entrance, a counselor was handing out cups of …. Yes, yes, bug juice. I took two. I was energized, recharged now and on my way back to the mess hall.

The race seemed like hours, but clearly it was not. I was running alongside the lake now. "No girls," I thought to myself. Then I saw them, a group of runners just ahead. They were fighting for position before we entered the forest.

Coming up behind them I shouted out, "see any bears?" As they turned in my direction, I passed them by, all of them. "What the hell?" I heard as I entered the forest.

"Think of the swing. Think of the swing." I kept pushing on. I was feeling good. And then I was at the top of the dirt road leading down to the mess hall.

Looking at the camp director, the group of counselors and many camp kids gathered at the finish line, I realized there was no one in front of me. No one. They were all cheering. I heard one counselor say, "I don't believe it."

And there was the yellow ribbon, stretched across the dirt road. That must be it, I thought, the swing set, the finish line. It snapped as I ran through it.

A couple of months ago, I turned 80. For some unknown reason I decided to open an old box of childhood items my mother gave me many years ago. An old baseball glove, a book of the planets, a jar of sand from a beach in Florida, birthday cards, an old lunch box, and there, near the bottom I found it.

A blue ribbon, with my name on it. On the back was handwritten:

First Place, Olympic Meet, Long Distance, Camp Sigorria, Summer 1948

I held it up to the light. All the memories of that day came rushing back. Every last detail. From start to finish. It wasn't the Olympics, but to me it was just as good. It could have been.

I pinned the ribbon to my shirt and walked into the kitchen. My wife looked at me and smiled. "Wow, a super star," she said. "Shall we celebrate?"

Reaching back to that summer day in 1948, I replied, "sure let's celebrate. Do you know how to make bug juice?"

You've Got to Know When to Hold 'em

Holding up the X-ray, he turned to me. "This one's bad. Compound fracture. How did you do it?"

Should I tell him the truth or make up a fantastic story. I quickly conjured up a few beauties in my mind. Speed skiing down a black diamond course, breaking up a nasty bar fight single handedly, lifting a car off a pedestrian.

"I tripped over the garden hose."

He laughed.

As the nurse started preparing the paste for my second cast this year, I wondered if this was just me, was I just unlucky.

Luck, what is that? Oh, I knew the dictionary definition, but why does it happen and why does it not.

"Color?" It was the nurse.

"Excuse me?"

"Would you like a particular color this time? We have many you can select from." The nurse was smiling, my doctor was still laughing.

"Does Medicare pay for a color cast?"

"No, but it's not that much more."

"Let's go with the standard color and I'll save the difference for my coffee at Starbucks."

"Suit yourself, but we do have some fantastic colors, and some even glow in the dark."

"I'll stick with the off white, thank you."

As the white paste started to harden on my arm, I wondered, why are some people luckier than others, especially luckier than me?

Las Vegas, now there's a good example.

I've never won there. At least nothing to brag about.

When I visited, my mother-in-law and I used to sit next to one another at the machines. Poker usually.

"Another full house, a straight flush, a royal flush." Frances would say over the course of an evening. "How are you doing?"

"As usual," I would tell her, as I watched my credits dwindle to zero.

"Perhaps you need to try a different machine. Perhaps that will change your luck."

But it never did. All that ever appeared when the cards turned over was a losing hand. My luck, it seems, was never willing to show its hand.

It took a long time before I realized that sometimes you needed something other than luck in life. Like a gambler perhaps, a feel for the situation. Nothing to do with luck, a real gambler would tell you.

I was ready to celebrate my cast coming off.

We had stopped at a cowboy bar for something to eat. It was our first date, and, trying to impress her, I thought it would be a cool place to stop.

"Ever been here?" I asked. I could tell she was not sure about this place. Perhaps it was the row of motorcycles parked outside.

"Never," was all she said.

It was smoky, crowded, noisy, and poorly lit. We sat at the bar.

"Two cheeseburgers and two beers, please." I ordered for both of us. I thought that was a cool thing to do. I had seen Humphry Bogart do that in a movie. But of course, he was cool to begin with and it was only a movie.

Suddenly I was overcome with doubt. Jesus, I wonder if she's a vegetarian. Perhaps she really wanted the pulled pork special instead, or hates beer. It would just be my luck.

"Is that okay with you?" I asked her, thinking that Bogart wouldn't even care.

"Perfect," she said, "perfect."

The floor behind us was packed with pool tables. Every table was occupied.

The juke box was playing cowboy songs. I knew many of them.

Johnny Paycheck's, Take this Job and Shove it, Dolly Parton's, I Will Always Love You, Marty Robbins', El Paso, Johnny Cash's, Ring of Fire, Willie Nelson's, Always on my Mind.

Then, John Denver, my favorite. Rocky Mountain High.

I started singing along with John. I couldn't help myself.

"Colorado Rocky Mountain high ..."

Suddenly I felt his hand on my shoulder.

"Hey John Denver, you up for a challenge?"

Turning on my barstool, I came face to face with him. A real cowboy? The hat, the shirt, big belt buckle, dirty jeans and pointed boots. Needed a shave. Yes, he could be for real.

Taking a slow draw on his cigarette, and then flicking the long ash to the floor, he spoke again.

"I said, are you up for a challenge? 20 bucks to the winner."

He was trying to look mean.

"Excuse me."

"Don't you want to impress your lady friend?"

I didn't know what to say. Sure, I was trying to impress her, but at a game of pool, no way that was going to happen.

"We're just having lunch."

"Sure, just trying to avoid my challenge." He laughed and his friends followed. They were all wearing cowboy hats.

He was pressing the issue. Jesus, just leave me alone. But he wouldn't.

"Afraid, if you lose, your lady will walk out of here? Perhaps with one of us?" he said, waving casually to his buddies behind him. They were nodding their heads in agreement.

My God, just go away, please, I thought.

"Besides think how impressed she'll be if you beat me. You might even get lucky tonight."

I was getting angry now. He must have sensed it even through my silence.

"Of course, if you lose, she may see you for what you really are. A loser. A guy down on his luck."

Down on my luck, that did it.

"Okay, challenge accepted, except ..."

"Except what, John Denver, except what?"

"A hundred."

"Hundred?"

Getting off my barstool, and standing close enough to smell the whiskey, I said, "A hundred bucks, to the winner."

He looked at me and backed away, slowly, almost tripping over a pool cue on the floor. His friends were suddenly silent. Others in the bar were now looking our way. The whole bar grew silent.

"A hundred dollars, are you nuts?"

"You heard me. That's my offer. Take it or leave it."

He turned to his friends. They were waiting for his response. Everyone was. I picked up the pool cue from the floor and walked to the closest table. I was smiling now, and I wanted him to see it. He did.

"Should I rack them?"

He looked at me, over to my lady friend, then back to his friends.

"I said, should I rack them?"

"Shit, no way."

He stormed out of the bar and as the front door slammed behind him, his friends broke out in laughter. They didn't follow. The bar returned to its previous noisy setting, and I returned to my lunch.

Turning to her, a familiar song came over the juke box. It was Kenny Rogers, The Gambler.

You've got to know when to hold 'em
Know when to fold 'em
Know when to walk away
And know when to run

"Impressive," she said, "a hundred bucks worth of impressive. Were you that confident? Or just lucky?"

Feeling like a real gambler, I answered, "no, not lucky, I just knew what to do."

"Yeah, but I'm willing to bet that you would have beat that guy."

I smiled but didn't answer her. I didn't want to tell her that I had never played pool in my life. I just knew when to hold 'em and when to walk away. It really had nothing to do with luck. Nothing at all. Just being a smart gambler. Perhaps that's what Kenny Rogers was trying to tell me. Perhaps that's what life was all about.

The King

The flat rock skipped across the calm waters.

"If you get one to the other side, you win and the game is over," Jimmy said.

After many bounces, the rock abruptly stopped and sank to the bottom. In its wake, a series of circles, all that was left of its journey.

"Not even halfway."

"Jesus, Jimmy, we've hardly ever made it halfway. What makes you think we can skip one to the far end?"

"Someday. Someday, it'll happen, Michael. I just know it."

"Well, not today," I replied, looking down at my depleted pile of flat skipping rocks.

The pond, where we fished in the summer and skated in the winter was not more than 50 yards across. But all summer we had not been able to reach the other side. As hard as we threw, all our skipping rocks fell short.

"What you doing tonight?" Jimmy asked.

"Nothing."

Nothing was the usual response. After all, in our small rural town in upstate New York, there wasn't that much to do. There was school in the winter and spring. But in the summer, nothing to do but get into trouble. And trouble we got into. Jimmy and me.

"Well, I managed to find the white paint."

"And brushes?" I asked.

"Yeah, I got two of them."

"What time?"

"How about after dinner. I'll meet you at the bottom of the road."

The road. A dirt road that skirted past the pond, down a slight hill, to the real road that ran through our village. Route 82.

"Sure, I'll be there."

"So, what are you and Jimmy up to this evening?" My mom asked between bites of her fried chicken.

"Just hanging out. No real plans."

She looked at me like she didn't believe me, so I quickly changed the subject.

"This chicken is so good, mom. Thanks for making it."

"Too bad your dad's not here. He had to work late tonight. Home after dark I suspect."

After dinner, I bolted out the front door. Making my way down the dirt road, I saw Jimmy under one of the big maple trees.

"I was ready to give up," he said with a slight anger in his voice.

"I had to help with the dishes. I got here as soon as I could."

"Okay, are you ready?"

"Oh, yeah."

Ready? We had been planning this since school let out. "More than ready," I laughed.

Route 82. Not much traffic this time of the evening. Perfect time for what we planned to do.

"Here's your brush."

"Let's do it."

And so, our artwork began. Well, really not artwork. Neither of us could draw. But we could spell.

Five letters, spanning both lanes of Route 82.

We stood back and admired our work.

"Perfect," Jimmy said.

"Yes, it is."

"Quick a car is coming. Get behind a tree."

As the headlights approached, we dashed into the cluster of trees.

The driver must have seen it. How could he not. The car slowed then stopped. Just in front of the five letters.

We were giggling now.

"Not too loud, we don't want to get caught."

The driver opened the car door and moved to the front. In the headlights I could see him. Looking down at the letters. He looked up and looked around. Jesus, it was my dad coming home from work.

He shook his head.

The car started up and pulled away.

"Better get home," I said.

"Don't you want to wait for another car?"

"You can, I'm headed home."

Walking in the front door, I saw my mom and dad at the dining room table.

My dad looked up.

"How was your day, Michael?"

"Just skipping stones."

"Really. And this evening?"

"Just hanging out with Jimmy."

"Why don't you come join us?"

As I pulled up a chair, I saw it. Oh God, there's white paint on my shirt.

"Just hanging out, huh?"

"That's all."

My dad was looking at my shirt. He knew, I could tell he knew. I was in trouble now.

"Didn't have time for Presley?" My dad asked.

"What?"

"You know the singer, The King as you call him. Hound Dog, Heartbreak Hotel, and all that rock and roll stuff."

Oh God, he knew.

My mother turned to my dad. "What are you talking about, John?"

Looking directly at me, a big smile came over my dad's face. He started laughing too.

"You'll see in the morning, Edna. You'll see it."

And she did, and every driver passing through our village for years to come saw it. Even when it faded slightly from the summer sun, one could still make out the name, the name of The King of Rock and Roll, that stretched across route 82.

ELVIS

In large bold white letters.

ELVIS

Pluto Returns

The wheels of the Boeing 767 touched down. A bump, a loud squeal, and we taxied to the terminal.

"Sorry for the detour." It was the pilot. "We shouldn't be long."

The flight from London was a rough one. A strong headwind tossed the plane around like a rag doll. Many of the 200 or so passengers on board had been sick, including me, so being on the ground for a while was fine with most of us.

"We need to refuel," the first officer said about 30 minutes before we started our descent into Keflavík International Airport. "The headwinds were much stronger than we anticipated. We'll need to refuel to make it to New York."

"Iceland," it was the passenger next to me.

"Excuse me."

"I've always wanted to visit Iceland, but I didn't think it would be like this. A refueling stop."

He had been so chatty for the entire flight. An American, returning from a conference in London. Typical New Yorker, I thought at first, until he told me he was from Cleveland. An astrologer from Cleveland, who had been the main speaker at last week's annual international conference of astrology in London.

I fully expected him to analyze my astrological sign, or whatever it is these people do, but he didn't. Instead, it was mostly about himself and why most people thought astrology was pure nonsense. I didn't have the heart to tell him I was one of those people. But I really didn't have an opportunity to do so, even if I wanted to, as he was sucking up all the oxygen on the flight with his nonstop lecture. I was just an unfortunate audience of one. Trapped against the window in seat 27A.

Thirty minutes passed, then an hour.

I looked to see if there was an empty seat I could move to. Unfortunately, all 216 seats were occupied. I was stuck.

"Ladies and gentlemen, this is your first officer from the cockpit. The good news is we have completed refueling. The bad news is we are experiencing a mechanical problem with the aircraft. We will keep you posted."

Another hour passed.

My fellow passenger had fallen asleep. I didn't dare wake him for fear of another lecture.

But his sound of silence was not that long. He woke with a snort with the next announcement from the cockpit.

"Ladies and gentlemen, it's your first officer again. I'm afraid we're unable to correct the mechanical problem tonight. A replacement aircraft will fly in mid-morning. Sorry for the inconvenience. But you will all be put up for the night in local hotels."

"Oh sweet," he said as he woke from his nap. "My horoscope said to expect an unanticipated event. And here it is."

Horoscope, smoroscope, I thought. What about the rest of us? Did all our readings say the same thing? Unanticipated event? Mine probably said you will spend time with a bag of hot air.

He tapped me on the shoulder.

"Are you into horoscopes?"

"Can't say as I am."

"Well, what's your sign?"

"Sign?"

"Yes, your sign?"

"I have no idea."

"When were you born?"

"February first."

"You're an Aquarius."

"A what?"

"An Aquarius. You're independent, fun around friends, willing to take a risk, and willing to fight for a cause you believe in."

"Interesting, but I really don't think those apply to me."

"And are you ready for this?"

"What?"

"Best of all, the most prominent Aquarius trait is that they are great listeners."

"Jesus, I don't know what to say."

He laughed. "Don't say anything, just listen."

I wanted to tell him that's what I've been doing since the Boeing 767's wheels lifted off the runway at Heathrow Airport. Listening, not talking. But of course, I didn't, I couldn't. I could only listen.

"Ladies and gentlemen, your first officer again. Due to the limited hotel space in Reykjavik, we will have to place a few passengers into small inns. The flight attendants will be coming through the cabin to give you your assigned accommodations."

Oh God, I thought, please don't match me with you know who.

Well, my appeals to the Heavenly Father were apparently not heard as the flight attendant stopped at our row and with a big smile said,

"You two gentlemen will be rooming together in the North Star Inn."

I wanted to ask her if I could stay in seat 27A for the night, but before I could, he tapped me on the shoulder and said,

"Let's go roomy, we might as well see Reykjavik."

Once we boarded the shuttle bus, it was only ten minutes to the inn.

"Welcome to the North Star Inn." She was short and stocky. Thick eyeglasses, soiled on the inside by her long eyelashes. A friendly smile that was overshadowed by a missing front tooth.

The lobby, if you could call it that, was the bar of the inn. Only a few customers remained. Probably too drunk, or too tired, to make their way home.

"You're in room 3. Upstairs. Shared bathroom down the hall. Hot water comes on at eight in the morning. Breakfast down here from 9 to 10:30. If you're hungry now, I have some salted cod."

Room 3 was small. Twin beds, an old desk, and a lamp. One window, with a long crack down the middle, that looked out on to the back yard.

"Thank goodness, it's only one night," I said, as I crawled into the lumpy bed.

"Huh?"

It was clear he hadn't heard me. He wasn't listening. I wanted to ask him if his sign were not good listeners. So, I tried again,

"Only one night. I think I can deal with this."

"Yes, only one night. But the night Pluto returns."

"Pluto?"

"In Roman mythology, the planet Pluto is known as the god of the underworld, assumed to have powers of transformation and change. Also perceived as representing death and rebirth.

"Jesus, I always thought the planet was named after the Disney character," I replied trying to inject some humor into the conversation.

"Oh no, not at all," he said with a serious tone clearly not picking up on my attempt at humor.

"Oh. But what did you mean by Pluto returns?"

"Pluto takes about 240 years to complete one orbit around the sun, 248 actually. So, for Pluto, it's takes 248 years to complete a natal chart."

"A natal chart?" what's that I asked.

"A natal chart is an astrology birth chart, a map of where a planet was on its journey around the sun on a particular date. A natal chart is usually applied to the birth of a person, but can also be applied to a country, or even the whole world. The birth and death and rebirth of a country, or the world itself."

"And how does this relate to anything?" He could tell I was hooked now. I had become a real listener.

"Well, for example, take the United States. In June 1772, the first naval attack of the Revolutionary War took place in Providence, Rhode Island."

He turned and looked out the window, and continued,

"And we all know what that led to, the eventual creation of the United States. That was 248 years ago. So, 1772, is seen as the natal date for the birth of the United States."

"And what about the world? Did anything happen in 1772 as a natal date for the world?" I asked.

"Again, in June, a court case in England found that slavery was unsupported by English Common Law. The decision sparked the birth of a long global abolitionist movement."

He looked at me to see if I understood. I did, but suddenly I was more interested in getting some sleep. Plus, I figured he would continue his lecture on our flight to New York.

"Thanks for the interesting story," I said, as I pulled the covers over my head.

After a breakfast of salted fish and extra strong coffee, we boarded the replacement plane for the journey to New York.

The flight was smooth and since my fellow passenger didn't get much sleep the night before, he napped most of the way. I was actually disappointed, as I had many questions for him.

So, I spent the next five hours staring out the window and thinking about his Pluto returns comments last night.

The 767 touched down at JFK in mid-morning. It was late January, and a fresh layer of snow covered the ground.

As we disembarked, I decided to celebrate my return to New York with a real coffee. My fellow passenger was just behind me.

"I'm having coffee, would you like to join me?" I asked, turning towards him.

He didn't answer, but instead was focused on a CNN news bulletin which had just appeared on one of the many TV screens in the concourse.

"I said, would you like to join me for a cup of coffee?"

Still there was no reply. He continued to stare at the large TV screen just above us. His mouth was wide open. He was shaking his head.

I looked up to see what was so important. Then I saw what had attracted his attention.

"2020." He finally said, turning away from the TV screen and looking directly at me.

"What?"

"It's 2020, the year Pluto completes a full natal cycle. 2020, the year that begins a new cycle of …"

He didn't finish, so I did,

"This is the year Pluto returns?"

"Yes, yes, exactly, Pluto returns from where it was 248 years ago. 1772."

We both looked back to the TV. The commentator was reporting on a strange virus that had just been identified in China. Wuhan, China. No one on the CNN panel had an opinion about what this virus would do. What it would mean for the United States, or for the world. They were all in the dark.

But we knew. Both of us knew. We knew because Pluto had returned. A new natal cycle was beginning.

I Should Have Listened
to Uncle Joe

· ·

I looked both ways on the platform. The train's engine was almost silent now. Passengers were rushing for the exit. They were excited to be home. Above me hung the station sign, Napoli Centrale.

I always wanted to come here. To Naples. And here I was, at last.

Naples, or, according to the Italians, Napoli. The guidebook summed it up, a beautiful coastal town, but be careful.

"Be careful, Jesus, that's an understatement," my Uncle Joe said when I told him where we were going.

"Naples, really? Watch out for cab drivers, tour guides, little children, old people, waiters, policemen, street hawkers, housekeepers, anything with legs. Jesus, Naples."

It started almost immediately. Getting off the Rome to Napoli express at the Napoli Centrale Station, just after we passed underneath the Welcome to Napoli banner. Here we were, standing in the middle of the city's main train station. Probably looking like the lost confused tourists that we were. Yes, lost and confused.

"Can I help you with your bags, a ride to your hotel, want to buy lira, my sister has a jewelry shop, need a cheap place to stay, my brother's restaurant has the best pizza in Napoli, need a guide for Pompeii, interested in night life, a boat to the Blue Grotto." And then, "first time to Napoli?"

"Yes, it is, our first time."

He was short and stocky. His attire did not qualify him for best dressed cab driver of the year. Shirt splattered with wine and pasta stains, baggy pants, and sandals whose best days were long gone. His five o'clock shadow was running into days, weeks perhaps. A distinct smell of garlic and wine as he moved closer. And his long, grey hair. That was the most curious. After close inspection, I assumed his pillow simply determined his hair style for the day.

He reached out. "Please let me get your bags. They look heavy."

Heavy was an understatement. Why did she need all that stuff for three days in Napoli?

"Hair dryer," don't you think the hotel will have one.

We were packing for our adventure to the "be careful city" in the south of Italy.

"And do you really need this hair curler? Why three pairs of shoes?" The questions went on and on, until I was sitting on the suitcase, watching her snap it shut, and resigned to dragging it to Naples and back.

"You don't understand. I need all this stuff," was the only explanation I got.

"Where are you going? What is the name of your hotel?" He was three steps ahead of us and was dragging our two wheelless suitcases across the dirty marble floor of the Napoli Centrale train station.

"The Napoli International," she replied, looking at me and pointing to our bouncing suitcases.

"Very nice hotel, you will like it. But too far to walk, I will take you in my cab."

Remembering the section in the guidebook about taking cabs in Napoli, I asked, "How much?"

"Oh, not much, Signore, you'll see. Besides, you can't walk there with these heavy suitcases."

And that was the only explanation as we got into the back of his cab. She looked at me and her lips moved. Silently. But I understood. "How much?" I just shrugged my shoulders.

10 minutes later we were at the entrance to the Napoli International.

"Thank you, Antonio," I said. "How much do I owe you?"

"Twenty-five dollars. No lira please."

Handing him a twenty- and five-dollar bill, I said, "seems like a lot for about ten minutes."

"Oh no, Signore, standard rate, fair rate, very good rate. Look at the meter."

Of course, the meter was in lira. 43,600 Lira to be exact. Not quick at converting currencies, I simply said, "oh."

Antonio was clearly done with us. He pulled our suitcases out of the trunk, dropped them at our feet, hopped in his car, waved goodbye, and shouted, "ciao." Then he was gone.

"Back to the Napoli Centrale Station, I'm sure."

"Strange fellow," she said.

"Not really, just a typical Neapolitan."

Neapolitans, as the English call them, Neapolitano, as they call themselves. Residents of Napoli, a city which can trace its origins back 3,000 years to its founders, the ancient Greeks.

Residents, who their Italian neighbors in the north, say are loud, overly emotional and worse. But, in their own view, are simply passionate, proud, and food loving.

Naples, the city that introduced pizza to the world when Antica Pizzeria Port'Alba opened its doors in 1830.

Naples, the city which is in the direct path and thus constant threat of Mount Vesuvius, which erupted in 79AD burying the towns of Pompeii and Herculaneum creating a world-famous modern-day tourist attraction.

Napoli, a city with a reputation.

"They'll rob you blind," my Uncle Joe would say. Of course, his father was from northern Italy, near the Austrian border. "The civilized part of the country," he would add. "Not like those crooks in the south."

Napoli and the Neapolitano. 140 miles south of Rome. One hour and seven minutes on the high speed ItaliaRail from the Roma Termini to Napoli Centrale.

The clerk behind the desk spoke English. "Welcome to the Napoli International." His English was perfect. I was relieved.

"Would you like a room with a view of the harbor or one with a view of Mount Vesuvius?"

"Mount Vesuvius." We both answered at the same time. We did that a lot after 35 years of marriage.

Handing us two keys to our room, the clerk said, "your room is on the top floor, overlooking the city and Mount Vesuvius. A wonderful view. Enjoy your stay."

Room 1313. "Lucky number 13, doubled," she said as I opened the door.

Running to the window, she shouted, "come here. Hurry. You must see this view of Mount Vesuvius. It's spectacular."

Dropping the two suitcases, I walked to her side and looked out the large window. Out over the city and the famous volcano.

"Spectacular. Right?"

I didn't answer. I couldn't.

"Can't speak? It's so magnificent. Isn't it?"

Pressing my face closer to the window, I let out with "I don't believe it."

"I know, it's unbelievable."

"No, not that, it's the …. the…"

"What, what is it?"

"Uncle Joe."

"Uncle Joe? What the hell are you trying to say?"

"It's the damn Napoli Centrale, just across the street. Just across the street. The damn train station. We could have walked here in two minutes."

The City on the Hill

Potenza. The sign was so old and faded that I had to mentally fill in a couple of letters. But I knew I was here. Potenza. A long overdue visit to this city on a hill in southern Italy.

The guidebook was not kind. A good place to change trains. Uninviting weather. Few historical buildings because of the war and earthquakes.

But I wasn't coming here for the weather, or the buildings, or to change trains.

Stepping up to the car rental counter, she had pleaded "But it's less than 100 miles, and the train is only $12.00."

"But this way we can stop along the way if we want to," I replied.

She wasn't convinced. "Driving in Italy is so..." she struggled for the right word.

"Crazy?"

"That, and terrifying at times. Did you know that Italians have the highest death rate from automobile accidents in all of Europe?"

"Where did you read that?"

She didn't answer, but instead appeared resigned to a road trip.

"Italians, they're so wild behind the wheel of a car," she finally offered.

Yes, they were, I thought. But why? They are so mellow otherwise. In those small cafes, sipping coffee, chatting with friends. Strolling through city parks, playing with their grandchildren. Enjoying a pizza or a plate of lasagna and a glass of wine. Not a care in the world. And then they get in their cars and a whole different person emerges. Like Doctor Jekyll and Mister Hyde.

"Don't worry, we'll be fine."

Looking at her facial expression, I knew she wasn't buying into it.

187

"Besides, according to Ancestry dot com, I'm 80% Italian. That should count for something."

"Yes, and that's what worries me too."

The drive to Potenza was uneventful, unless you consider the Audi that passed me on that mountain curve, almost pushing us off the road, the Fiat that sped through that four way stop and missed us by inches, the funeral procession I mistakenly joined, and the two mopeds that passed me on the right shoulder.

Then there was the policeman who pulled me over.

"Stai guidando troppo lentamente."

After asking him what he said in English, I learned I was driving too slowly. Too slow! Jesus, only in Italy. For the rest of the day, I wondered if a casual mention of my DNA results would have avoided that ticket? But all I could muster was "mi scusi." Jesus, all I could say was "excuse me." Yes, uneventful.

After what probably seemed like a day and a half of white-knuckle terror to her, we were coming into Potenza.

Potenza, 2,700 feet above sea level. Overlooking a lush valley below. Potenza, referred to by some as the city of "100 stairs."

I wanted to say, "I told you we'd make it okay," but seeing that frown, I simply said "welcome to Potenza."

Our hotel room was quite charming. "I hope you enjoy our town," the clerk had said, handing us two gigantic room keys.

"I'm certainly not going to walk away with these," I said.

She laughed. We were good now. Of course, we were out of the car and on solid footing.

Standing in front of our hotel, I said, "Are you ready to explore?"

"Yes, but only on foot."

Again, we both laughed, perhaps too loudly, as the young Italian couple sitting on the bench next to the hotel, and who were clearly engaged in a romantic moment, turned and looked our way.

"Mi scusi," I said, thinking that was a much better time to use mi scusi than my pathetic response to Patrolman Rizzo.

"Wait here, I need to get a map of the city."

Walking up to the hotel desk, I asked the manager for a city map.

"Oh yes, you will need one. Where are you going?"

"To the city center and the old cemetery," I replied.

"Do you want me to call you a taxi?"

"Oh, no. We like to walk."

"Well," he said, "good luck."

He must have seen my sudden look of confusion, and so he elaborated.

"There are three ways to get to the city center. First, by taxi, second by walking, which will take you a little over an hour, and..."

"Did you say an hour?"

"Yes, to work your way up and around the side streets to the top of the city."

"And the third way?"

"The elevator, just across the street. 1 euro. Three minutes and you're at the top, at the city center."

"Thanks," I replied, thinking they should change the city of 100 stairs to 10,000.

"What did he say? How do we get to the city center?"

"Take the elevator over there."

"Elevator?"

"Yes, the elevator," I avoided telling her about the hour walk.

Three minutes later we stepped out of an old, smelly, creaky elevator and looked out onto the Piazza Mario Piagno, the large city square.

Some youngsters on the square were involved in a game of soccer. Suddenly, an errant kick came my way.

"Watch this," I said.

I approached the oncoming ball, ready to show my skills to all those kids. I suspected they would cheer me after.

As I started my kick, the ball took an unexpected bounce and went over my swinging leg and into the open elevator. As the elevator door closed, I raised my hands as if to signal a score. The kids were not impressed and there were no cheers. Mostly groans. And it would now cost them 1 euro each way to retrieve their soccer ball.

"Best we move on," I said. "Quickly."

"Indeed."

She must have laughed for the next five minutes, while I looked for a coffee shop.

"Due espressi per favore."

The expresso went down quickly. That's the way Italians do it. 80 percent DNA, showing me the way, I thought.

"I'm ready to find the cemetery."

Using the hotel's map, we quickly arrived at the Cimitero di Potenza.

The search took about an hour, even with the English language cemetery map. But finally, we were there.

The entrance to the mausoleum revealed its age. The heavy iron doors were rusted and difficult to open. The crypt was damp and cold. The only light in the room came from the open door.

White stone caskets lined the three walls. Using my cell phone as a flashlight, I read the names of the family members. Rocco, Margarita, and then Michael.

She came up behind me and put her hands around my chest.

"Is this the one?"

Tears were slowly running down my cheeks. They were tears of happiness.

"Yes, Michael Pomponio, my great grandfather."

My long search was over. My lifelong commitment to visit the city where my great grandfather lived, where my grandfather was born and where he immigrated from, where my 80 percent DNA was born.

I was home, to Potenza, the city on the hill that my grandfather told me about, the city he loved, that he begged me to visit one day. That I promised I would. The city he told me I would love too. And I did. Yes, I was finally home, and I could imagine my 80 per cent DNA saying, "grazie, Michael, grazie"

My Best Friend

It was that voice, again.

"You won't find it in there."

"What? What won't I find?"

I glanced down at the floor.

It was resting at my feet.

"What? "I repeated.

"The solution, that's what."

"Who said I'm looking?"

He was silent. At last.

I reached down to pick it up but lost my balance.

The hardwood floor rose up and hit the side of my face.

Or did it just seem that way?

Sometimes the floor rose up. Sometimes my face fell down.

It was getting harder to tell the difference.

Not that I cared.

All I knew was that I had joined the almost empty bottle of Jim Beam on the hardwood floor.

As the sweet smell of bourbon reached out to me, he returned.

"Isn't it obvious?"

Now it was my turn to be silent.

"I said, isn't it obvious? What you're looking for?"

Don't respond, I thought. Perhaps he'll go away. Jesus, if only he would leave me alone.

But I knew he wouldn't. He never did. He always returned.

"You do know that I'm not going anywhere, at least until we settle this."

"What if I don't care? What if I don't care if it's ever settled?" I shouted back.

"How can you be so selfish?"

"What are you talking about?"

"How many times do I need to tell you?"

"Just stop it. Stop blaming me."

"Well, it's certainly your fault. Who do you expect me to blame?"

"Well, I'm tired of it, just stop it, or …"

"Or what? More threats?"

"I'll do it this time. I mean it. You're pushing me too far."

"Right, you say that every time."

"But I mean it. Enough with this."

"And what would you do without me? Did you ever think of that?"

Suddenly I realized that I hadn't thought of that. What would I do?

"No, I haven't."

"I thought so. Never considering your actions, especially on me."

"But why should I consider you? What have you ever done for me?"

"Again, with that selfish question. It's all about you, never me."

"Of course, it's all about me."

"And so, this discussion never ends. There's never a closing."

"I could close it if I wanted to. Close it forever."

Closing it, I thought. It would be so simple. So easy. So permanent.

But what would I do without him? Again, that question.

I had no answer.

"Well then do it. Close it. Damn it, do it."

Sitting there on the floor, staring at the now empty bottle, I tried to imagine how I could do it.

"I'm thinking. Give me time."

"Time, that's all you've ever had. And how you've wasted it. Thrown it away. You're pathetic.

"Well, you've been no help. All you do is criticize me."

"What did you expect?"

"You could say something nice sometimes."

He was looking straight at me. And then he started laughing. A slow, rolling laugh. Like he was teasing me. Yes, he was teasing me."

"Something nice? You must be kidding."

"Huh?"

"When have you ever done something nice?"

"I ... er ..."

"Yeah, I thought so. There's nothing. See, you're so pathetic."

"But I've always ..."

"What? Always what?"

"Liked you."

"What?"

"I like you."

"How could you?"

"Because ... you're my only friend."

I started crying. I finally told him. It felt good to finally say it.

"But after all I've done to you?"

"In fact, I think I love you. Yes, I'm sure I do."

"I don't know what to say. This is a complete surprise. I had no idea you felt this way."

"And you? Do you like me?"

He looked down, then back up at me. I was afraid of what he might say, but I knew I wanted to know."

Then he spoke,

"Yes, I do like you. Very much."

"Really?"

"Yes. And I would miss you if you left me."

He was crying now. We both were crying. Our shoulders were heaving up and down with each sob.

I wanted to reach out and touch him, hold him, hug him.

As my arms moved forward, his did too.

Our crying grew louder. Rivers of tears were running down our cheeks. We grew closer.

I smiled, he smiled.

I started laughing, so did he.

Our hands were almost touching. This is what I had been dreaming of for so long. Me and my best friend. Together at last. I was so happy. I knew things would be different now. I knew I would change. I would be better, yes much better.

Closer, and closer. We were about to connect.

And then ...

My fingers touched the mirror.

Southern Hospitality

"What's this?"

My mother turned to me, "what's what?"

"This," I replied, holding a brochure in my hand.

We were on an extended family vacation. Driving from upstate New York to the Florida Keys.

I had never been south of New York City. I was ten and so looking forward to this. We had just crossed into Florida and had stopped to get gas.

"I'll explain that later," she replied. Then she glanced over at dad and shrugged her shoulders. He just nodded back.

Back in the car, that brand new 1950 Ford station wagon, the four of us were on our way. Christmas holiday vacation in the Florida Keys.

"So, what are these? They were in that display stand at the gas station." I was now holding at least a dozen different brochures.

"I'll explain later, your sister's sleeping now. We don't want to wake her."

How does she do it? I wondered. She can fall asleep anywhere. Even with this bumpy highway. US Route 1, one of the oldest highways in the United States. I read somewhere that it was built in the 1920s and ran from Canada to Florida. A two-lane highway, noisy and bumpy. And she could sleep.

After a couple of hours, my mom turned to the backseat. "You two hungry? Ready for lunch?"

Cathy immediately woke up when she heard that question. How does she do it? I wondered. The mere mention of food.

"Yes, yes." Cathy was wide awake. I just nodded yes.

"There's a diner up there," my dad said. "Shall we try it?"

Pulling into the parking lot, the sun's glare bounced off the structure's stainless-steel siding. I could barely make out the sign...

GOOD EATS DINER

... in big red letters.

"This must be a popular place, look at all the cars."

"And even a line to get in," my mom noted.

Jumping out of the car, I could feel the heat. "Not like New York in December," I said.

As we got in line, I saw it. Off to the side of the diner was a small run-down shack. I wonder what that is, I thought.

Then the line moved. Soon we were at the entrance to the diner. Then I saw it. The sign by the entrance.

NO COLOREDS

Tugging at my dad's shirt and pointing at the sign, I asked, "What's that?"

As he bent down to talk to me, those in the line behind us suddenly looked in our direction. Were they waiting for his reply? He must have noticed too, as he put his finger to his mouth and whispered. "Not now, son."

Stepping inside, we were greeted by a waitress wearing a blue checkered dress with a small white apron. "Welcome to Good Eats. The counter or a booth?" She asked with that southern drawl I had heard for the first time a day earlier.

"A booth, please."

Walking between a row of booths along the front wall and floor mounted stools at the counter, I looked down at the floor. A checkerboard of black and white vinyl tiles. So cool, I thought.

Motioning to an unoccupied chrome trimmed table, she said. "I'll be back shortly to take your order."

As the four of us settled into the booth, I looked across the table. "Okay, now, what was that sign all about?"

"Not in here, son. Please wait until we're back in the car." I could tell my dad was uncomfortable with me asking. My mom too.

"So, what would you folks like to order?"

My mom went first. "A cup of coffee and a hamburger."

The waitress smiled and said, "you're not from around here. Up north?"

My mom laughed, "yes, it's the New York accent. A dead giveaway I guess."

"First time in Florida?"

"Yes, in fact our first time south of New York with the children."

"I hope you enjoy your stay." Again, that southern drawl. I liked it.

The rest of us ordered. Hamburgers and French fries all around. Ice cream for dessert.

It was time to leave. While dad went to the cashier, the three of us went outside.

Then I noticed it again. That small run-down shack. My mom and sister started walking towards the car. But I was drawn to the old shack.

As I approached, I saw an old rusty sign on the front of the shack.

FOOD ORDERS AND PICNIC TABLES
AT THE REAR
COLOREDS ONLY

Then I saw him. He looked about my age, perhaps younger, but a little smaller. He hesitated. I smiled. Then I noticed the dog. Walking over to him, I could tell he didn't know what to do.

"Your dog?" I asked.

Shaking his head yes, he took a step back.

"Can I pet it!"

He looked around, and seeing no one, he replied, "yes, if you'd like to."

Of course, I would. I loved dogs, all dogs.

I reached down and started petting him. Just a mutt I thought, but so friendly. "What's his name!"

"Rocky, sir."

Sir? What's with that? "it's Michael." I replied. "What's your name?"

"Justin." He smiled and seemed more at ease now. He moved closer.

"Do you live around here, Justin?"

"No, just passing through. On our way to Georgia. What about you?"

"Just on vacation. We live in upstate New York. Getting away from the cold and snow."

"Never seen it."

"What?"

"Snow. What's it like?"

"It's like white rain, but frozen."

"Must be nice. Is it always white?"

"Never seen it otherwise."

"Oh."

"Did you eat at the diner? I asked. "The hamburgers are really good."

Justin looked down; I noticed he was barefoot. He was searching for the right words. He looked uncomfortable. He looked embarrassed.

"Did I say something wrong?" I asked. As I did, I reached out to him. Just then, we heard it. A big booming voice from behind me.

"Hey, get away from that white boy."

I turned. I recognized him from the diner. He was sitting at the counter when we sat down.

He was big and tall. Stepping between us and looking down at me he said, "Son, is this boy bothering you?"

I stood there, in silence.

"I said, is this boy bothering you?" The tone in his voice frightened me.

"No, we were just talking. I was playing with his dog."

Spitting at the ground just missing Justin's bare feet he continued, "Where are your parents? I saw you with them in the diner."

Pointing to the car, I said. "Over there. We're on vacation."

"Yea, damn Northerners coming down here. Disturbing our ways."

"But I was just..." He cut me off.

"Why don't you and your parents get in that car and head back north?"

"I ...." Again, he spoke before I could continue.

"We don't like your kind down here. Bring your northern way of life, putting ideas in the heads of blacks."

Then he turned to Justin.

"As for you, boy, get back behind that shed with the rest of your kind and finish your fried chicken."

"Yes."

"Yes, what?" he shouted

"Yes, sir, yes sir." Justin's voice trembled. He looked like he was going to throw up. Or cry. Or both.

"Damn right, it's sir."

"As for you, get back to that God damn car."

As he spoke, he moved his jacket ever so slightly. Just enough for me to see the gun. Justin saw it too. I started shaking. Justin just stood there.

Now it was all clear to me, the brochures. Motels, restaurants, and more:

Whites Only Motels
Theaters For Colored People
Picnic Grounds for Colored
The Best Hotels for Colored
Restaurants for Whites Only

"Did you hear me? Back to your damn car."

"Yes, sir." I made sure to emphasize the "sir." He was grinning now, but not a friendly grin. Probably the "sir," I thought.

Turning, walking, then running, I made it back to the car.

Everyone was waiting.

"What was that all about?" Mom asked.

"Oh nothing, just playing with a dog."

As the car pulled out of the parking lot, I looked back. Justin was waving. I could see tears in his eyes. I wondered if he could see mine.

The Eclipse

The solar eclipse of the century, the astronomers proclaimed.

"Are you driving south to see it?"

"Thinking of it as I've never seen one before. I mean a total eclipse, never seen one."

"Yeah, according to the local news, it'll only be 75 percent here."

"200 miles south should do it."

It was a rainy day in Seattle. Late October when the temperatures start to fall, and the leaves start to turn. Grey skies from dawn to dusk. Low clouds hiding Mount Rainier. Not my favorite time of the year.

"Salem, perhaps."

"Huh?"

"Salem, Oregon, it's about 200 miles south, and according to this eclipse map it will be within the total eclipse path."

"And does the map take into account weather?"

Oh that, the weather. The Pacific Northwest weather this time of the year. The time of the year when the sun takes a six-month holiday.

"Perhaps Idaho Falls or Casper. They're both in the total eclipse path."

Looking at my road map, I focused on Idaho Falls. It was closer than Casper.

The total eclipse path. That small track about 50 miles wide. I needed to be in that path, otherwise just stay put in Seattle.

Idaho Falls would be perfect, right in the middle of the path.

"Did you know that for any given location on earth, a total solar eclipse only happens about once every 100 years?"

"What, are you the expert eclipse person now?"

"Well, I did do some reading."

"Are you driving?"

"Yes, if I leave later this evening and drive all night, I could be in Idaho Falls about an hour before the eclipse.

"And the weather?"

"According to the newspaper, clear, sunny skies."

So, Idaho Falls was my destination. I had never been there. Never even spent any time in the state.

"It'll be an adventure. Idaho Falls and a 7-minute full solar eclipse."

It was 1956, I was in my mid-forties, a professor at the University of Washington. Twenty years removed from Southern California, I still had problems driving on the winter roads in the northwest.

And my car. A 1956 Chevrolet Corvette, Turbofire Special V8, 225 horsepower, five speed. Bright red and, of course, a convertible.

"This is a car more appropriate for cruising the beach neighborhoods of LA," my colleagues told me. "Hardly a car for the weather and road conditions here. You need an Oldsmobile 98 or a big Buick station wagon. Those cars live for the rain and snow."

And they were right, but I didn't care. I needed to retain something of my early years in San Diego. And this bright red Corvette was that. Besides, when the weather was bad, I simply walked to campus. My Corvette never went out in bad weather. Never.

The sun had set over Puget Sound. It was 7:00. The rain had stopped, replaced by a soft, cool breeze, and the sky to the west was ablaze with the fire of the departed sun. The evening sky above Seattle was aglow with the early city lights. Stars were appearing in the darkening sky to the east. This was my favorite time in Seattle. This is what kept me here.

The Interstate Highway Act had been passed earlier in the year, but construction was just starting. Thus, the only route to Idaho Falls would be on Highway 20, the Oregon Trail Route.

Driving south out of Seattle, a hundred miles to a nondescript junction just north of downtown Newport, I turned eastward on highway 20. 770 miles, 12 hours to Idaho Falls. I should be there by 8 in the morning, an hour before the eclipse.

Highway 20 nicknamed Big Daddy. The longest highway in America. 3,365 miles, through 12 states, from Newport, Oregon to Boston, Massachusetts. My route to a seven-minute eclipse!

The drive east was fine at first. A two-lane blacktop highway along the northern banks of Beaver Creek. Little traffic. Good weather. The Corvette was eating up the miles.

Starting up the Cascade Mountain Range, the weather quickly changed. And not for the better.

The westerly winds from the Pacific Ocean cooled as they were forced from the lower coastal elevation to the 4,800-foot summit at Santiam Pass. As they did, the humidity rose, and snow fell. Soon it was a blizzard.

The small towns of Shotpouch Butte, Menagerie, and Tombstone were hardly visible as the Corvette pushed its way to the summit. Then as the blizzard worsened the road gradually descended into the high desert of central Oregon.

The windshield wipers struggled to keep up with the blowing snow. The road markers were plastered with ice and snow. My last highway reading occurred just before Santiam Pass. 640 miles to Idaho Falls.

The road was empty now. No cars in either direction. But the snow was piling up. I started to question why I was doing this. For an eclipse. Jesus, I could have watched it live on TV from the comfort of my apartment overlooking Puget Sound.

Crossing the Harley Valley to the town of Buchman, I decided to stop for gas. Buchman, home to Ota Tofu Company, which advertised itself as the oldest tofu shop in America, located on the banks of the Willamette River.

One gas station was opened. Even in the raging snow, the circular iconic Texaco star sign and the bright red pumps stood out.

I pulled up to the Sky Chief Premium tank and turned off the engine.

The office was dimly lit, and I could barely make him out. 40 watts, I muttered out loud. No more than 40 watts.

He was standing behind the glass of the front door. Probably wishing I would just drive away.

I flashed my lights, twice, and he opened the door and started walking towards me. The blowing snow knocked his cap to the ground.

Rolling down my window, he came over to my side of the car. Brushing the snow from his cap, he leaned in.

"What ya need?"

"Fill it up please."

"And I suppose you want me to check the oil." His wrinkled face showed nothing but displeasure. He didn't want to be out in the storm. I didn't really blame him, but the gas indicator was approaching empty.

"No, that's not necessary."

"Hell of a night to be on the roads. What in hell's name you doing out here?"

"I'm on a mission."

"I hope it's worth it."

I wanted to tell him more but decided I was getting too cold, and he probably didn't give a damn about my mission.

"Where you headed?"

"Idaho Falls."

"A mission to Idaho Falls." He started laughing.

"I guess you could say that."

"Well, be careful of the construction at Cairo Junction. It's a real mess there at the junction."

"Cairo Junction?"

"Yeah, Cairo Junction just after the Stinkingwater Mountains."

"Huh?"

"Stinkingwater Mountains from the foul-smelling mineral springs in the creeks along the highway. You'll know when you're there, even with your windows up."

As I pulled away from the Texaco station and back on to snow covered Highway 20, I glanced in the rear-view mirror. He was shaking his head. Probably thinks I'm crazy driving in this stuff. Well, perhaps he's right.

Stinkingwater Mountain lived up to its namesake. The inside of my car now smelled like rotten eggs. Damn sulfur springs.

As I approached Cairo Junction, I could see the construction. Large trucks, bulldozers, construction trailers and equipment of all types lined the now gravel road. Rows of flashing yellow warning lights seemed to run in every direction. The blowing snow didn't help.

Midway through the construction, I encountered an intersection. I stopped and searched for directions. All signs had been blown over; some were buried in the deep snow.

One road went south and the other continued east. East, I thought, Idaho Falls is east. Depressing the clutch, I slowly eased the car into first.

The tires started spinning, then they caught the loose gravel. The car lurched eastward, into the storm, with the howling wind at my back.

Hours passed; the storm weakened. The winds subsided.

Another hour and I was out of the storm. It was still dark, but the road was dry. Time to push on, I thought, as the car accelerated. It would be smooth sailing from this point on all the way to Idaho Falls. To take in the full solar eclipse of the century.

The sky started to lighten as the sun broke the horizon. I glanced at my watch. 90 minutes before the eclipse. Plenty of time to reach Idaho Falls.

Not a cloud in the sky. Perfect viewing conditions. I felt like a little boy waking up on Christmas morning, jumping out of bed, rushing downstairs, to my presents under the tree. Only this time, the present would be a wonderful solar eclipse.

I was close now, but there was enough time for coffee and something to eat. The restaurant was just ahead.

Sitting at the counter, I looked around. Not many people in here. They must be in Idaho Falls setting up to view the eclipse. But that was not for 45 minutes, so I was going to enjoy my breakfast.

"What's your pleasure, honey?"

She was on the other side of the counter. I guessed in her 50s. Messy hair and a dirty pink apron. She looked like she just woke up.

"Coffee, black and your biscuits and gravy."

"Sure, honey." She smiled and then popped the gum she had been chewing.

The coffee was black, and bitter. Almost impossible to drink. I reached for the sugar.

The biscuits were stale and the gravy, cold.

"Everything fine, honey?"

"Oh yes, very nice."

She smiled, turned, and popping her chewing gum, strolled down to the far end of the counter.

Returning with the glass coffee decanter, she stopped in front of me. "Refill, honey?"

"No thanks, I'm fine."

"I'm curious, honey, what are you doing in these parts."

"I'm on a mission."

"Well, you must be lost. There's not much to do or see up here."

"There will be in about 30 minutes."

"Oh."

"You'll see when the sun goes dark, and the stars reappear."

"What are you talking about?"

"The eclipse, the eclipse of the century."

"The eclipse?"

"Yes, that's right. Best viewed in Idaho Falls. That's why I'm here."

"Idaho Falls?"

"Yes, Idaho Falls."

"No Idaho Falls here, honey."

"Huh,"

"That's 200 miles south."

"Oh, God."

"Are you okay, honey?"

Then I noticed the TV on the wall."

"Can you turn that on? I'm sure some station will be broadcasting it."

The old TV, with a grainy black and white picture, could only receive one channel. It was a live broadcast from Idaho Falls. An Eclipse Special.

The eclipse of the century was about to begin.

I closed my eyes. My imagination took hold.

The sun was burning brightly in a cloudless blue sky. As the moon's black disk slowly blocked the sun, consuming a larger and larger chunk, the temperature began to fall.

The sky began to darken. Birds, believing it's the onset of dust, grew silent and flew closer to the ground. Many birds took shelter for the 'night.'

In the moment before totality, a bright flash of light could be seen. Then there appeared a spectacular corona encircling the darkened disk of the moon. It was the Diamond Ring. Bright red and pink spots, caused by jets and loops of gas arising from the sun's surface.

The sun, now completely hidden, with its corona's light streaming out into space like ghostly whispers. Thin fingers, stretching millions of miles into space.

In the darkened sky, planets and brighter stars appeared. Venus, the morning star, was the most prominent.

Glancing away from the eclipse, I saw the horizon, where a partial eclipse was taking place. A narrow band of light.

It was even cooler now and a slight wind blew in from the east.

Then after about 7 minutes, the moon's trailing edge began to move off the sun. As the sun's rays shone through the moon's mountains and valleys, a sparkling necklace-like effect, called Bailey's Beads, was visible.

Moments later the sun re-emerged in a burst of brilliant light. And it was over.

I opened my eyes. The TV was still on. The broadcast showed Idaho Falls engulfed in a raging snowstorm. The announcer was offering his sympathy to the viewers. Given the unexpected weather, the total eclipse had not been visible. Not one second of it.

"Another cup of coffee, honey."

"Sure, why not."

"What's with the big smile."

"It was beautiful. Everything I imagined."

"What?"

"My first total eclipse."

I took a sip of the coffee. Strangely, it didn't seem bitter this time. In fact, it was very good. I thought of ordering another plate of biscuits and gravy.

It's all Part of the Experience

"Jesus Christ, I wish those cars would get off my ass."

"Just slow down, let them pass."

Driving through Croatia's countryside was more than I bargained for.

Rolling hills, beautiful scenery, narrow roads, and drivers from hell.

"Why do they drive so close?"

"Pull over, let them pass."

There were four cars behind me, and we were exceeding the speed limit.

"There's no place to pull over." My hands were sweating now. The steering wheel was getting harder to grasp.

"Turn on the damn air conditioner. It's too hot in here."

Croatia in August. Hot, hotter, hottest.

"I thought Simone said the weather would be perfect?"

Go to Croatia, he said. Get away from the fast pace of Italy. Relax.

She missed the AC button. Heat poured through the car's vents.

"Sorry."

"My God, it's like an oven in this damn car."

"I guess it's all part of the experience," she laughed, trying to ease my frustrations.

"And to think, we could be sitting on a beach in southern France. Why didn't we listen to Dominic? I wonder if Simone has even been to Croatia?"

The narrow road was now winding through the mountains.

SHARP CURVES
NEXT 10 KILOMETERS

Jesus, I didn't need to see that road sign.

Funny, why did I suddenly think of the Beatles? I started humming 'A Long and Winding Road.' It didn't help, the drivers behind me kept pushing. Closer now.

"They're not going to be happy, until they're in my trunk."

Finally, as I navigated what appeared to be the last curve, I could see a stretch of straight road ahead.

"The long and winding road is over," I said, again thinking of the Beatles.

"Paul McCartney would not be pleased," she replied.

"Well, he could think of it as just part of the experience."

The road straightened. Time to put some dust between me and these local drivers.

As I pushed on the accelerator, I saw him. Two of them. They were off to the side of the road standing next to their police car. The drivers behind me saw them too, but they didn't react. Still on my ass.

Oh Jesus, the red paddle. The tall one was waving that red paddle and pointing at me.

"Better pull over," she said.

Pulling off the road, the four cars behind me continued on. I thought I saw one guy wave. Really?

I rolled the window down as the tall guy walked towards me. Jesus was it hot. Thanks Simone.

"Hello officer, was I doing something wrong?" I hoped that playing the dumb tourist would help my case.

"Can you please get out of the car?"

"Yes, sir." Now I was hoping the "sir" would help.

It didn't.

"Come with me."

Walking across the road to the police car, I noticed the other officer. A young woman. Surely, she would be more understanding. More sympathetic.

Holding a radar gun, she said. "You were speeding."

"I... I didn't..."

"Fifteen kilometers over the speed limit."

Searching for a reasonable excuse, I settled on. "But those cars behind me were pushing me to go faster."

Clearly not buying into my attempt, she countered. "You could have slowed down."

She was right, I thought, so that strategy isn't going to work, perhaps I should try a different approach.

"But, how come you didn't pull over all of us?" Surely, she would see the logic in that response, I thought.

"Because you were in the lead, and I only had the radar gun on you."

Could it also be that they were locals, I wondered. Perhaps that driver behind me was waving to the police. Yes, that must be it.

"Can I see your driver's license?"

Handing her my international driver's license, I said, "the countryside is so beautiful. My wife and I are really enjoying your country."

She didn't buy into that approach either. "The fine is 350 krona."

The other policeman turned to me and said, "do you have 350 krona?"

"No, I don't," I replied, pulling my pockets inside out.

"What?"

"Sorry I don't, my wife carries all the money." I was laughing, hoping a humor strategy would work.

It didn't. "Go check and see if she has 350 krona."

"What if she doesn't?"

"Why are you giving us such a hard time?"

"Because I think it's unfair that you only pulled me over."

"As I explained to you, the radar ..."

"And I'm from New York, New York City. I'm a New Yorker, and we just naturally argue when we think we've been wronged."

"But we pulled over a driver from New York yesterday and he didn't argue. He was very nice, actually."

"I bet he wasn't from the city," I countered. "Probably from upstate."

I couldn't tell if they were confused, or angry, so I quickly moved on.

"I'm sure she has 350 krona; I'll get it."

Returning with the 350 krona, I could see she was writing out a ticket.

"Is that necessary?"

"Of course, we need a record. Don't you want one too?"

"Why, why do I need a record?" I asked.

Her reply was perfect. I wanted to laugh but hesitated. Then they both laughed, and I followed. I shook their hands and turned to my car.

"What did she say? Why were you all laughing?

Fastening my seat belt and handing her the speeding ticket, I replied, "She said it was all part of the experience."

Checkmate

It was the day of my birthday. 30 years old. The day when I felt the shift.

Yes, it was like a shift.

That's how I would describe it.

The moment seemed to stop, and then reverse.

It didn't feel like time was reversing, just me. Something about me was going backwards.

It was a terrifying feeling. I tried to stop it but couldn't. I had no control over it.

I was terrified too. Terrified of where I was going, and more terrified of where I would end up.

Memories and visions of the past started playing back.

At first, I was back to yesterday. I was finishing my assignment at the lab. Forecasting global weather.

The weather prediction project, called the Deep Learning Weather Prediction, was completed yesterday. It had taken 2 years to develop.

Given the importance of accurate longer term weather forecasts to many sectors of the economy, like energy demand and disaster preparedness, our team's assignment was to predict weather in a 2-week to 2-month time frame.

There was a sense of accomplishment and relief among team members in our ability to finally roll out useful global weather forecasts on an ongoing basis. "Job well done," the team leader said.

As one member of the team, I felt that sense of accomplishment, joy actually, but not relief. I wondered why.

The two years had gone by so quickly. Every day it was a challenge, and it appeared I fed on challenges. "Grew on challenges," my team leader commented. Now that it was over, I was satisfied with the accomplishment, but was more anxious to start a new project, with new challenges. More than anxious, I thought, I desperately needed a new challenge.

Then suddenly I was back to 10 years earlier. I was in a math department at a major university. MIT. Our department was working on unsolved math problems.

The most challenging math problem was the Diophantine equation, sometimes known as summing of three cubes. It was shown as $x^3 + y^3 + z^3 = k$, with k being all the numbers from 1 to 100.

What remained unsolved for over eight decades, stumping the smartest mathematicians in the world was the solution for k = 33 and k = 42.

Our math team at MIT decided to take on the challenge and find the solutions.

Working, what seemed like around the clock for 3 years, we were able to solve the equation for k = 33. K = 42 remained a mystery for some other math department. It was at that point that I was recruited to be part of the Deep Learning Weather Prediction team.

Suddenly I was back another 10 years. Ten years before joining the math department at MIT.

I was in a large room with a lot of small tables and many people, some young, some old. The room was buzzing with conversation. Other people were watching from a raised balcony. A large clock on the wall was approaching twelve noon.

There were two people to a table. As the large wall clock struck noon, conversations stopped, and the entire room fell into a strange silence.

Then there was a single cough, someone clearing their throat. About to speak perhaps.

"Ladies and gentlemen welcome to the thirteenth annual California open chess championship."

There was a smattering of polite applause. Then silence.

"As you know, this year we have opened the contest to all ages, as well as ..."

He stopped, perhaps just pausing to catch his breath, perhaps collecting his thoughts.

After a few uncomfortable seconds, he continued.

"This year we have 100 contestants and not just from California."

Again, he paused, but there was no applause. Just a few squeaks from contestants shifting in their folding chairs.

"So, our contest has become truly global, with contestants from Japan, Canada, and Europe."

"And for the first time in the history of the California open chess championship, we can say it is truly open."

There was laughter, then shouts of yes, and then applause.

"So let us commence play. The rules are simple. The loser at each table must leave the competition hall. The winner remains to take on the next challenger. Chess moves must be made in 30 seconds. Failure to do so will result in disqualification. An alarm will signal the completion of each 30 second interval."

"I would ask those of you in the audience to refrain from unnecessary noise, or movement. The contestants need silence so they can devote all their attention to the chess board."

Some in the audience nodded in agreement. We were ready to start.

"Players be at your ready."

One piercing tweet from the judge's whistle and the games started.

For the next two hours, as the alarm sounded every 30 seconds, losing players rose from their chairs, left their tables, and walked silently to the exit at the far end of the old convention hall. Most simply shook their heads as they did.

Finally, a few contestants remained. Perhaps 20.

The main judge called for a short recess.

"Time to revise the rules," he said.

"Contestants will now be required to make their moves in 15 seconds."

A collective gasp could be heard coming from the balcony.

"Players be at your ready." It was the head judge again. Whistle in hand.

With the sound of the whistle, the games resumed. But now the pace was faster and more intense.

Within 20 minutes, only two contestants remained. And after another couple of minutes, checkmate, only one was left.

And that was me. On my very first entry, I had won the California open chess championship.

The applause slowly eased and suddenly I was back at the beginning. My beginning.

I heard that some could remember the moment of their birth, that instant when one's existence begins. It's rare, but it happens.

And I remembered. For me it was like a bright light turned on. Actually, a flash of light.

And then I was there in that light.

But now that bright light was dimming. I was still reversing, back before my birth.

It was almost dark when I heard them speaking. Those voices I had first heard 30 years ago.

"Such a shame," one said.

"Yes, but what an accomplishment. Amazing."

"We never thought that it …"

"It would last this long."

"Yes, thirty years."

"For the IBM 2000."

"Yes, the first artificial intelligence machine."

"And what a success it was."

"Chess champion, mathematics, and weather forecasting. More than we had anticipated."

"But the new model, the IBM 2020 should be even more powerful."

It was almost dark now, a small dot of light remained.

But one final thought surfaced.

"New model, hell, I thought. I bet I could beat it at chess …"

The Border

. . . .

The sun had completed its journey to the west. It was dark now. Night had arrived.

Off in the distance were the lights of El Paso. The city lights flickered like diamonds and created a welcoming glow in the moonless sky.

I stopped to take in the view. I never tired of it, El Paso.

My horse was anxious to start moving again. I held the reins tight to signal to stay. He groaned as the bit dug into his mouth. He was not happy, perhaps in pain. I eased up on the reins.

"Good boy." I reached down for his mane. The long black hair was smooth to the touch, almost human my dad would say. I rubbed his neck. He snorted, letting me know he was happy again.

I was southeast of El Paso. A couple of miles. On my left the Rio Grande, separating the United States from Mexico. Further down across from the lights of El Paso, on the other side of the river was Ciudad Juarez with fewer lights. The border town Juarez, on the Mexico side.

The head lights behind me flashed, twice.

"Anything?" The voice from behind me broke the peaceful silence of the evening. It was Daryl.

"Nothing here." I replied.

We were on a slight rise overlooking El Paso, the Rio Grande and Juarez. Dust from the dirt road swirled in the slight wind, but the bandanna protected me.

How many times had I rode this way? Southeast from El Paso along the banks of the Rio Grande. About thirty miles, then back again, with Daryl, in the van, following closely.

We had just passed the La Equis, on the Mexican side of the Rio Grande. The massive red towers, nearly 200 feet tall, intersecting in an X

217

shape to represent the merger of two cultures in Mexico, the indigenous Aztecs, and the Spanish. Unfortunately, it was also the scene of many drug related conflicts and fatalities. Far too many.

And that's why we were here. Me and Daryl. Looking for drug traffickers.

La Equis was also a favorite crossing spot for those simply seeking a better life in America. Not drug traffickers, just ordinary people.

"Okay guys, your job is to catch those God damn drug traffickers when they cross over. Toss 'em in the van and bring them to the holding cell for processing. We'll take care of them after that." It was our commander, in charge of DEA activities here the El Paso area. An aging ex-military guy, who wasn't happy with his pension and even less happy with Mexicans. Hardly the kind of guy one would want in command, but here he was with all this power and all his hatred.

I was assigned the horse detail given that I grew up on a ranch in Wyoming. Daryl grew up in Detroit. I used to tell him he didn't know the difference between a horse and a cow, so that's why he drove the van. Still, we were good friends and worked well together.

"No action tonight," Daryl said as he drove the big white van up alongside of me. "The traffickers must be taking the weekend off."

Well, it was more than the weekend. It had been about two weeks since we caught any drug traffickers. Not surprising either. But the damn commander wouldn't listen. He just chewed us out when we didn't bring him any to interrogate. It was all numbers to him, numbers to make him look good and to pad his pension.

"Jesus Christ, guys, are you letting them slip through? Get out there and do your jobs." He was pissed, as usual, but not willing to acknowledge the changing times. I told Daryl he was too stupid to understand. Daryl said he was just stretching out his time because he was pissed about his pension. I think we were both right.

December 8, 1993, the date that changed everything. NAFTA, the North American Free Trade Agreement. Signed into law and went into effect less than 30 days later.

With NAFTA there was no longer a need for countless numbers of drug mules, poor young Mexicans looking to earn some money, smuggling drugs across the border by foot. Now they could use trucks. Some used airplanes.

So, trucks by the hundreds crossed the border at Tijuana and Juarez carrying tons of Colombian cocaine into the U.S. Their biggest and most profitable market.

Even the 1993 death of Pablo Escobar, head of the Medellín cartel, which was the world's largest and most powerful drug cartel in the 1980s and early '90s, did little to slow the flow of cocaine from Columbia, through Mexico, into the United States.

New drug lords simply replaced Escobar. The Sinaloa cartel based in Mexico, under the ruthless guidance of Joaquin "El Chapo" Guzman was one of them. El Chapo achieved his fame by pioneering the use of long tunnels under the Mexico U.S. border, which enabled him to distribute more drugs, especially cocaine to the United States than any other trafficker in drug history.

Using trucks and tunnels, the drug traffickers no longer needed mules, and certainly didn't need drug runners to wade or swim across the Rio Grande.

"Did you see that?" Daryl was pointing to the river.

"No, what did you see?"

"Motion, something moving across the river, heading to our side."

It was dark and hard to see, but I did make out some unusual movement. Like a frantic splashing.

"Well, perhaps it's a carp or catfish," I replied. "Those are about the only ones you'll find in the dirty slow moving waters down there."

"Na, there was too much splashing for a fish. Let's check it out. Maybe we have a mule. That should please the commander."

Daryl cut the engine and I dismounted. With our guns drawn we walked towards the river. The bright spotlight on the van, pointing the way, casting our shadows almost to the river.

It was a steep decline. In front of us, a chain link fence. Someone had cut a hole in it. Just enough room for a person to fit through. As fast as we repaired them, they were cut again. It was like a game with no ending, no final score.

"I better call that in," Daryl said as we reached the fence.

"Why bother? It'll be cut the next day."

"Yeah, but it'll keep the damn fence crew busy."

For years there had been talk of building a wall, a real wall. But this was 1997, and it was only chain link fence where we patrolled. Darryl and I, part of the Border Control, traversed along this side of the 15-foot chain link fence at night, looking for drug mules.

Suddenly they appeared. A family of three. A man, a woman, and a boy, probably in his teens. They were wet to the waist and frightened.

Daryl shouted, "you're under arrest, come forward."

They were on the Mexico side of the fence, but of course they didn't know that. So, as usual we took advantage of them.

As they squeezed through the fence, I turned to the man.

"Habla usted Inglés?"

"Si, señor, I speak English."

"What is your name?"

"Pedro."

His weathered face concealed his age, but not his hard life. Perhaps he was a farmer.

"Pedro, do you have a weapon, a gun?"

"No, señor."

"The boy, what is he carrying?"

"Just a backpack, señor. That's all."

"I have to search you, Pedro, all of you."

"We have nothing señor. Nothing."

"Well, Pedro, I still have to check."

Pedro emptied his pockets. They were empty except for a piece of paper with an address.

"What's this?" I asked holding the worn piece of paper in my hand.

"An address."

"Whose address?

"My brother in El Paso."

I handed it to Daryl, and he held it up to the light from the van. Then he turned to me.

"Not sure the commander will be pleased with this, but perhaps it will lead to something."

As Daryl handed me the piece of paper, I noticed the woman was carrying something in a blanket. She was holding the blanket close to her breast.

"El bebé … a baby?" I asked.

She shook her head, "Si señor, la niña, a baby girl."

Turning back to Pedro I asked, "are you the father?"

"Yes, and the father to Juan, too." He placed his hand on the shoulders of the young boy. That's when I could see the blood on his hands, on the side of his face too.

"How did that happen, the blood?"

"Some strangers, wanted our money, but I fought them off."

"The backpack? Did they try to steal that?"

"Yes, but my son ran ahead like I told him to, to the river."

"Well, I need to open it."

"Please senor, it's all we have left. Just enough to get us started here in El Paso."

Daryl grabbed the backpack out of Juan's hands. "Now I'm intrigued. Let's see what's in here. What's so damn important."

Daryl opened the backpack and turned it upside down.

Small charms fell to the ground. Dozens of them. Angels, crosses, a few horseshoes.

"Milagros, senor," Pedro said. He was forcing a smile, but it was a nervous smile.

Daryl reached down and picked up a cross. "What did he say?"

"Milagros. Spanish for miracles. Religious charms that are carried for protection, good luck and good fortune."

"Si, señor, for our trip to the United States."

"Hey Daryl, is there anything else in that pack?"

"Just some clothing, and Jesus, what do we have here?"

Daryl slowly pulled the package from the backpack. The contents came into the light.

A brick of cocaine. About 2 pounds in a sealed plastic bag. Daryl started shouting, "We've got ourselves a mule. Jesus, about time, a God damn mule."

"Please señor, let me explain."

"No explanation, Pedro. This speaks for itself." Then Daryl turned to me, "what do you think this brick is worth?"

"$15,000 give or take."

I turned to Pedro, "would you like to explain this?"

Pedro looked down, then over to his wife.

"Marie, por favor … please … show them."

Marie slowly unwrapped the thick blanket from around her baby.

"Jesus, what's that?" Daryl shouted.

It was a small baby, sickly looking. Pale and waxy complexion. Underweight. Dark sunken eyes. Gasping for breath.

"Pedro, what's wrong with your child?"

"We don't know, señor. The doctors in Mexico won't help her. They say she is cursed. That's why we have come to the U.S. To seek help for our child."

"But what about the cocaine, Pedro. What about that?"

"We were told it would cost mucho dinero to have her treated in your country."

"So you …" before I could finish, Pedro broke in.

"Stole it from some Sinaloa drug traffickers. I would sell it to pay for my daughter's…"

"But Pedro, you know that's against the law here."

"Si señor, but what could I do? My daughter, she is dying. She needs help. She's my daughter."

"But still, it's against the law."

"But señor, do you have children? If you do, you would understand."

Children, I thought. Yes, I would. But too busy with my career, unhappy marriage, then divorce. And now, patrolling this God damn chain link fence. No wife, no children, just a small cluttered apartment in El Paso.

"Pedro, is that what the fight was all about?"

"Si, señor, they fought me for it. Some drug traffickers from the Juarez cartel."

Daryl turned to me, the brick of cocaine in his hand. He was grinning and I knew why.

"Jesus, I vote to take them back to the commander. Perhaps he'll stop bitching to us if we bring him some mules."

"I'm not sure, Daryl. Look at that baby. She needs medical attention, now."

"So, what do you want to do?"

"You take the family to the El Paso Children's Hospital. They'll take care of her."

"And the cocaine? What about that?" Daryl asked.

"I'll take the brick to the commander."

"But how will you explain it? Jesus, just a brick, no mules."

"I'll say we found it near the fence. I'll say, someone probably dropped it when they saw us approaching. That they must have run back into the river. Back to Mexico."

"Shit, you know he's going be pissed, really pissed that we didn't capture the mules. Numbers, that's what he wants."

"Well, what would you do, Daryl?"

Daryl looked at me. Then he turned to the family. The mother was on her knees. The boy was crying. Pedro had his head down. Then Daryl handed me the brick of cocaine.

"Just make sure you stand at least 6 feel away."

"What? Why Daryl?"

"I doubt if the commander's pissing range is more than 5 feet."

Olé

．．

Standing on the red dirt, I could tell that it had just rained. My toes sank into the cool soil.

But how did I get here? I remember a long dark tunnel and before that sunshine. Plenty of sunshine. Green grass.

And where are my friends? We were running through the green grass but now I'm alone. So alone.

I called out for my friends. "Where are you?"

But they didn't reply.

What was that? The noise was unlike any I had ever heard. Over and over. Louder and louder. All around me.

I don't like that noise, it scares me. Instinctively I kicked the cool dirt under my feet. The noise stops.

The sun was shining in my eyes now. And my vision blurred. I was thirsty. So thirsty.

Then the noise returned. Even louder.

Something was in front of me. Colorful. Tall and straight. Should I run? Before I could, it was behind me.

Scared. I called out for my mother. "Mother. Where are you? Help me."

But she didn't reply.

The heat from the sun was more intense now. I was sweating. Thirsty. Angry too. Why am I here?

The pain in my shoulder was sudden and intense. The noise returned. Was that blood running down my back? Oh God, please not blood.

Looking down, I saw it. First a small spot and then more and more, into a bigger and bigger circle. The ground beneath my feet turned bright red. Blood. My blood.

Where was my father? He could stop the bleeding. He would. "Father," I cried out.

But he didn't reply.

The sun had disappeared behind the clouds. It was cooler now. Afternoon.

It was long and shiny. Just above me. The noise grew louder. Louder than before. I was terrified. What was happening?

Shooting through my upper back, the pain was more intense than before. My knees buckled. My face hit the red dirt. The taste of blood. That god awful taste of blood. Was all of that mine?

For one fleeting moment I could see and hear. One sound, over and over.

Olé, Olé, Olé

Then,

Bravo, Bravo, Torero.

So tall, so colorful, with his short jacket, a waistcoat, and skintight trousers of silk and satin. His outfit beaded in sparkles of gold and silver.

He was kneeling before me. Reaching down, he cut off my ears with a small knife. I felt nothing. The noise grew louder. Cheering. They were all cheering El Torero, the brave matador, for he had just defeated me, the bull.

A Lesson in India

The pain was intense.

"Stop feeling sorry for yourself," my wife said. "Work your way through it."

Of course, the back injury was my own doing. "You're not in your twenties, so stop acting like you are," my doctor lectured me. She was referring to the fact that I had done the same thing less than 6 months earlier.

God, I hate getting old, watching my ability to do things which were so routine slip away. Naps in the afternoon, many unplanned, just falling asleep, many times in the middle of a movie. Hearing and eyesight, too. Reading glasses all over the house. Hearing aids and boxes of hearing aid batteries. All monuments to aging. My aging.

Driving at night no longer pleasant. Oncoming headlights burning into my eyes, blinding me for the road ahead. Yes, it's time to head home, the sun is setting, seemed to be a common theme when visiting friends.

Spicy foods, which I long enjoyed, now necessitated a prescription pill prior to eating. And sometimes they didn't work. Gastric reflux, the doctor said. Gastric hell, I replied.

At least you have your hair, my friends would tell me. Yes, I did thanks to my father's DNA. But his DNA was now presenting me with diabetes. "Pre-diabetic," my doctor tried to reassure me. Just one more thing, I thought.

Sitting in my easy chair one day, I was reflecting on my past. I do that a lot now. Much more now, thinking about time gone by, more than about the time in front of me.

I felt myself getting depressed. Was it the pain, was it my age?

"Stop feeling sorry for yourself. Work your way through it." Her words were consuming me. But she was correct.

Thinking back again.

I was in India. I had gone there to experience the country, the culture, the people.

"It will change your life forever," the travel agent said.

I never could have imagined how much, until I returned. A month, just a month, and I felt reborn, almost a different me. At first the lessons learned were so subtle, but gradually they replaced my old ways of doing things and old ways of thinking. But over time, the lessons seemed to fade. Why, I wondered? Why couldn't I recapture those lessons.

I thought again about India.

One afternoon in particular stands out. It may have been the most important afternoon of my life, certainly at that age. I was in my late twenties and had decided to walk to the park overlooking the river. I was in the city of New Delhi, Old New Delhi actually.

Delhi is a mixture of old and new. The street network of Old Delhi, where I decided to stay, reflected the defense needs of an earlier era. Streets irregular in direction, length, and width discouraged earlier invaders.

Narrow and winding paths, alleys, and byways rendered much of Old Delhi accessible only to pedestrian traffic. The streets also resulted in many confused and lost visitors.

The clerk in the hotel told me it was best to avoid the beggars. "Pay no attention to them, just walk away, and never give them anything," he said.

That afternoon, I found out what he meant. As I walked through the narrow streets, trying to find my way to the park, a young boy approached me. He held out his hand. His arm was covered in dirt, his feet too. He had no shoes. His shirt was faded and torn, but I could still make out what it said, Welcome Home.

He didn't speak very good English, but I knew instinctively what he was asking for. I didn't have any money with me as I had left my wallet in my room. Again, on the advice of the hotel clerk.

But I did have a candy bar. A Milky Way.

I handed the boy my only candy bar. He smiled and then he shouted out to his young friends. Before I knew it, I was surrounded by young kids, reaching out to me, shouting "please, please."

I broke away and continued my walk. After many wrong turns, I was finally at the park. Overlooking the Yamuna River, the park was full of Neen shade trees, with their low hanging pale yellow fruit.

I saw only one empty bench and decided to sit. All the other benches were occupied, and I wanted to be alone, especially after my experience with the Milky Way. It was shaded by a large Neen tree, so it seemed like a good place to rest.

But I wasn't alone for very long.

"May I join you?" he asked.

"Of course."

He looked quite old, but then I could never really tell the age of anyone in India. He was wearing a traditional Sherwani, a long below the knee jacket styled coat, studded with colorful beads. His pants looked like tight fitting pajamas. For shoes, leather sandals, and of course, no socks.

"Are you an American?"

"Yes, I am. Have you been to America?"

"No, but I know about America."

I was curious, "what do you know?"

"America, the land of engineers and entrepreneurs."

"And what about India, how would you describe India?" I asked.

"That's easy," he said. "We're the land of philosophers."

He smiled, and then I asked about the red dot between his eyebrows.

"The tilak," he said. "It represents a third, inner eye. Hindu tradition holds that all people have three eyes, the two outer ones used for seeing the outside world, the third one focusing inward on God. The red dot serves as a constant reminder to keep God in the front of a believer's thoughts."

We talked for a long time, before I asked him what I wanted to, after he described India as the land of philosophers.

"What is your philosophy of life?"

He leaned close to me. He was smiling, like he expected my question.

"Life. Life is just a journey. Sometimes it's a long journey, and sometimes it's short. We never know how long it will be when the journey first begins."

"Like a walking journey, a pilgrimage?" I asked.

"No, more like a journey on a train."

Of course, a train, why didn't I think of that, the most common form of transportation in India.

He continued.

"When we leave the first station, we get to see all these new things. We meet so many different people on our way. It is a delight, a wonder for us."

"As we stop at stations along the way, some passengers get off the train, never to be seen again, but some stay, and new passengers get on. And the scenery, our experiences, change as the train pushes on."

"Eventually, the train breaks down, in need of repairs before we can continue our journey. Sometimes the repairs are minor, but sometimes they require much effort to repair."

"Along the way, we may decide to get off our train, and board a different train, which may be going in a different direction. But from time to time, it too will be in need of repairs along the way. There will be breakdowns."

"During your journey, you will come to realize there is still much to see, more people to meet, perhaps more trains to catch. You are continuously filled with wonder and excitement for the journey ahead."

"Over time, the speed of the train slows, the number of passengers disembarking increases. Fewer passengers are on the train with you. The scenery is still new, but sometimes you wish for that scenery past. Sometimes you wish to return. But the train is only one way, there is no return ticket. And the breakdowns and repairs become more frequent and perhaps more difficult, until they cannot be overcome."

"Finally, you hear the conductor's voice."

"Last Stop Ahead."

"You get up from your seat and reach for your baggage in the overhead. But there is no baggage. Everything you have collected along your journey is gone. As the train pulls into the last station, you notice old friends and old family members on the platform. They are waving at you. Some are holding signs. Welcome Home."

He was done speaking. He looked at me and smiled. He started to get up.

"That's an amazing way to look at life," I said.

He put his hands together, bowed slightly and said, "thank you."

I reached out to shake his hand. "May I?" he said, as he reached out to me. "Yes, of course," I replied, as he gently applied the tilak to my forehead.

"Appreciate your journey. Appreciate, every day you get to spend on your train." Then he turned and walked away.

Now in my eighties, thinking back to that day in India, I realized that I had changed stations many times, met so many passengers along the way, had to endure delays because of breakdowns, and been exposed to a diversity of scenery. I also realized that the conductor had not yet shouted, "Last Stop Ahead."

Clearly it was time to stop feeling sorry for myself and continue with my journey.

The Script

"Where were you last night at 11?"

The detective was clearly annoyed and upset with me. The interrogation was not going as he had anticipated. Perhaps he needed another cup of coffee.

"Home watching a movie on TV."

Witnesses? Any witnesses?"

"Just Bosco."

"What?"

"My dog, Bosco."

"Your dog? Bosco."

"Yes, he likes to watch movies. Any movies with dogs. Bosco just loves those."

"What the hell kind of name is Bosco?"

Yes, Detective Jones was angry now. He started shouting and pounding on the old wooden table. I wondered if the legs would hold. He needed to calm down, I thought. No more coffee. Perhaps pot. Yes, some strong weed would be helpful. If only we were at my house, I would offer him some. But not here. Definitely not here. Although I'd bet, they have some really good stuff in the evidence room.

"A drink."

"What the fuck are you talking about?"

"My favorite drink when I was a kid. Bosco. A chocolate syrup mom would put in my milk. It was really …

Raising his hand to stop me, he asked, "How long did you know Mr. Smith."

"Well, we worked together, so a long time. Twenty years, perhaps more."

233

"And during that time, you never had a disagreement?"

"Of course, we did."

"And did they ever become violent?"

"Violent?"

"Yes violent, damn it, violent." His voice rose on each word until he was shouting. "Violent."

"Depends."

"Depends? On what?"

"Your definition of violence."

He was pissed now. His fists came crashing down on the table. Hard. Really hard. The table shook and the empty coffee mug fell to the floor. Its broken pieces slid across the barren floor like marbles. Now that's violence, I thought. No wonder his wife left him.

"Do you think this is a fucking game we're playing here? Do you?"

"No, of course not." But I thought if it were, I'd be winning. Yes, it wouldn't even be close."

"Okay, tell me about some of your disagreements."

"Well, as you know, we both worked in the national weather forecasting department. So many of our disagreements would involve things like tomorrow's high temperature, amount of snowfall, or the chance for rain. I think the most violent disagreement ended with me throwing a magic marker at him once when we argued over a moving cold front."

"Listen, wise guy, I've about had it with you and your crap replies. We happen to know that you two were seen together two nights ago and were having a pretty heated argument. And we have multiple witnesses."

"Unlike Bosco, I hope they can speak," I said.

He jumped from his chair, almost knocking the table over. He was really mad now. I had probably pushed him too far. I could tell he was also stressed. This must be difficult for him, I thought. After all, Mr. Smith was his stepdad. And now, Mr. Smith was dead. Murdered they said.

"Jesus, what's with you?" A man is dead, and you're joking around."

He came around to my side of the table. He was furious. Lowering his face close to mine, he whispered, "if we weren't in this room, I'd be tempted to beat the crap out of you."

"Don't let him get the best of you, Detective Jones." A second detective walked into the interrogation room. He was carrying a thick folder in one hand and a cup of coffee in the other.

"Here, take this," he said as he handed me the cup.

Reaching for the coffee, I looked at his badge. Detective Brown.

"You must be the good cop," I said. "I guess that makes Detective Jones the bad cop,"

"Can you believe this guy?" Jones shouted. "A real clown."

"But without a big red nose, like you," I replied. I could see I was getting to him. His entire face was turning red. His hands were shaking too. He wanted to hit me.

"Jesus Christ," Jones yelled, "in the good old days, we wouldn't have to put up with this shit. God damn rules now. No physical contact. Cameras everywhere. Shit."

Detective Brown opened his folder and in a calm voice said, "please tell us about your meeting with Mr. Smith two nights ago."

"Jesus, now we have to ask please," Jones was sneering as he walked to the far end of the interrogation room and glared into the one-way mirror.

"What do you want to know?" I asked.

"Well for starters, what was the conversation about and why did it get heated?"

"It was personal, Detective Brown. Very personal."

Jones turned and bolted back to the table. Grabbing the coffee cup out of my hand, he screamed. "Give me one minute with this shit, Brown. I'll get all the answers we need."

"I wouldn't drink that coffee if I were you," I said in the calmest voice possible.

"Why," he said taking a big gulp.

"I may have spit in it trying to cool it down."

Coffee flew all over the table, on my shirt, over Detective Brown's open folder.

Jones's hand clenched into a fist. Yes, he wanted to hit me. I was winning the game.

"Let's get back to my question," Brown quickly interjected. "Please tell me about that evening?"

Rolling his eyes, I could see Jones mouthing the words fuck you. Who's he referring to, I wondered? Probably both of us. Both Brown and me.

"Well, like I said it was personal, but I guess it might be helpful if I did tell you."

Both detectives were sitting across the old table now, looking directly at me.

"Smith was concerned. Said he was growing more afraid of someone by the day. The person was becoming more violent too. Not physical yet, but his tone of voice. Very threatening tone of voice."

"But why did you argue?"

"He wanted to work it out. I wanted him to go to the police. That's what we argued about."

"Did he give you a name?"

"No, not directly. He refused. He wanted to work it out."

"This is a joke," Jones said. "No names. Just his stupid story."

"Well not exactly, "I said, "there was a name."

Brown leaned in, "well?"

"Mary, over and over he used the name Mary."

Jones jumped to his feet. Clearly angry, but also concerned. Yes, I could tell he was concerned now.

"What the hell, now we're supposed to believe that someone called Mary killed my stepdad. Jesus, can you believe this guy?"

"I didn't say Mary killed your stepdad."

"Well, what did Mary say?" Brown asked.

"Mary warned him about this guy. Said, he was trouble. Big trouble. Told him to avoid him."

"This is nothing but crap," Jones screamed pounding on the old desk. Suddenly one of the wooden legs broke. The desk toppled over on its side. The papers in Brown's folder spread across the floor.

"Jesus, calm down," Brown ordered. "What's got into you?"

"Yes," I said, "what?"

Jones looked at both of us. He was quiet now.

"Did Mary tell Smith anything else?" Detective Brown asked.

"Yes," I replied. "She said that was why she left him. She was afraid of him."

Detective Jones shook his head. "This is crazy," he said. "We're supposed to believe this guy?"

"Why not?" Brown replied. "Why shouldn't we?"

Jones said nothing. He was looking down at the floor, all the loose papers around him. Then he noticed. There was a picture of Mary. Jesus, she looked so beautiful. So happy.

"Can you think of a reason not to believe him, not to believe Mary?" Brown was looking at Jones now.

I was silent now, too. Just watching the game play out. Just watching. It was coming to an end. Did Jones realize that?

"No, I can't," Jones finally said. I could tell he was down to his last out. The game was almost over.

"Why did she leave me?" Jones said. Crying now. "Damn it, why did she leave? I told her I would control my temper, but ..."

He stopped speaking. He was just staring at his open hands.

"But you didn't stop. You kept hitting her," Brown said. "Didn't you?"

"Yes, I couldn't stop. I wanted to, but I couldn't."

"And then Smith told her," Brown continued, "he told Mary to leave. To leave you."

"Yes, he did, damn it. He ruined everything."

Finally, I broke my silence. "Your stepdad told Mary to leave you because he feared for her life. He wanted to protect her from you and the violence."

"Yes, God damn it. He told her to leave me. He ruined everything." Jones slumped to the floor. He knew the game was over. He had lost.

"So that's why you killed him, your stepdad?" Brown said. Not a question, I thought, just a statement.

"Why did he tell her to leave me? I could have killed him for doing so. I could have ... I mean I did, I did."

Two other officers came into the room and escorted Jones out. He was in handcuffs.

Detective Brown walked over to me and reached out to shake my hand. "So, how's the acting career going?" he asked.

"Well, just doing commercials now. Mainly for prescription drugs. Heartburn, muscle aches, erectile dysfunction. But at least it keeps me in front of the camera."

"You probably miss the old days."

"Oh yes, working on movies and TV. Columbo was my favorite.

Working with Peter Falk, now that was exciting. That was acting. Unlike erectile dysfunction commercials."

"Well, as usual, thanks for helping out with this one."

"Anytime, just get the script to me in advance."

"Will do, take care."

"I think I would have liked them," I said heading for the door.

"Who?"

"Mr. Smith and Mary, of course."

To Be or Not to Be

"To be or not to be, that is…"

"Stop, stop." It was John the director.

"Say it like you mean it, like you are searching for an answer. Should you take your own life, or not? That's the answer you're searching for."

"Sorry."

"Okay, take it from the top. Act 3, Scene 1."

"To be, or not to be, that is the question.

Whether 'tis better in the mind to …"

"Stop, stop. William it's nobler, not better."

"Sorry."

Jesus, what was I doing here anyway? I didn't even want this part. The role of Prince Hamlet. Why was I chosen?

"William, concentrate. I know you can do it. Just concentrate on the dilemma facing Prince Hamlet. To be, or not to be, that is the question he is confronting."

John wasn't upset. He was trying to help me. I realized that, but why was I resisting his help? Always, resisting.

"Take it again, from the beginning."

I took a deep breath, then,

"To be, or not to be, that is the question.

Whether 'tis nobler in the mind to suffer

The stings and arrows of…"

"No, no William. It's slings, not stings."

"Sorry."

"Okay everyone, let's take a 30-minute break."

We had been rehearsing this part, Act 3, Scene 1 all morning. The opening scene with the soliloquy by Prince Hamlet, where he's bemoaning the pain and unfairness of life but at the same time recognizing that death might even be worse. Thus, his dilemma.

"To be, or not to be…"

I sat down on a hard metal chair. We were in a circle. All the performers and the director, John.

"Perhaps it's time we discuss this scene in more depth." John was talking, but I felt he was really speaking to me. "Everyone, please pick up the book in front of you."

Selected Works of William Shakespeare. The cover was ragged in places. The binding was loose.

I gently opened my copy. The pages were worn. Some had handwritten notes in the margins. Different handwriting too. I wondered how long these books had been used and how many had used them.

Turning to Hamlet, Prince of Denmark, Tragedy in Five Acts by William Shakespeare, 1600, I flipped the pages to Act 3, Scene 1.

Hamlet is Shakespeare's longest play, with 29,551 words. Set in Denmark, the play follows Prince Hamlet and his planned revenge against his uncle, Claudius, who has murdered Hamlet's father in order to seize the throne and marry Hamlet's mother.

John was speaking, "So what is Hamlet contemplating in this scene?

"To be, or not to be, that is the question.

Whether 'tis nobler in the mind to suffer

The slings and arrows of outrageous fortune,

Or to take arms against a sea of troubles.

And by opposing end them? To die: to sleep."

"What do you think is the philosophical meaning of to be, or not to be? The deeper meaning?" John was probing us for answers.

"William, what is your take on this scene?"

I was looking down, hoping John wouldn't call on me. Perhaps that's why he did.

I hesitated, shuffling my feet, rubbing my head, and answered,

"I think he's pondering the nature and consequences of being and nothingness."

"Excellent, Willian. That's it, exactly. What else?"

"I think he's flirting with suicide and perhaps trying to work up courage to do it."

"Okay, William, but Hamlet never mentions I, or me. So, do you think it's just about him, or is he just raising a philosophical question?"

God, I wanted to scream, "who cares?" I suspect we all wanted to scream. But as usual all of us remained quiet.

John continued, "Let's all think about this. Let's consider that perhaps Hamlet is exploring the ideas of being and nothingness by articulating a basic truism that we are born, we live, and eventually we die. All of us."

"But perhaps it's more frustrating to Hamlet when he realizes that …"

"No traveler returns, puzzles the will."

"What does that mean to you William?"

"You tell us, John. I'm sure you want to," was my reply.

"Well, perhaps he's lamenting that since no one has returned from the dead, we remain ignorant of what death really means, or what it is, or what it's like."

He paused for a moment and then continued,

"So, perhaps Hamlet's dilemma captures several universal human questions. Questions we have been asking since the beginning of time."

"How do we act in the face of a sea of great troubles and sorrow?"

"Do we merely wallow in the suffering and passively accept that we must endure them."

"Or can we end our troubles by opposing them?"

"And lastly, what is death? In death, do we experience a restful sleep, or in death's sleep do we find no rest at all?"

John stopped, put his book down, and looked around the room at each of us.

Jesus, I couldn't take it anymore. I pounded my hips. Everyone turned in my direction.

"John, why the hell are we doing this? My god, it's just a play. A damn play. Hamlet wants to end it, he chose the side of nothingness, of death. That's all it is. Don't make any more out of it. Let him do it."

"Really William, is it just a play? That's all? Or, William, can we find meaning in Hamlet's words and thoughts? Meaning for our everyday existence?"

"Who cares, John. Hamlet should do what he wants to. We all should."

"And just what is that, William? Do we really know for sure what Hamlet wants to do? Or what we want to do? What you want to do?"

John was looking directly at me now. It was like we were the only two in the room.

Then he continued.

"Perhaps Hamlet wonders whether death is nothingness, and as he says,"

"Will end the heartache and the thousand shocks that flesh is heir to."

"So, William, it looks to me like first he questions whether death will end thinking, knowing, and remembering. End his suffering. That death will bring him lasting peace."

John paused, took a deep breath, and spoke.

"But then perhaps, Hamlet pauses and reconsiders death when he admits that,"

"Ay, there's the rub. For in that sleep of death what dreams may come, when we shuffled off this mortal coil."

"So perhaps, William, now Hamlet is questioning the very nature of death and he ponders,"

"Do we sleep in death, or do we cease to sleep, thereby finding no rest at all?"

"William, that is Hamlet's philosophical dilemma. And he has no answer, just questions and fears. Just like us, he has no answers, just questions. Fears."

"And, William, in the end Hamlet's biggest fear is the,"

"Dread of something after death, the undiscovered country from whose bourn."

"Maybe he fears that, in death, he will be haunted by bad dreams of life itself, by his memory of fear and pain and suffering. By his,"

"Slings and arrows of outrageous fortune."

"So perhaps William he concludes that however bad life is we hesitate from doing anything about it by fear of the unknown that death presents. That we,"

"Must give pause."

And when we do pause and consider, we choose life over death. Perhaps that's the takeaway, William."

"Jesus Christ, John," I was standing now, waving my arms. Everyone was looking at me.

"Enough with this philosophical crap. No one cares. Don't you get it? No one here cares. Let's do the damn play and move on."

"Move on? And just what are we moving on to, William?"

"John, you tell me, you tell all of us. Isn't that the way it always is?"

"I'm not sure I know what you're referring to, William. We're just a group working on a play. Hamlet, and it just happens to have one of the most famous lines of any play, to be, or not to be."

"Bull shit. And stop calling me William."

"But that's your name, isn't it?"

"No, it's Bill. Only my mother calls me William."

"Okay, Bill, calm down."

John turned to the group. His voice was suddenly soft and reassuring.

"Perhaps that's enough for the day. I think we're all exhausted. Let's meet back here tomorrow after breakfast."

And so, another day in the theater ended. Back in my room, lying on my bed, gazing up at the white ceiling. I started thinking about Hamlet's soliloquy:

"To die, to sleep;
To sleep: perchance to dream: ay, there's the rub!
For in that sleep of death what dreams may come
When we have shuffled off this mortal coil,
Must give us pause: there's the respect
That makes calamity of so long life"

Just then there was a knock at my door.

It was John.

"Feeling better, Bill?"

"Yes, I think so."

"Well, we hope this play acting is helping."

"I'm not sure. But sometimes I think it is."

"In what way?"

"Well, I was just thinking about the lines about giving pause to suicide and wanting to live."

"And what do you think about that?"

"It's starting to make sense."

"Wonderful Bill, you continue to think about that."

"John, can we remove these?"

"Soon Bill, soon."

I was looking at the restraints. Confining me to the bed. The tight leather straps on my arms and legs. Holding me securely to the bed.

"But when?"

"That depends on you. Entirely, on you."

I glanced again at my arms and the tight wrapping on my right wrist. Yes, that. Where I tried to end it all with that deep cut. The knife wasn't sharp enough. All I did was make a mess of my mother's kitchen.

"John."

"Yes?"

"It's okay to call me William."

"Thanks William."

"No, thank you Doctor John. Thank you."

Doctor John closed the door. I was alone again. I started thinking, and then I started talking, softly so no one would hear,

"To be, or not to be, that is the question."

The Light

"There it is again."

My voice drifted off into the space around me, but of course no one replied.

It was dark, completely dark, except for that strange flashing spot of light.

Reaching out in the darkness, I could feel nothing. And except for that flashing spot of light, I could see nothing. Absolutely nothing.

I tried to remember how I got here. Here to this place of darkness.

But my memories are as blank as the darkness in front of me. The darkness all around me.

I was lost, with only that flashing light as my company.

"Again the flash," I muttered to myself.

I had counted the time between flashes.

Thirty seconds. A constant thirty seconds.

I wonder how far away it is? Miles, perhaps.

But, in the darkness there was no way to tell as I had no reference points to measure by.

And the spot of bright light was so small. If I didn't know where to look, I wouldn't see it.

Not sure how I saw it in the first place, as the flash was so brief. Just lucky, I guess.

I looked for other lights. Perhaps there were more in the darkness.

I focused in different directions, but none appeared.

Only the single bright flash broke the darkness.

Every thirty seconds.

"I guess it's you and me." I said as the light once again revealed itself.

"But what are you? "I asked not anticipating an answer.

245

And of course, there was none.

Again, I tried to focus on the past. Perhaps if I can reconstruct the past, I can figure out where I am and more importantly how to leave this place. This place of darkness.

But as before, I could pull up no images of the past.

I was trapped in the present. In the darkness.

I could feel panic setting in accompanied by a churning feeling in my stomach.

The beginning of a panic attack, I wondered.

My breathing was becoming faster.

"Where the hell am I?" I suddenly shouted in desperation.

"Is anybody out there?"

But nothing. Not even an echo. Just that God damn flashing spot of white.

I was cold now. Shivering.

Panicked thoughts started running through my head.

Am I being held captive? Is this a nightmare from which I can't awake? Have I gone blind? Has the world come to an end?

And more ominously, have I died? Is this what what death is? Alone in the darkness with a flashing spot of light in the distance?

But I could feel my breathing, so I guess I'm not dead. Or at least I hope so.

And what if I try to reach that light? What would I find?

Of course, I had no answers.

The cold intensified. I was shaking all over.

I rubbed my arms to try to warm up. But my cold hands didn't help.

The thirty seconds were up.

The light returned. For a split second. A small bright flash. No sound. Just that white light.

Perhaps I've gone crazy, I thought.

Think, think, who am I, what is the month, year?

Okay, I got my name and month, I think, but not sure of the year. Jesus, what's happening?

My legs are going numb, arms too. Is it the cold, or something else?

Nausea sweeps over me. I fight to contain it. I gag.

Dizzy and lightheaded now.

Dear God, please don't faint. Not now.

I feel like I'm losing control. I'm just being carried along by my negative emotions and physical ailments. No control.

Perhaps I've caught a mysterious disease. Yes, that could be it. A mysterious disease. Probably deadly too. Just my luck.

I could be in a hospital. Isolated in a dark room. Some contagious disease. Very deadly.

The flashing light is monitoring my condition. When it stops flashing, I have …

No, no, stop playing these mind games. Try to calm down. Take deep breaths. Slow, deep breaths.

Now what the hell was that mantra I learned in that meditation class? I certainly could use it now. Shri something. Or Sur something?

Oh God, did something just touch me? I felt something on my foot. I'm sure I did. Perhaps a wild animal? A poisonous spider or a snake.

Jesus, get a hold of yourself. Try to focus. Yes, focus.

You're okay. No snakes, no mysterious disease, no hospital, none of that. Just darkness and that stupid light.

That God damn stupid light.

There is goes again.

So quick.

So small.

So bright.

Perhaps it's a signal? From a distant lighthouse.

No, don't be so stupid, there's no water here. Or is there? How would I know for sure? Perhaps out in the darkness there's a large ocean.

Perhaps there is a lighthouse out there surrounded by swirling water.

Swirling water. Cold water.

I feel like I'm being pushed underwater. I'm drowning and every time I come up for air another wave quickly throws me back under. Under the cold water.

Yes, that must be it, a flashing beacon from a lighthouse. Every thirty seconds. Warning ships. Warning me of a deep ocean on the horizon. Of treacherous currents and rocks.

But of course, I can't see the horizon, so I better stay here.

Here where I'm safe.

Here, in the cold. Here in the darkness.

Strange, I just realized there is no sound. No sound of a wind, no sound of any animals, no sound of that ocean. My God, the only sounds are the words spinning around in my head.

The words spin in a constant loop. And I can't break the cycle.

My sobbing breaks the silence. At least I have that. That's real.

The tears running down my face only add to my misery, and they are cold against my skin. Like the cold ocean.

I want to scream out, but what good would that do? I mean, I could just alert predators to my location. And of course, I wouldn't see them until it was too late.

Yes, better to remain silent.

Stay silent and wait.

But, what am I waiting for? And why in hell am I here?

I close my eyes to escape the darkness. Of course, I can't.

I am trapped, physically and emotionally. Trapped in this darkness.

My heartbeat becomes faster. I feel the thumping in my chest. Is it going to explode? Can hearts explode?

My throat tightens and I struggle to breathe. But the air is so heavy, and suddenly it carries a terrible smell. Like rotting wood.

Could I be in a forest? Perhaps a rain forest, with damp air and the smell of moist trees and grasses.

My God, listen to yourself, why the hell would I be in a rain forest?

Why me, why the hell is this happening to me?

Okay, try to relax, think of someplace you'd like to be. A calming place.

Jesus, I can't. I can't do that.

Another thirty seconds.

God damn light.

Then darkness. So dark. I start shaking, violently.

Suddenly a memory surfaces.

I was seven, I am in a closet. Playing hide and seek.

Suddenly I hear the closet door lock.

I stay silent. Hide. It's the game.

It's dark except for the room light under the door.

Then that light goes out.

How long am I in the locked closet? I've lost track of time.

No one comes. I am alone in the darkness. Complete darkness.

I am scared. The darkness scares me. It always has.

The memory fades, I'm no longer 7, I return to the present and I see the flashing light.

But something is different.

The darkness is slowing lifting.

It gets lighter and lighter.

I wait for the flash of light. The small, bright light.

I count to thirty.

And there it is.

I can see clearly now.

I can see it, just above me.

There is no lighthouse,

No ocean,

No rain forest,

No hospital,

No snakes,

No spiders,

Just a smoke detector on the ceiling above me.

I am lying in bed looking at the smoke detector in my bedroom.

The battery indicator light flashes and will again in thirty seconds.

The Deer

I was running through the woods, only occasionally looking back. Darting between the tall trees for cover. Stumbling over fallen branches, decaying branches hidden beneath the deep underbrush.

The fall leaves crunched beneath my feet. Normally I liked that sound, but not this morning. It was too loud. Too revealing.

I could sense someone's presence, perhaps more than one, in the woods with me. I shivered at the thought. What might they want? Why were they in the woods? My woods?

"Jessie, wake up," he was shaking my arm, "you've fallen asleep."

"Huh."

"You need to stay awake."

I recognized the voice. It was David, my best friend.

"Sorry. I'm just so damn tired. I must have dozed off. Having a strange dream too."

"Strange dream?"

"Yeah, running through the woods and being chased by someone."

"Well, you're not running through the woods."

"But it was so real, I really could feel the ..."

"Hey, I'll get some coffee for you. Perhaps it will help."

"Thanks."

As David stood up to get the coffee, I could feel my eyes closing. Damn I was so tired.

Suddenly I broke into a clearing. The dark forest was at my back. I thought the fear of being chased might ease. But it didn't.

In front of me a slow stream emptied into a small lake, and then it continued its lazy winding journey to the valley below.

I lowered myself at the lake's edge and reached into the water. It was

251

cold and so clear. I gently rubbed the water across my hot forehead down to my cheekbones. I closed my eyes as I felt its cooling effect on my face. It was so refreshing. I almost forgot about the woods, the unknown stalkers. Almost.

Strange. My shirt was damp and heavy, but my throat was dry.

All that running through the woods, I thought.

I reached down to cup some water in my hands.

"Damn it, Jessie, stay awake." It was David again, shaking me, bringing me back to the present.

"Sorry Dave, I don't know what's got into me. I'm just so sleepy this morning."

"Well, I know it's been a long night, but damn it, stay awake."

"I'm trying, Dave, believe me, I'm trying."

"Okay, drink some more coffee. See if that helps."

The coffee was lukewarm now. As I sipped it, I felt my eyes closing, again. I was dozing off.

My hands broke the surface of the cool water, but something was not right.

Looking down at my reflection in the lake, I noticed that the color of the water had changed. It was no longer clear. I shook my head in disbelief and continued looking down.

A dark red pool at the lake's edge was growing larger and larger and spiraling outward.

Streaks of red were being carried away by the slow-moving stream, heading to the valley below.

A sense of foreboding, actually panic, washed over me as I watched the lake turning red.

"Jessie, Jessie," it was David again, "if you can't stay awake, we're leaving."

"Dave, sorry, I don't know what's gotten into me."

"Christ, Jessie, if you want to pack it in, just tell me. We'll leave."

"Dave, please …"

"Damn it, Jessie, you were the one who wanted to do this."

"Yes, I know …"

"But if you're having second thoughts, let's head out."

"Dave, I'm sorry. I don't know why I can't stay awake."

"Okay, just try to. Otherwise, we're just wasting our time. Otherwise..."

David's voice faded into the early morning. I was dozing off again.

I stood up and looked at the changing color of the lake.

My wet shirt clung to my chest like an extra layer of skin. Sweat. Sticky sweat.

I started to lift the shirt up, to remove that extra layer of skin, when I realized what was happening.

Seeping through my shirt, fresh blood. I watched as large drops fell into the water in front of me. My blood was turning the clear lake water red. Bright red.

I turned away from the lake and looked back towards the forest. I thought I saw something move. Was it them?

"Jessie, do you see it?" Dave was whispering.

"Where?"

"Over there." He was pointing to his left.

I didn't want to tell him I had dozed off again, so I simply replied, "oh yes."

Of course, I didn't see anything.

"Just wait, Jessie. Be patient. Don't move."

Don't move. That was easy for me. Lying here. That's all I had been doing. Lying here and dreaming. So tired. And then it started again as I dozed off.

I was struggling, but finally I managed to tug the blood-soaked shirt up over my head.

Blood was oozing from the top of my shoulder.

Perhaps I punctured my shoulder on a low hanging branch in the woods. Yes, that's the only explanation. A deep cut from a branch I didn't see. I was in such a panic to escape from whoever was following me, that I neglected to notice that branch.

Suddenly Dave was whispering in my ear again.

"I told you this was the place. The perfect place."

David's muted voice did little to conceal his excitement. I was surprised he was able keep the volume to a whisper.

"Is it time, Dave?" I asked.

"Almost. Almost, Jessie."

Time slowed down as I waited for the signal from David. Lying there at the edge of the woods. I yawned, then I felt my eyes closing.

The injury on my shoulder was deep, the blood flow wasn't letting up. I need to be more careful in those woods, I promised myself.

I focused my attention to the spot where the woods began. Where I thought I had heard movement.

I heard some sounds, but I didn't recognize them. Strange sounds indeed. I remember hearing something similar when I was in the woods with my father. He told me those sounds were sounds to be afraid of, to run from.

Suddenly there was a loud, booming noise, accompanied by a bright flash of light.

I just stood there, looking at it. I couldn't move.

The sharp pain in my side was intense, and then blood appeared. Like a river, cascading down my leg. I let out a scream.

My vision was waning. Everything around me was turning dark. I felt dizzy. Weak.

I was frightened. What was happening?

My legs started to give way and I slowly fell into the lake.

As my face hit the cool water, my eyes suddenly opened, but all I saw was the color red.

Suddenly Dave was shaking me. I opened my eyes.

"Jessie just look at those antlers. He still has them."

"Is that a white-tailed deer?"

"A buck, Jessie, we call male deer a buck."

"Jesus, he's looking right at us."

"Might have heard us talking. They have good eyesight and damn good hearing."

"Oh."

"And look at his white tail. See it wagging from side to side?"

"Yes."

"Well, they do that when they sense danger."

"Hey Dave, look, he's bleeding."

"Must have hurt himself in the woods."

"He's losing a lot of blood, Dave."

"Well, he's going to lose a lot more when you finish him off. Are you ready to shoot?"

"I don't know, Dave, the poor animal is hurt."

"Jesus Christ, if you won't shoot him, I will."

"No Dave, I've changed my mind. Let's leave."

"Fuck you, Jessie."

"I won't let you, Dave. You can't do it. I think I know that deer, yes, I think I do."

"What the hell are you talking about? You know that deer?"

"Yes, we know one another and ..."

"Well say goodbye to your friend, the deer."

As David reached for his rifle, I jumped to my feet and started running. Running in the direction of the white-tailed deer.

I knew what I had to do.

The deer stood there looking at me. He didn't run.

Our eyes met. His big eyes looked so familiar, almost like I was staring in a mirror.

He understood. Perhaps he had the same dream. Yes, that must be it. The same dream.

"Run, run," I shouted. "Get out of here."

Then, I heard the sound of a gun. A flock of birds took flight.

The bullet ripped through my side.

I stumbled and then fell into the lake.

Everything was red.

Everything was so cold.

David was pulling me out of the water.

"Jesus Christ, Jessie why the hell did you run into my line of fire."

"The deer," I mumbled, "what about the deer?"

"Oh, I forgot to mention, white-tailed bucks are good swimmers too. He's on the other side of the lake, looking back at us."

"Really. Good swimmers. That was not part of my ..."

I hesitated.

"Part of what, Jessie?"

"Oh nothing. Just dreaming Dave. Just a stupid dream."

Broken Promises

We could just barely see them in the distance. They were on horses and riding away from us. That much we could tell.

The freezing wind was whipping up the last of the sage brush.

While our bandanas protected our noses and mouths, the blowing snow felt like needles against our unprotected eyes.

It was miserable.

"It looks like about ten of them."

"Do you think it's them?"

"Can't rightly tell. But if I had to guess, I'd say yes."

We were low on food and low on morale.

It had been two weeks since we left El Pueblo Fort in search of the Ute Indians. Two grueling weeks in the middle of winter.

The troops were starting to question why we were here. My explanation didn't seem to convince them. Some threatened to turn back. They were exhausted. And angry.

The El Pueblo settlement, which was a trading post rather than a military base, had long encouraged trade between white settlers and the Ute Indians in the region.

Strategically located near a prominent bend in the Arkansas River where trails and roads converged. The settlement consisted of an adobe brick structure on the border of two nations, and so it became a natural trading location, offering such items as contraband liquor, cultivated crops and domestic livestock.

But El Pueblo had come under attack. Those same Ute Indians, who would trade here, stormed the settlement.

The raid was unexpected, quick, and bloody. Nineteen traders were killed, and two boys taken hostage. Three traders managed to escape during the raid, but two of them died soon after.

It was Christmas, 1854. The locals referred to it as a massacre and they were angry, and they wanted revenge.

In response, we, cavalry troops from Fort Massachusetts, were in pursuit of those Ute Indians who were involved in the Christmas Day attack.

For two weeks as we headed south from the Arkansas River Valley in southern Colorado into Mexico, we had not seen any Utes. But we did see evidence of their retreat.

"And what the hell are we supposed to do once we catch up with them."

"Take them prisoners and return them to Pueblo to stand trial," I replied.

"Good luck with that."

It was starting to get dark. And the temperature was falling.

"Best we stop here for the night. Make camp and start a fire."

I could hear the mumbling, the groans. Clearly, they were not happy. I wasn't either, but I couldn't tell them. I was in command.

In the morning we woke to overnight snow. Just what we needed. Sleeping bags covered with fresh powder.

And it was damn cold.

Slipping my feet into frozen boots, I shouted.

"Be ready to leave in 30."

More groans, only louder this morning.

After 30, the ten of us saddled up and headed south.

The Christmas Day attack was unexpected. Throughout the preceding decade, the Ute Indians were seen as peaceful, at least when compared to other tribes in the area, especially the Apache and Arapahos.

In 1849, the Utes signed a peace treaty with the U.S. Government.

However, as more and more settlers came into the area, intruding upon Ute lands, hunting became difficult. As the wild game became depleted, the Utes took to raiding the settler's villages for food.

In the years leading up to the attack, the U.S. Government made many promises to the Ute Indians. The U.S. agreed to provide the Utes with food, to recognize their ancestral territory, and to protect them from Arapaho raids.

But the U.S. Government reneged on its promises.

The last straw occurred after a meeting in the summer of 1854, when the Ute chiefs met with the Governor of the territory.

At the meeting, the Ute chiefs were infected with smallpox, and all died upon returning to their village. The disease was quickly spread among members of the tribe, with many dying.

The tribe was convinced that the blankets that were given to the chiefs by the Governor were the source of the disease.

New Ute leaders rose to take charge.

With the Utes suffering from starvation and this deadly disease, the new leaders decided to take revenge on the settlers who had settled on their lands, including the traders at El Pueblo Fort.

"Can't say as I blame them." It was my second in command.

"Who?"

"The Indians. After all those broken promises and worse."

"Doesn't excuse what they did."

"Just saying. I would have been angry too."

By the early afternoon, the wind had eased. The sun was out and the sky a deep blue. The fresh snow sparkled like diamonds.

"Beautiful country."

"Sure is."

"I can see why it was special to them."

I didn't need to reply, I knew who my second in command was referring to. And in a way, I agreed with him. So best to say nothing, I concluded.

The fresh snow also revealed their path south.

"I think we're closing."

"Yes, I think so too. Their tracks are undisturbed. They were here recently."

"Shall we pick it up?"

"That and we'll push on tonight. The full moon will show the way."

The Utes were sure to be in our sight within a few days. In sight of our eyes and our guns.

The Utes were the oldest residents of Colorado and travelled throughout Colorado's mountain ranges.

One range in particular had become a sacred site. The Utes called it Sun Mountain, because its highest peak was the first to catch the rays of the morning sun.

But, in 1806, the American explorer, Zebulon Pike, named it Pike's Peak. So much for the sacred Sun Mountain.

A growing number of European settlers took notice of the territory, especially its bounty of timber, wildlife, and abundant water. Unfortunately, as they established their settlements, they failed to recognize that the land had long been inhabited by the Ute Indians and that these Utes considered the land sacred and their rightful home. All part of Manifest Destiny the settlers said.

"How's our ammunition?"

"Much better than our food supply."

Over the last two weeks, the focus on our pursuit, combined with the harsh weather, had affected our ability to restock with the local wildlife. Just a few days left of supplies.

"After we capture the Utes, we'll take time to restock our food supplies."

As we pushed further south, the temperature warmed, the snow melted. The ground was soft with vegetation. The mountains were far behind us. We were now riding through gentle green valleys.

We had been riding for three days. Then, on the fourth morning as the sun rose, we noticed the smoke. Columns of white smoke on the horizon.

"A camp?"

"Possibly."

"Well, we should know in a couple of hours."

The terrain was rich with trees and flowers in bloom. Wildlife grazed, occasionally looking up in our direction. We crossed many streams. The water was clear and full of fish.

"Not like Pueblo." My second in command observed.

"Strange," I replied.

"Huh?"

"This territory. It's never been explored. Never been settled. And it's so ..."

"Blessed."

"Yes, so abundant and so blessed."

We were approaching the crest of the hill. On the other side, we expected to see them. The Utes who had murdered the settlers at El Pueblo Fort. The Utes, who were probably more willing to die in a gun fight then be escorted back to Pueblo. The Utes who had lost so much with the white man's arrival. The Utes who had seen so many promises broken.

We dismounted and slowly walked toward the crest of the hill. With about 50 feet before reaching the peak, I instructed everyone to stay back. My second in command and I would go alone and observe what was on the other side. Then we could settle on a strategy.

The grass was like a soft mat. We finally pulled ourselves to the crest of the hill.

Looking down we saw them.

It was a large village of Utes. Men, women and children, hundreds of them. Some were gathered around open fire pits. Others were fishing. The children were running and playing. There was a wealth of livestock and fields of planted crops.

The Utes had established their new home in this unoccupied territory. It looked so peaceful, like it was meant to be.

"What are we going to do?" It was my second in command.

"I'm thinking."

Suddenly I knew. This was their new sacred land.

"Let's head back."

The troops were waiting for us. Their guns were at their sides. They were ready to attack.

"Well, captain, what are we doing?"

Looking back at the peak and the rising smoke, I said, "nothing, we're doing nothing. Saddle up, we're headed back."

"What? Why?"

"There's nothing there, just some abandoned fires. No Utes to be seen. We're done with this search. Time to go home."

I looked at my second in command.

"Isn't that right? There's nothing there."

"Yes, absolutely, nothing."

On our way home, we stocked up on food supplies. The abundance of wildlife made it easy. It was a perfect place, I thought. This new sacred land. It was perfect, but, I wondered, for how long.

The Flight that Might have Been

The clouds were starting to separate. I could see mountains below.
Suddenly the big airplane shook.

"Rising air currents, warm air pushing up from the green forests," the
pilot laughed.

He was used to the bumps, the turbulence, in fact I thought he enjoyed
them. As for me, I never did like them.

"Weak stomach," my buddies would say, as I vomited in the airsick bag.

"Only in the air," I replied, then I would remind them how I could
drink them under the table when I was on solid footing.

How long had we been flying? I lost track. Watching the ocean below
I lost track of time. But not our mission. We were all curious about that.
What were we doing?

"Anyone for lunch?"

"What do we have this time?"

Lunch time already? Well, I guess we had been flying for some time,
I thought. We did have an early breakfast before we left. It was still dark.
Biscuits and gravy. No way, I was having that before the long flight. If I
did, I would need extra airsick bags.

"Ham and cheese sandwiches."

"Jesus, that's all? Just ham and cheese sandwiches?"

"I guess that's all the damn Air Force could afford."

The plane shook again. Worse than before. No sandwich for me. I'll
have to wait until we get back for something to eat. Of course, that assumes
we get back.

Our mission was a mystery until we were in the air. Each of us was
given a sealed envelope when we boarded. On the outside of the envelope
in bold print the statement.

Not to be opened until over open water

Why over open water, I wondered.

"Who didn't get a sandwich?"

"I don't want one," I shouted over the roar of the four engines.

Open water. Perhaps if we didn't make it, the instructions would be lost in the vast ocean? That way, no one would ever know.

"Okay, I have one more sandwich, thanks to lieutenant weak stomach. Who wants it?"

"Give it to the fish."

The contents of the envelopes detailed what each of us were to do on this top-secret mission. Since I was the photographer, I was instructed to take pictures before and after the event. That's all, I thought? This is top secret?

"One hour to target," the co-pilot announced.

The flight was bumpier now. Morning heat. I hated this part of the flight.

I returned to my printed instructions. Take pictures. Jesus, what were they expecting? Then I noticed more information. Put on protective face mask when instructed.

"Hey, has everyone read their mission instructions," the pilot asked.

"Hey, captain, what's this protective face mask stuff?"

"Yea, what is the mission all about?"

"And why top secret?"

The reply came back. "Later guys, I can answer those questions later. For now, just do as you're told."

Well, that's the military, I thought. Do as you're told. I guess we shouldn't be surprised.

The clouds were all but gone now. The land beneath me could have been anywhere. Mountains, valleys, rivers, lakes, occasional towns. So green, so peaceful. I could be back home, hiking through the Cascades. Through Stevens Pass, then along the Wenatchee River, to the small town of Leavenworth, where I ran a whitewater rafting company. Yes, I could be home. But I wasn't. Instead, I was airborne, over some distant country on a top-secret mission to take photographs.

"Thirty minutes to target. Time to try on your protective masks. Make sure it fits tight."

Jesus, what is this thing, I thought, as I pulled the bulky face mask from my assigned pack. Made of metal with a rubber seal and with a really dark eye shield. Designed to cover my eyes and nose. As I pulled the straps to tighten it, I felt like I was blocking out everything around me.

'Who the hell came up with these?"

"God, why are these so heavy?"

"Damn, how long do we have to wear these things?"

Again, no answers. Not that I expected any. My eyes adjusted to the dark lens. Like walking the Sauer Mountain Trail at night. How many times did I do that, especially in early winter after the whitewater rafting season was over? That was my favorite hike. Especially with a full moon lighting the way.

"15 minutes to target. Take out your maps and familiarize yourself with the target area, especially the drop point."

The plane started a slow descent. The sky was cloudless. I could see a mountain range ahead. Looking at the map, I could tell that the target was just beyond that mountain range. It was almost 8 in the morning. I'm sure birds below were just starting their early morning songs. Just like in Leavenworth, I thought. Those beautiful early morning songs. How I used to love those in the morning.

"How do you pronounce this target city?"

"Christ if I know."

"Hero something."

Just another target, I thought. How many have there been? How many more until this is over? How many more before I'm back home, preparing for the whitewater rafting season? Before, I'm back with my girl. Jesus, how long?

We were above the mountain range now. In the valley just beyond, I could see a large sprawling city. It was just after 8, people were probably headed to work, kids to school, mothers going shopping. Just another day.

The plane descended more. The captain's voice broke the silence.

"Everyone in position? Masks on?"

"Co-pilot, aye."

"Navigator, aye."

"Radio operator, aye."

"Flight engineer, aye."

"Turret gunners, aye."

"Tail gunner, aye."

"Bombardier, aye."

"Photographer, aye."

Holding the heavy Bell & Howell Eyemo wind-up movie camera in my right hand, I felt I was ready. But what was I ready for?

I looked again at the map and the city. Then I shouted to the rest of the crew.

"It's Hero she ma. It's pronounced Hero she ma."

"Hero whatever."

"Let's get this over with and get back to base."

I looked back down at the city below us. So many wooden structures, I thought.

"Bombardier, the plane is now under your control."

"Acknowledged, I'll take it from here."

I looked at my watch. 8:13. Then I pointed my camera straight down.

"Drop target sighted."

My left hand was positioned on the crank that would film the event. But what event, I still wondered. Why all this top-secret stuff? Why didn't we know what the real objective of this mission was?

"Armed and ready for release," the bombardier shouted.

I started cranking the camera not knowing what to expect.

Suddenly, the radio operator started yelling.

"Abort, abort."

"Why? What's happening?"

"They've just surrendered. The war is over. Japan has surrendered. Do not drop the bomb."

The B29 Super-fortress banked to the right. The pilot was again in control of our aircraft, the Enola Gay.

"You can remove your face masks. The mission has been terminated. Navigator, take us back to base."

As I removed my bulky face mask, I decided to take a picture of the city below. It looked so peaceful. I wonder if they knew the war was over. I wonder if they knew we were just above them.

Monday Morning

It's Monday and it's the peak of the morning rush hour as the young man makes his way to his destination. He's 19 years old, and still not sure how he got here.

He has spent another sleepless night as loud sirens sounded one after another. Even this morning, about an hour ago, there was one.

It is 74 degrees, and the winds are calm.

People are off to work, children make their way to school, housewives clean the morning dishes.

The city of 245,000 people is beginning another day.

An early morning fog had lifted. The sun is shining.

The city buses and local trains are packed with morning commuters. It is a typical busy beginning to a new week.

The young man reaches his destination.

Shops are opening their doors for the day.

His memories suddenly come rushing back. He begins to tell his story. I am ready to listen. Anxious, actually.

"I was outside at an army training ground," he says.

Suddenly above him, there appear two large airplanes. There have been many of them lately, so he is not concerned.

The sky is clear blue, and he feels the warmth of the sunny August morning. It feels good.

But then,

"When I looked up at the sky, it suddenly disappeared. It turned white."

Strangely, he hears no sound. Just bright white light all around him.

He doesn't know what to make of the strange white light.

It was 8:15 in the morning in the Japanese city of Hiroshima. An American B-29 bomber had just dropped the first atomic bomb in war.

The atomic bomb created a wave of heat that momentarily reached over 6,000 degrees Fahrenheit on the ground.

Hurricane winds roared through the city. The flash of light from the bomb was 10 times brighter than the sun, instantly blinding those unlucky enough to be staring at it.

Suddenly an enormous wave of wind hits him.

"I immediately fell to the ground."

As he attempts to stand up, he realizes that his clothing is on fire. He manages to slap out the flames.

"I was injured, and my shoulder was burnt."

Looking around he is surprised to see that,

"All the buildings around me were destroyed. The wooden ones were on fire."

He doesn't know it at that moment, but an atomic bomb had just exploded 2,000 feet above him in a blast equal to about 15,000 tons of TNT, immediately destroying five square miles of the city.

But he is spared even though,

"I was about a mile away from the point where the bomb exploded."

Later it will be estimated that more than 80,000 lives were lost from the initial impact. By the end of the year, 60,000 more would die from burns, injuries, and radiation effects from the bomb.

About 60% of the city's population would be dead.

But not him, he will survive.

Looking around he can see that,

"Everyone was burned or had sores on their skin."

"Seeing so many burnt people, I was shocked."

It begins to rain, but it's a rain he has never seen.

"Soon black rain began to fall."

The black rain reaches the ground as sticky dark water.

The intense fires created by the bomb carry large quantities of ash into the atmosphere. The ash has the effect of seeding the clouds and the result is a black rain. This rain, which has the consistency of tar, is a combination of the ash, water, and radioactive fallout.

He tries to remember how he got here, to Japan.

He was only five years old, and the memories are fuzzy. They have always been fuzzy. But he can remember some things.

He remembers being on a farm in Fresno, California. He, his three brothers, and his parents.

His father died and his mother sent him and his younger brother to Japan on a big ship where he is raised by an aunt. His two older brothers remain behind. He often thinks of them and wonders if he will ever see them again.

He has no explanation as to why he was sent to Japan. It is a mystery and will always remain so.

But now he is in Hiroshima, wandering for hours through what remains of a once bustling city, helping others.

The atomic burst created a fireball, which began at 850 feet in diameter and kept expanding on its way down, engulfing the sky above the city. The intense levels of heat from the fireball consumed everything below it in fire.

Within half an hour, almost every building within a two-mile radius of the hypocenter was in flames. About 90% of the city's 76,000 buildings were partially or totally incinerated, or reduced to rubble. Of the 14 square miles of land considered usable before the bomb, 40% was reduced to ashes.

There is utter destruction as far as he can see. Nothing remains except a few buildings of reinforced concrete. For acres and acres, the city appears like a dark desert except for scattered piles of brick and melted roof tile.

"It's like a burnt field of darkness."

He thinks of his brother and eventually learns that,

"My brother, who was many miles away when the bomb exploded, came to the city to find me."

"But he can't find me."

He assesses his physical condition and concludes,

"Luckily, my injuries are minor, and I am able to walk."

But he observes that the intense heat has produced a frantic need for drinking water, and so,

"Everyone was searching for water."

Many are so desperate for drinking water that they scoop up the radioactive black rain which has collected on the ground. Of course, they have no idea of the deadly consequences of doing so.

But it's more than water that people are searching for.

Panic and chaos are rampant as people struggle to find medical assistance, friends, and family.

Around him a procession of ghost-like figures, with faces and lips swollen and blackened with soot, covered in blood, with their clothes in shreds, are searching for an escape from what remains of Hiroshima.

By the evening, the sky is red with flames and the sound of crying and groaning is heard throughout the city.

The young man eventually makes his way home, to Etajima, which is about 20 miles from the explosion.

There he meets up with his brother.

"Luckily, my brother seemed to be okay. I don't think the bomb had any effect on him at that time because the distance was too far."

The young man is Kasumi Furukawa. In later life he is referred to as a Hibakusha ("explosion-affected person").

Over time, Kasumi becomes one of the dwindling numbers of the survivors of the Atomic Bomb.

Kasumi, however, manages to lead a long life.

Five years after the atomic bomb, he marries and raises a family.

Initially he works on his family's rice farm, but admits that,

"Life was quite difficult."

Kasumi never returns to the United States, but his brothers come to Japan to visit him. Even his mother visits once.

About 30 years ago I had the privilege of meeting Kasumi Furukawa.

I am immediately pulled in by his kind and gentle simile and his infectious laugh.

He doesn't speak English, so we communicate through interpreters.

It was a family reunion of sorts as one of his older brothers had come to Hiroshima to meet him. This older brother was my wife's, father, Jack.

I was there, along with Charmaine and our young son, Sean.

On that day my long friendship with Uncle Kasumi began.

Over the years every time my wife and I returned to Japan, we made the journey to see Uncle Kasumi. Every time we did, I would ask him more questions about that Monday morning. He was always willing to answer them.

This year's visit to Japan was to be no different. But on August 15th, Kasumi Furukawa passed away. He was 96.

I never got to say goodbye.

Author's Notes

The quotes in the story Monday Morning are Kasumi Furukawa, as told to me (through an interpreter), or as told to his son.

The one quote that stands out for me was the answer Kasumi gave me 30 years ago when I asked him what his thoughts were that day after the bomb was dropped. He replied,

"Thank goodness, the war is over."

About the Author

Michael Palmer was born in 1941 in New York City.

For 47 years, he was a professor at the University of Colorado in Boulder. During that time, his publications consisted solely of academic research papers.

When he retired in 2013, he continued to teach as a visiting professor in Japan, Italy and Germany.

However, when the pandemic took hold in 2020 those opportunities quickly ended.

Tired of watching tv reruns, his wife, Charmaine encouraged him to find something more exciting to pursue.

Remembering that his father published two books when he was in his 80s, Michael decided to try his hand at writing short stories. Before he realized he had written over 100.

Friends and family encouraged him to publish some of these stories. So, in January 2023, his first book, The Last Green Flash was published.

Continuing to write, but now focusing on events in his life to form a story, he put together his second book, No Cappuccino in the Afternoon.

As the reader will see, many of the short stories in this second book reflect his travels and early childhood experiences. Others of course, are pure fiction.

Michael lives in Boulder, Colorado and when not writing, he and his wife enjoy traveling.

Printed in the United States
by Baker & Taylor Publisher Services